17 95

8 95

6 95

Memory

Harry

By may

June 25, 1952

*This
book
stinks!!*

THE DREAM GATE

The Dream Gate

by

MARCUS BACH

THE BOBBS-MERRILL COM
INDIANAPOLIS   *Publishers*

To
ROSEMARY

*In every life there is a dream gate
through which one ought to go with all his
wishes, soon or late, and take the free road
where it leads.*

THE DREAM GATE

CHAPTER 1

~~~~~~

*T*HE wheat was like the people who had planted it. It pushed up defiantly between stones and dried-out stump roots. In patches of sand it struggled, stunted but eager to fulfill what the sower had expected of it. In fertile spots it stood resolutely as if to say, "Give me half a chance. You will see how strongly I put down my roots."

Little Mike walked through the field with arms spread wide and allowed the bristling amber tops to caress the palms of his hands. Sometimes he walked on tiptoe. He was keeping his eyes intently on the two sharply contrasted figures striding ahead of him. Always in the lead was the stocky, black-jacketed form of his father, walking possessively, swinging his arms. The stranger, in his blue Sunday suit, was slender and tall; he walked slower and hardly swung his arms at all. The men left a swath behind them that closed up fast. The wheat was alive. It snapped back into place just as Little Mike came along to brush it aside with a bold, wading motion of his bare arms. Sometimes he ran a few steps to catch up with the men, but for the most part he walked as his father walked, owning the earth. Words and phrases drifted back to him, and he wrote them on his mind, adding new knowledge and wonder to his ten years.

11

"There's been hard work here," the stranger was saying. "I remember twenty years ago when this was all scrubland."

Little Mike saw his father snatch a handful of the grain with a strong motion and thresh it between his palms.

"If we were all like you, Joshua Volkner," Michael Neumann asserted, "this would still be scrubland today."

His words cut through the throbbing stillness of the Sunday afternoon and seemed to set the wheat bobbing in a motion of agreement.

"I only meant that many a tired back has gone into this improvement," Volkner corrected genially. "Now if you had machinery——"

"We have machinery," Michael interrupted.

"Where?" Joshua wanted to know. "A few used pieces. You will not become modernized. You will not come up to date. No, that would be making a concession to the world. That would be admitting that something in the capitalistic system has value. So you buy a few secondhand pieces in the hope that the curse of newness has at least been taken off."

"Hard work and the good life go hand in hand," Michael Neumann vowed, brushing the wheat husks impatiently from his hands. Then he pushed his black hat back on his head and set his bearded face in stubborn survey of the wide, undulating sweep of yellowing grain.

"From the colony buildings to where we stand is sixty acres," he said shortly. "We redeemed every foot; swamp and timber."

Little Mike's eyes traveled over the ripening field to where the cluster of thirty colony buildings stood irregular in height and shape. They were the mighty fortress about which the pastor often spoke. They were the dwellings of God's people. Some of the houses were old, some were newly built, but they all huddled together as if each needed the other's strength. This was the commune which held the world at bay. This was the Hutterian kingdom whispering its security to Little Mike's heart. The sixty acres were but a small part of the commune. If the stranger would walk westward through the yard, he would find a thousand acres and orchards and apiaries and gardens.

"Find a place with water and a mill," his father was saying, calling Joshua's attention to where the rough-hewn, two-story mill stood in respectful Sabbath silence. "You remember how the fathers said that in Russia long ago? 'Find a place with water and a mill.' Well, here it is! Right here in South Dakota." Michael's words rushed forward with the river. "Everything a man wants and needs is here! Must I remind you, Joshua Volkner, that when the fathers came here in 1874 they came without machinery, without the capitalistic system and without an automobile? The mill had been abandoned. Hutterian communism made it work. Homesteaders said they couldn't get enough wood for building. The fathers found the chalk cliffs across the river. They were here seventy-five years ago. They were still here when you ran away from our community in favor of the world. Chalk blocks built the first commune home and the first barn, and there are enough left for you today, Mr. Worldling, if you are thinking of coming back."

"I am back!" Joshua laughed and took off his hat in a gesture of welcome. "I am back—for a visit!"

"And after the visit," said Michael bluntly, "it's back to the husks and the swine."

"Yes, back to the system." Joshua sighed.

"See, you are sick of it!"

"Oh, everybody gets sick of it at times. But I dare say you get tired of colony life sometimes too."

"Never!" Michael vowed.

Joshua smiled and followed Michael Neumann's steps to the edge of the wheat field. Little Mike looked back over the rolling acres. The snug, weathered roof of the old barn seemed to hug the tops of the heavy wheat. The barn was like a huge gray hen and the roofs of colony houses and shops were its brood over which it kept a solemn, endless watch. He wished that Joshua Volkner would look back, too, at the big sight, but his father was calling the stranger's attention to the deep pits and the gray-white walls of stone on the other side of the river.

"There's the chalk quarry," said Michael, "which God put there for us Hutterians."

"And I suppose you still cut the blocks by hand?"

"Why not? Isn't that the way the fathers did? And we haul them over on the ice with a stone bolt just as they did too. Today the Missouri is a river. In winter it's a road."

The river captured Joshua's thoughtful gaze and carried it westward until the willows drew a curtain across his view. Then he turned to Michael with a glint of mischief in his eyes.

"And where does the river rise, Michael? How far does it go?"

The question struck Little Mike with concern. He had thought of the river only in terms of the colony acres through which it flowed. Born within sound of it, wading, swimming, playing in it, watching the men of the commune set nets and haul up fish for food, he had thought of it simply as "our river." Did it come from anywhere? Did it go anywhere? If so, did his father know?

Michael Neumann grunted in disgust at Joshua's question. Then he stopped, plunged his hands into the roomy pockets of his homespun black pants and stood with legs spread solidly on the slope. Shrewdly he said, "If you followed that water from where we stand here in Old Portage Colony, you would go a thousand miles upstream, 'way into Montana state where it rises. And if you followed it downstream, you would go a thousand miles also, 'way through Missouri where it empties into the Mississippi. Such is the river that waters our land."

Joshua smiled. "Well, then, you do depend on the outside world! The schoolmaster never told us that in the olden days."

Michael Neumann replied prophetically, "America is a big country, Joshua Volkner, but we are the seed of a new society. If the river nourishes us, well and good. That does not mean that we must be carried either upstream or down. There are roots that hold us right here, no matter how many thousand miles the waters run."

Half-hidden and forgotten at the edge of the field, Little Mike plucked absently at the wheat heads while his blue eyes scolded the river for coming such a great distance. A thousand miles! How far was that? When the Town Man went beyond the commune grounds to Tabor, that was five miles. Yankton, to which the colony pastor or the Householder occasionally went on business, was thirty miles. That was far into the world and no boy or girl in the commune had ever made that trip. The colony truck was strictly for business. The colony gate was opened

only by permission. "Our river" ran a thousand miles upstream and a thousand miles down. Could it travel that far
in and out of the world and still be a good river? For the
world was that wicked place about which the pastor
preached every evening of every day when the community gathered for Evensong. The world was the dreaded
place of private ownership and private enterprise which
were rapidly bringing men to ruin. There was only one
true and right way to live: the Hutterian way; the way of
the colony; the communistic way. For the first time the
Missouri was a stranger and a deceiver. Did it flow through
the world of sin and still do the good work of turning the
mill's huge wheel? Did it open its own gates and cross
strange lands without being punished at all? Could there be
other people, and good people, too, a thousand miles upstream and a thousand downstream even though they did
not live under the Hutterian system? What were they like
and why did God watch over them—if indeed He did? Little Mike's truant thoughts were shattered by a stinging
blow across his knuckles. His father stood over him, a
blunt stick in his hands.

"Don't stand there pulling off the wheat! Waste is of
the Devil."

Little Mike gasped. Not because of pain or hurt. Not
because of anger. Nothing his father ever did to him was
undeserved. His father was boss and Little Mike understood discipline. The shock sprang out of the frightening
knowledge that he had ventured in thought far beyond the
commune grounds. He had slipped through the forbidden
gate. He had pierced the curtain that hung between the
colony and the world.

Solemnly he brushed his burning knuckles on his faded blue shirt, then wiped his hands in his tousled brown hair. His eyes grew large with a plea for forgiveness, but his father was already walking away. Little Mike looked himself over as if to assure himself that he had fully returned from his mental flight. He noticed that some of the hooks and eyes on his shirt were unfastened. He fixed them. The visitor's coat had buttons. That made Joshua Volkner different from the men of the commune too.

Michael Neumann led the stranger along a soggy cow-path that ran between the deep ruts of a wagon road. Little Mike walked in a rut so narrow and deep that he had to balance himself to stay in it. His bare feet, scratched by the trek through the wheat field, touched softly against the cool, moist earth. He stopped and rolled up the legs of his Sunday pants, then galloped on. The men's voices lured him on; his father's voice led him just as Little Mike sometimes led the colony pony on the bridle strap. He was tied to his father like that and it was pleasant—just as it was pleasant to listen to his father's voice and hear so many wise and fearless words. Last night when Joshua's big black car drove into the commune yard, Little Mike had crowded around with the men and the children of the colony. The men who remembered Joshua greeted him; others held back as if not knowing what to say. But Michael father took the newcomer's hand with the ready words "Well, Joshua Volkner, is it welcome home?"

Little Mike remembered how those words brought a silence over everyone. They were stern, startling words, spoken with the blunt strength which was his father's way.

The stranger dismissed the greeting lightly. "Well, for

the little that has changed here, I should surely feel at home," he said.

"I wouldn't have known you from a million other men in the world," Michael told him hopelessly.

Little Mike gazed at the stranger with serious eyes. Joshua Volkner was straight and tall, and there was a suggestion of calm authority about him that was as strong as the bold manner of Michael father. None of the men had kissed the newcomer. Pastor Kunz did not come out of his room to greet him, and at the Sunday-morning church meeting he made no mention of the visitor, even though the man was at the service. Then, after dinner when the men filed from the eating house, Volkner, in a lost sort of way, walked over to the house bench where Little Mike's father and mother had just seated themselves.

Volkner said, "I've got a Sunday afternoon on my hands. Have you suggestions, Michael?"

Michael's eyes had roved critically over the man. He groaned at the colorful necktie and the clean-shaven face, measured him from his shining black shoes to the top of his summer hat, then turned to glance around the commune where other families sat on house benches or walked slowly in the yard. Suddenly Michael Neumann clamped his hands on his knees. "I'll show you around, Joshua Volkner, if everybody else is too busy."

"Oh, they're not too busy," Joshua said tolerantly, "but you see how it is. I'm the world."

"Well, that's not our fault," Michael told him.

"And the commune is still the kingdom. Yes, I remember the Sunday laws: no work, no play, no noise or activity. It might be a Sunday three hundred years ago in the Ukraine or in Moravia for all that has changed——"

"Stop taking pictures of us," Michael said wryly.

"—or it might be a Sunday right here in Old Portage commune when I was one of you."

"Yes," retorted Michael bluntly, "when you heard the world calling and you could not close your ears. When you saw the beckoning finger across the commune borders and you could not shut your eyes. When you heard the sound of an automobile and it said, 'You must have one, too.' When you turned your back on your people and your God."

"I wouldn't make it quite that strong——"

But Michael Neumann had already started on his way. Then without turning his head he called out, "Little Mike, come along!"

The joy of these words balanced Little Mike now as he walked with a playful, swaggering goose step in the narrow rut. He looked at his knuckles and said, "You don't hurt." He set his feet down with a rhythmic smack. He swung his arms wide and free and gave his shoulders the possessive, twisting motion with which his father walked. *Little Mike, come along!* He had wanted to ask, "May I come along, Michael father?" but no boy in the commune ever put such requests to his parents. The fathers had a saying, "Children should keep silent," and that is the way it was. The father's word was law. Over it was the word of the seven elders and the pastor. Over that was the word of God. Children and women had no voice in these things. *Little Mike, come along!*

The cowpath led into a narrow lane guarded on each side by a sturdy stone fence hung over with wild grape vines; behind it currant thickets huddled against an aging poplar windbreak. Michael Neumann strode on, but Joshua stopped and cocked his head. Little Mike stopped, too, a short distance behind him. He heard the familiar stirring, fluttering sound in the overhanging growth. He heard the nervous whispering of the birds, and he saw Joshua turn and look at him with a glance of friendly understanding.

"That sounds familiar," said the man. "You know what we used to call this path? The *Vogelpfad*."

Little Mike's heart leaped. That, of course, was what everyone in the commune called this sheltered corridor: the *Vogelpfad*, a path where one never failed to hear the birds morning, noon or night, Sundays or any day.

"Well, come on!" called Michael Neumann, waiting where the lane led to the meadow. He was taking stock of the huge basinlike expanse, its distant boundary fenced in by rows of trees.

"This is something new!" Joshua exclaimed as he reached Michael's side. "You've done good work."

"What the Lord doesn't provide, the hands must make," Michael boasted.

"I know," Joshua admitted, "but I remember how gnarled and stubborn the trees once stood here and how the gravel washed in when the river was high. . . ."

His words trailed off as Michael Neumann stalked on with firm steps and swinging arms. He led Joshua and Little Mike forward. The boundless pastureland made Volkner breathe deeply. He spread his arms as if to own some part of what he saw and felt.

"Freedom!" he confessed.

"Notice these clumps," Michael ordered as he strode into one of the generous islands of extraordinarily high and thriving grass that studded the meadow. "Good wood chunks came out of bad timber and even better firewood out of the roots. Where the trees came out, in went grass, and you can tell where the trees once stood by the patches. Every one of them speaks of hard work and grubbing and planting. Like colony haircuts these grassy spots look! As if somebody had put a bowl over them and cut them off all the way around with a big shears!"

Little Mike laughed happily and ran his hand around the rim of his thick brown hair.

"And there are the cattle," Michael stated, pointing off into the distance. "Three hundred head. All Angus, as you see."

"Yes, yes," marveled Joshua. "After bad years the good years, shall we say, Michael? I remember the burned earth and the struggles we had when I was here. I remember the time of the cattle disease that cleared the pastures and the mornings that you and I went out with the Cattle Boss and the Farm Boss. They worked with the dying animals and even prayed over them. I remember the winters when it was not cattle, but people, we were praying for. Nobody knew that, for the Hutterians always had great pride. No one ever became a doctor or a veterinarian. People or cattle, the problems were always brought to the Lord. I remember the floods and fires and famine and the First World War when they drove our stock from the fields."

"And that is the world you went into. I will never understand it. What was it you wanted, Joshua?"

"Freedom, Michael," the onetime Hutterian exclaimed. "I thought of that when I saw the young people in the commune and heard them singing. Yes, singing they were, but what if they should say, 'We want to go out and see how

other people live. We want to live our lives as we please.
We want to be free to come and go as we please.' What
then?"

"Wild animals, Joshua Volkner, think they have freedom, too. But they have none. The jungle makes them
fear every moment. Here we have contentment and
brotherhood. Here we are doing God's will. Of course,
after twenty years I do not expect you to remember Scripture, but you can read it any time and find it has not
changed. 'All that believed were together and had all things
in common.' "

"My wife and I have often discussed the meaning of
that text——"

"Your wife and you! And would you please tell me
what does a woman know about these things?" Michael
swept the question aside in disgust. "Where is she? Did
she come to South Dakota with you?"

"She is in Chicago with the children."

"Children?"

"Two."

"I've got six. Five girls and Little Mike."

"So I hear. And I congratulate you on a nice family."

"Really we would have seven children, only that Little
Sarah died."

"Yes, I know," Joshua answered, half turning away.
"The first-born died, didn't she?"

"You know, Joshua," Michael exclaimed, "if you had
listened to us you would not now be wandering lost in the
world."

"Lost?" Joshua echoed. "I'm not lost at all."

"But you are not happy,"

"Indeed I am."

"No man is happy who turns his back on the truth," Michael told him. "No man is happy who chooses the way of private ownership over the way of the commune. He may think he is happy, but in his honest moments he has to say, 'It is gone. I have lost something. The world has nothing to make up for it.' Have you one really true friend in the world? Come now, tell me! Have you any-one who does not think first of himself or how he can get something out of you? Have you security and peace? Oh, yes, I know you have made money, but so did the rich man in the Bible and you know what happened to him."

"Oh, well," Joshua replied lightly, "you Hutterians al-ways picture the world worse than it really is."

"That," said Michael shortly, "is impossible."

He walked deeper into the pasture swinging his arms. "Well," he exclaimed, "the land runs to the clump of trees to the north and to the fence at the south. That pond in the low grass is perpetual. If the Cattle Boss were here he could round up the herd for you."

"Yes, I'd like to see them up close."

Little Mike stood near his father in the thick, fertile growth. His eyes lighted expectantly as he watched the black, glistening herd stolidly gazing toward them across the open field. "I can get them over to you, Michael father!"

"So?" grunted Michael without looking at him. "Are you Cattle Boss today?"

Little Mike felt the touch of gentleness, slight, veiled, suppressed, but welcome as a soft caress. "Not Cattle Boss, Michael father. But I know the call."

The father's bearded face remained expressionless. His hat pulled low over his eyes, his hands stuffed inside the waistband of his pants, he stood as immovable and stubborn as the Angus. A hasty, single glance assayed his son's round, eager face and the tanned arms and legs which needed only a commanding word to fly into feverish action. Shortly he said, "Well, call them then."

Little Mike cupped his hands around his lips and took a deep breath. *"Mo-kaa! Mo-kaa! Mo-kaa!"*

The call swept over the field.

The cattle made no move.

"Mo-kaa! Mo-kaa!"

Little Mike glanced anxiously at the unyielding figure of his father.

"Well," Michael chided, "I thought you could round them over."

The boy looked up, wounded by the hint of censure in the words. He heard again, "Little Mike, come along!" He saw Volkner smile as if to say that rounding up cattle was a man's job. Strongly he felt his father's judgment. "A man should never boast unless he can fulfill his promise. Leave cheap talk for the world. Say nothing that you do not intend to back up." Such were the commune sayings that rose to torture him and caused him to spring forward with a cry, "I'll get them, Michael father!"

"Michael!" Joshua warned. "Don't you think the boy—?"

"Quiet!" snapped Michael.

"Mo-kaa! Mo-kaa!" Little Mike called as he ran, and the sharp cutting edges of grass under his feet drove him on. He was the Cattle Boss riding his horse into the herd. He

was a Hutterian doing what the world said could not be done. He was Michael Neumann afraid of nothing.

"*Mo-kaa! Mo-kaa!*"

The cattle lifted their heads. They stood defiantly in a solid pack, and Little Mike instinctively slowed to a walk. Then he stopped and picked up a stone, measuring the distance between himself and the herd.

"Mike!"

His father's voice sent a cold sensation through his body and his hand tightened over the stone. He dared not turn. He drew himself as tall as he could, breathlessly waiting.

"Mike! We don't stone the cattle!"

The words ran through him and pried open his hand. The stone fell to the ground. Once more he realized that his father could see everything. Even before a boy in the commune committed a wrong, the fathers knew about it. They were like God. They knew everything.

There was a tremor in the herd. Through the solid black walls a big steer shoved its massive bulk forward and stood with its head jutting out, its bulging, muscular neck tensed with unleashed power, its legs like rods of iron driven into the soft ground.

Little Mike stood with his open hands defenselessly at his side. He took a step. The steer began slowly swinging its head from side to side. Little Mike kept his frightened, breathless gaze on the large, bulging eyes. They were like two glowing coals in the blacksmith's forge. The swinging head made them roll and flame, and every step he took made them burn more fiercely. But something told him to go on. What was it the Cattle Boss said?—"A steer's natural look is stubborn and mad, but he's tame as the colony dog."

The Cattle Boss knows, Little Mike told himself assuringly. He knows and would not lie. No one in the colony lied. No man ever said anything that he did not know for sure.

He was close now. About the distance of the swing rope on the riverbank tree. Ten feet. The steer's head snapped up. A rope could not have pulled it up faster. Slowly the beast's front hoofs clawed at the earth. Slowly and threateningly its head swung from side to side. Little Mike held out his open hands. He had no sticks, no stones, nothing. His lips moved. Over and over he murmured his magic prayer, "*Mo-kaa, Mo-kaa!*"

The word died hopelessly on his lips. The hot breath of the steer was on his face. Panic seized him and his heart was begging God for help. He longed to look back for protection to where his father stood.

There was a movement in the herd. A sudden swift impulse told him to turn and run and he choked back a cry of fear. His father must never see what he felt. The magic power of his father's all-knowing must never guess.

He forced himself to turn and as he stood with his back to the herd, he whispered tremblingly, "*Mo-kaa, Mo-kaa,* come along."

He started to walk, praying that the cattle would follow him, but they made no move.

Far away, through a mist that was heavy tears, he saw Michael father standing with hat pulled low over his eyes, hands on hips, legs spread apart. He saw Joshua Volkner at his father's side. Then he heard a heavy thrashing sound behind him and felt a thunderous rumbling break over the ground. Suddenly the onslaught of black bodies swirled around him. Sunlight and darkness passed over him out of the dirt-filled air. The pounding hoofs were like the workmen's sledges breaking the white chalk cliffs. The cliffs were falling over him in the wild stampede. The herd was veering sharply as the black steer led them toward the far end of the basin. When Little Mike swung around and saw this, his voice returned. *"Mo-kaa, Mo-kaa!"* he shouted and started running after the cattle frantically. Faster and faster he ran, calling until he stumbled and fell and lay exhausted and weeping in the grass.

Slowly the hoofbeats faded away. Slowly out of the silence came the sound of firm, unhurried steps. He looked up and choked back the quivering in his throat. His father stood over him and held out his hand. "Hurt?" he asked shortly.

"No, Michael father."

"Can you get up?"

"I think so."

"Get up then."

Little Mike rose to his feet.

Joshua Volkner said, "There's blood on his leg. It's a deep cut, but if that's all there is, he's lucky."

Michael Neumann knelt down. "I'll tie my handkerchief around it. A hoof grazed it or maybe it was only the fall."

Little Mike put an arm around his father's shoulders while the red handkerchief was tied over the wound. "They didn't kick me on purpose, Michael father," he said. "The Cattle Boss always says that if you don't hurt them, they won't hurt you."

"Well, it's a cut of some kind." Michael shrugged. "You'll have many more before you're a man and maybe some more kicks, too."

"I wanted so much to bring you the cattle, Michael father," he said chokingly. "Why couldn't I?"

"They wanted to go the other way. Just like some people want to do. They knew you weren't the Cattle Boss so they went where they wanted."

"They wouldn't have gone the other way if I had really been Cattle Boss, would they?"

"Can you walk?"

"I think so."

"Come along then. You can take my hand."

His father's firm grip tightened over Little Mike's hand. He got up. The bottom of his feet felt torn and bleeding and every step was painful, but he would say nothing about that. It was bad enough that he had failed in calling the cattle, especially after having boasted that he could bring them in. It was bad enough that his father had seen him lying there with tears in his eyes and trembling.

Joshua Volkner said, "Well, Little Mike, you were a brave one."

"I see nothing brave about going after some dumb cattle," Michael Neumann corrected. "Especially when they've always been treated good. That big steer! I could collar him right now with one hand and ride him into the commune yard if it weren't Sunday."

"You Hutterians!" Joshua lamented. "Never show your feelings. Never let anyone know how you feel or what you feel. No, that would be too much like the world. That would be a sign of weakness and an admission that something is wrong with your way of life."

"You came to see the colony," Michael replied brusquely, quickening his steps. "All right, look! Over there is the potato patch and the berry garden and, if you keep your eyes open, you will also see we're going to have some watermelons. We have our own little world every day of the year, Mr. Joshua Volkner, and if you think private ownership is better, go to it! As for us, we'll take our communism and show you what it can do."

Little Mike felt his father's hand close protectingly over his. It was the strong clasp of security and guidance. He was hand in hand with the man he loved best and admired most among all men. He was walking through the *Vogelpfad* and the birds were singing just for him. Run, Missouri! his heart was saying. Go your thousand miles upstream and your thousand down. And run, Joshua Volkner, wherever you want to go! There is no better place anywhere in all the world than in the commune and no better life than the life of the Hutterians!

CHAPTER 2

*L*ITTLE MIKE lay in the soft dirt of the commune yard idly reaching out a hand to
rock his baby sister Leah in the homemade cradle. His
mother, seated on the house bench, was really rocking the
cradle with her foot while she knitted, and Little Mike
simply let the motion carry his hand along while he sang
snatches of a hymn which the colony members had sung
at Evensong a short time ago.

"Once more, O God, we near the end of day;
  The darksome night again is coming o'er us;
  But Thou, O God, dost still go on before us. . . ."

He paused and raised his head, brushed his hair from his
eyes and looked from the early evening sky to the familiar
commune.

"There's Michael father going over to talk to Joshua
Volkner."

Sarah's eyes lifted quickly like the hasty parting of a
curtain, then returned to her long wooden needles. She
gave the cradle an accented tap with her heavy shoe. "We
don't always report everything we see."

"Poor Joshua Volkner!" Little Mike sighed, and dropped
his head back into the dirt.

"Why poor? He's made a great lot of money, everybody
says."

"Yesterday when we came from the wheat field Michael father said he was poor," Little Mike replied. "So he's poor. And no one ever calls him Volkner Joshua—always straight out Joshua Volkner. That shows he no longer belongs in the commune or we'd call him first by his family name."

His sister Rachel came from the house and hastened to Sarah's side. "See how I am doing with the wedding apron, Sarah mother," she said happily, holding the apron against her body.

Her brown eyes swept the commune. She was looking for David Wiese, of course, and she hardly listened to her mother's comment. She bundled the apron into Sarah's hands and sat down on the bench. She took off her polka-dot head scarf and smoothed it out. Her dark hair was properly parted in the center and turned under to form a neat roll against her forehead. Now she folded the head scarf into its diagonal shape and put it on so that it covered her entire hair with the exception of the soft roll which framed her forehead. She tied the scarf carefully under her chin and it made her look very much like Sarah mother. But her mother's face was thinner and her features were sharper and her eyes did not have the eager light in them.

"There he is, Mother," Rachel whispered excitedly. "We're going for a walk."

She bounded from the bench, brushing some threads from her long skirt.

"Not out of anybody's sight," Sarah warned. "And, here, take the apron."

"Ruth is coming out soon," Rachel said, hurrying off. "She'll put it back safely into the wedding chest."

"Walk decent," Sarah counseled. "And be here before it gets dark." Then she added, "And don't hold hands when you walk together. Don't go outside the commune gate."

She fondled the deep-blue wedding apron.

Little Mike let the accelerated rocking of the cradle shake his hand. Dreamily he looked up to see pink-red sheaves of clouds gilding the colony acres. He rolled his head back and forth on the ground. With this motion he made the comune come and go, appear and disappear, chalk-stone houses, then sky; the big barn, then clouds; the women on the house benches, then endless space. With a slight turn of his head he could make realities vanish into dreams.

"You're here to stay, Sarah mother," he said, gazing up at her. "I won't make you disappear."

"Get up from the dirt," she told him.

Little Mike did not move. He knew from her tone that she did not really mean for him to get up. If his father had told him, that would have been different. He was glad he was a boy, glad he would be a man in the commune. Men had the say. "The man," said the Bible and Pastor Kunz, "is head of the house."

As he tried to comprehend this saying, he studied his mother. Sarah Neumann could have leaned against the house, but she would not. She sat upright, knitting. Her fingers were restless. He had often seen her at the spinning wheel, with Baby Leah on her lap, making the wheel sing and calling orders to his other sisters at the same time. *The man is head of the house.* Somehow his mother did not seem to mind. She had a manner of doing things that always seemed to fit in exactly with his father's plans. Her brisk ways and her quick words directed and ruled the household while Michael father really thought it was he who directed and ruled it.

"Sarah," Michael father would say, "look at Leah. Churchtime and you still have to wash her and put her to bed."

"Anna will do that. Anna's eight now and has good responsibility."

"Sarah, my socks. I can find nothing when I want it."

"They're on the bed, Michael, where you said you wanted them."

"Sarah, the children put something in my pocket. I told you that if they did a thing like that——"

"That's a sandwich I put there. You said yesterday that you get hungry walking in the timber looking for wood for the cabinet shop."

"Sarah, we ought to carry in water for the bath. Remind me of these things."

"Little Mike and I carried it in already."

Little Mike smiled when he thought how his mother was always just a little ahead of Michael father and yet how Michael father ran things with authority. *The man is head of the house.*

"I said get up," Sarah repeated. "Go and play with the boys. What's wrong with you tonight lying there in the dirt and making believe you are rocking the cradle?"

Her voice was always lively and she had a habit of beginning a sentence loudly and then letting the words fade away. This pattern was always exaggerated when she spoke with make-believe anger as now and he hummed the song as she glanced down at him.

"Foolishness!" she exclaimed in disgust, but behind the word she seemed to be smiling.

She sat knitting with the ball of yarn in the familiar honey pail at her feet. Just now she seemed no older than Rachel. The roll of hair turned under at the edge of her head scarf was like that of the older girls of the commune.

Playfully he said, "You're pretty, Sarah mother."

"Hush up," she said. "You'll wake Leah."

"You look like Michael father said he was sure Joshua Volkner's wife looked."

Sarah pressed her knitting to her breast and stared at him. "What kind of talk is that?" she probed.

"Michael father said he was sure that Joshua Volkner's wife painted her face because she's a woman of the world. And that," Little Mike explained with a hint of gaiety, "is just what the sunset is doing to you."

"You get up or I'll get the strap!"

But her fingers resumed their knitting and she put her face lower over her work, weaving her thoughts into the design.

"Your cheeks are so pink, Sarah mother."

"Well, it's not paint. Rouge or whatever they call it."

"Rouge," he repeated.

Pink and pretty was his mother's face as the sun tinted her high cheekbones and added a touch of color to her lips. Never had he heard his father say that she was pretty. Never did anyone say that anyone was pretty, but as he looked at her he remembered a picture on a calendar. Pictures were not allowed, but there had been a calendar once in the pastor's room with a mother holding a baby. Some said it was Mary and Jesus and the calendar was never seen again. Pictures of people were bad enough, the pastor said, but who would dare to make a painting of the Holy Child?

Sarah mother was like that picture. Her eyes were blue as her head scarf. Her long black dress was almost hidden by Rachel's deep-blue wedding apron which Sarah had spread over her lap. She was slender beneath her full black blouse. Only her hands looked old as she continued to knit and rock, knit and rock while Baby Leah slept.

"Ruth," Sarah called, "come and take Rachel's apron."

In a moment Ruth and Anna came out of the house and into Little Mike's line of vision. Ruth seized the apron with delight and held it against the faded-gray apron she was wearing. Her face shone as she asked, "How does it look on me, Sarah mother?"

"Wait four more years and I'll tell you," Sarah said with dismissal. "Don't get it in the dirt."

"Will I have as pretty a one when I get married?"

"Foolish talk!" exclaimed Sarah. "Fold it nice and put it in the wedding chest."

Ruth hurried into the house. Anna knelt beside the cradle and rocked it gently, giving Sarah's foot a rest. Little Mike locked his hands under his head. His sisters liked pretty things and so did he. Surely his mother did, too, though she made believe that it was best not to admire things at all. Of course, his sister Anna was too young to see anything attractive in the apron. She was a few years younger than he. As she bent over the cradle she looked like a little mother in her polka-dot head scarf and her long black skirt. She was barefooted and her feet were as dirty as his.

"Sweetheart Leah, sweetheart Leah," Anna chanted as she nestled her face against the baby.

"Now you woke her up!" Sarah scolded. "See if she's dry. Don't put her to bed wet."

"I'll take care of her. Come, sweetheart Leah, come!"

She lifted the baby out of the cradle and, crooning over her, carried her into the house.

Little Mike rocked the empty cradle, singing:

"Once more, O God, we near the end of day;
    The darksome night again is coming o'er us . . ."

"*Hovering* o'er us!" Sarah corrected in exasperation. "Sing right or keep quiet. Twice you make the same mistake. For the last time, get up from that yard!"

Little Mike sang happily:

". . . hovering o'er us;
    But Thou, O God, dost still go on before us.
    Both night and day obey Thy hand alway."

In a high, melodious voice, Sarah guided him on:

"With contrite heart I see night's shadow drawn,
    Throughout the day the world estranged me from Thee
    O Mighty God, be gracious in Thy judgment——"

"Little Mike! Up from that dirt!"

The spot in which Little Mike lay swirled with an instantaneous "Yes, Michael father," and he was on his feet, brushing the seat of his black pants, hurriedly pulling up the red kerchief that bound his leg and shaking the dust out of his hair all at the same time.

Joshua Volkner, amused at this exhibition of discipline, asked gently, "How is the leg today, Little Mike?"

The boy raised embarrassed eyes. "It never was bad in the first place," he said.

"Sarah," Michael announced, "Joshua Volkner stays with us tonight. That means somebody must get the washbasin from wherever it is."

"It's already in the room," Sarah informed him without pausing in her work. "With clean water in it."

"That so?" said Michael awkwardly. "Well, then it's attended to."

"Good evening, Sarah Neumann," Volkner greeted her.

"Good evening!"

"It's soon too dark for knitting, I would think," he observed.

"Sarah can knit in the pitch black," Michael boasted with an indifferent wave of his arms.

"I seem to remember that Sarah did that in the olden days," Joshua began.

"Well, then, you have a good memory," Michael grunted.

Joshua smiled. "Yes, I have, for things that made a special impression. And I find many memories returning now that I'm back in the commune once more."

"You were twenty when you left," Sarah ventured without lifting her eyes.

"When he escaped," Michael corrected her. "That's what he told us in the letter he wrote. Escaped? Ridiculous! Does anyone stand at the commune gate with a gun to keep us here? There's a better guard than that. God's will and God's law. You want to escape from that? Then, Mr. Volkner, you'll need a faster automobile than the one you have."

Little Mike stood at his mother's side and heard these words with admiration for his father's wisdom. But Joshua bantered good-naturedly, "I was going to say that I re-membered how Sarah used to knit long into the dark. You remember, Sarah, I told you once, 'You'll need glasses be-fore you're twenty.' I was wrong. You still don't look like twenty, but the *Stammbaum*, that stern genealogical chart which the pastor keeps, will very likely say that you're—— No, that can't be possible!"

"What can't be possible?" Michael wanted to know.

"That Sarah is thirty-eight."

"Listen to the worldling!" laughed Michael. "Age! That's the important thing in Joshua Volkner's world. There everybody must keep young. Women must paint their cheeks and spend their time under hair machines and get their faces fixed by a hundred artificial and devilish schemes. Think of it! An everlasting fight to stay young and go against nature. Here we're willing to be honest with time and even help time along. Here age is a blessing. Age brings wisdom and reverence. The *Stammbaum* may say I am thirty-eight, if that is what I am, but my beard can say I am fifty or sixty—I don't care. There's nothing worse in the world than the everlasting madness to stay young. Thank God that we Hutterians have more sense! Well, come into the house."

He started to the door and Volkner, with a hesitant glance at Sarah, followed.

The knitting needles paused. Sarah picked at a thread and pulled it into place.

Little Mike climbed up on the bench beside her, drew up his bare feet and wrapped his arms around his knees. Chil-dren moved in the commune yard. The Chore Men, with their black hats setting off their stoical, bearded faces, came from their jobs and entered their homes, letting the screen doors bang. Soon their wives went in, too, calling orders to the children. The pink-red clouds burned themselves out and now hung in the sky gray as ashes. The light was taken from Sarah's face as though the heavens were sorry that they had painted her like a woman of the world. Evening spread an autumn haze over the commune grounds, enveloping the buildings and drifting familiarly across the wide acres of colony land.

In the shadows Little Mike caught sight of Volkner's car standing alongside a commune home. Strange that it had been there all evening and all day and that only now he seemed to notice it. The boys had been warned to stay away from it, but there was no rule against looking as he looked now, straining his eyes until his imagination carried him across the yard and set him down inside, behind its glowing windows. He was reluctant to stay there even in his thoughts, for it was not a happy prospect to be carried out into the world. Yet in his inmost heart he wanted to go, even though he was afraid. Now he imagined that as he sat crouched in the car, Joshua Volkner came to take his place at the wheel. Volkner was "car boss"; and wherever he willed that the car should go, there it went. And Volkner was saying, "Come along with me, Little Mike." Where to? Over the river and out across the commune lines, far from the colony and the safe protection of the commune yard; far away from everyone he trusted and loved—from Michael father and the pastor and the elders, from Sarah mother and his sisters and the boys he knew—far away from all that was good, out into all that was bad, so far away that he could no longer hear the commune sounds or the singing of the old hymns at evening time. He snuggled against his mother and said half aloud, "Go away, Mr. Worldling, go away." Sarah trembled as if to shake off his words.

There was a long stillness as sometimes fell over the commune grounds. Then could be heard the squeak of a long-handled baby cart as a mother walked slowly to her home, pulling a child while leading another by the hand. Night sounds began to creep in from the fields as if warning that it was time for the kerosene lamps to be lighted in the windows. But Sarah sat on the house bench knitting, waiting with contrite heart the ending of another day as Hutterian women had done in Old Portage Colony for seventy-five years.

"Sarah mother, why did Joshua Volkner leave the commune twenty years ago?"

"Who knows that?"

"But why did he? Was it because he wanted to marry the girl from the outside?"

"It was the world," said Sarah shortly. Then she shrugged. "But he wishes now he could come back—that, anyone can tell just by looking at him."

"How?"

"How what?"

"How can you tell?"

"What has the world but trouble?" Sarah demanded, fortifying her own thoughts. "Wars and sin and private ownership."

"And the other that Michael father said, too."

"What?"

"Face painting and hair fixing and all that."

"Oh, that!" Sarah retorted impatiently. "That is most foolish of all."

"It is," Little Mike agreed. "Because you are pretty even when the sunset paint is gone. You are pretty as the calendar picture was."

"Silly!" said Sarah.

"Poor Joshua Volkner!" Little Mike sighed, with his chin on his knees. "And his father and mother are far away in a commune in Canada. Will he go to see them?"

"He telephoned to them, somebody said," Sarah admitted. "They have a telephone in that colony."

"If I would ever not see you and Michael father for even a day, I would be very sad," Little Mike told her.

"You just be good," said Sarah.

"How many communes are there in Canada, Sarah mother?"

"About thirty."

"And nine here in America," Little Mike announced in a voice of wonder. "I will be glad for the day when a new colony starts. I heard the Householder say that it might be soon, for we are nearly two hundred here. And when there are two hundred that's time to start a new place. I told Jake Linder that if always new colonies began, someday the whole world will be Hutterian. Wouldn't that be wonderful, Sarah mother, to have the whole world Hutterian? And if the whole world would be Hutterian, Joshua Volkner could not run away because there would be no place for him to run to. And to marry he could marry a Hutterian, as he should have done in the first place. Michael father just as good as told him."

Sarah's fingers moved the needles ever more slowly.

Soon they rested in her lap. The figures that moved through the commune yard were now part of the shadows, veiled in the darkness along with her thoughts. Evening had a way of gathering up half-forgotten memories and bringing them from the many tranquil corners of the commune back to their owners for the night. Could the boy sitting at her side know what she was thinking? Was it twenty years ago, that autumn night, after Evensong, when the pastor walked menacingly through the commune yard and stopped the Chore Men with a question, firmly asking the Farm Boss and the Cattle Boss and the elders, "When did you see him last? What did he say to you?" Was it twenty years ago that Joshua's parents sat in their rooms as parents sat tonight? "He was at supper, wasn't he? He must have gone during churchtime. He didn't leave a note. Not a word. Nothing. It's the world." They all said it was the world. Sarah Neumann, Michael's bride of three days, was sitting on a house bench that night, knitting. Michael was working in the cabinet shop. And now as Sarah remembered she leaned back against the house and closed her eyes. She stretched herself until her foot touched the cradle, Leah's cradle. Mary's. Anna's. Little Mike's. Ruth's. Rachel's. It should have been Little Sarah's, too.

She would never forget that night, the moving, searching lanterns, swinging in the hands of those who hunted through the quarries and the fields, those who would not bring themselves to believe that Joshua had run away. Plans were being made to drag the river when the news spread that a note had been found. Joshua had left a note concealed beneath the hymnal in his parents' room: "I am going into the world. Do not worry about me." The children who talked about it were sharply rebuked. Women gathered in groups in the commune yard. The men milled around the pastor's home, armed with parables and axioms from the wisdom of the past.

Sarah remembered how Michael came from the shop that night very late and found her sitting on the house bench. Breathlessly she watched him approach. She remembered the sound of his shoes in the yard, the sight of the shadowy figure swinging his arms, the ominous movement with which he dropped down beside her, and she thanked God that the night hid her face from him. She recalled the tense moment before he spoke, the eternity of waiting while he leaned back against the house, tilted his hat over his eyes and thrust his hands into his pockets.

"What a thing to do! He has turned his back on all of us and spit into God's face. I stopped in to see Adrian and Martha Volkner. There they sit with their other children. 'One black sheep cannot spoil six whites,' the Cattle Boss said. But there the poor parents sit and there's nothing to say. There's nothing to do. He could have been Farm Boss someday, just as I will be Carpenter Boss if I do good work and the elders agree on it. He wants the world. So we will let him go. Good-by, Joshua Volkner, good-by to you."

They sat together for a long time that night while Michael philosophized and consigned Joshua to the judgment. He never asked Sarah for her opinion. He had the say and she was glad for that. She was glad that the families which moved about the commune yard that night kept saying, "He'll come back." But Michael spoke of him as one who had died. Vividly she recalled how they went into the new quarters and how Michael scratched the match on the bottom of the table and lighted the kerosene lamp. His face was dark with a three-day growth of beard. In keeping with colony tradition he had let his beard grow from the day of their marriage. Resolutely he hung his black hat on a peg. "Joshua is gone. It's the world. The bait hides the hook. The Devil's long, lean fingers have finally come in between the wires of the commune fence. Joshua is gone."

She remembered how he looked at her with a love he never seemed to express, a love that was deep and compassionate behind his matter-of-fact and sometimes boastful manner. They got ready for bed and Michael knelt down to pray. He prayed long and earnestly, telling God all about Adrian and Martha Volkner who had lost a son. He assured Him that the Michael Neumann family through the years would keep the commune gate secure. And he prayed for Joshua, lost and roaming, homeless and alone. There was no song after the prayer that night and Sarah was thankful, for she wanted only to lie quietly in the feather bed in the dark while her thoughts ran wantonly out into the world. Wildly they carried her far beyond the reach of prayers or songs, but always she returned with the knowledge that firmly clasping her hand was the one she had promised to love and serve and obey until she died.

Little Mike was speaking. "Look, Sarah mother, how big and bright the moon is coming up! Pastor Kunz calls it the lantern of God. He says it is always shining somewhere even if we don't see it in the commune. Just as God is always everywhere even if we don't see Him."

The moon rose majestically, showering the commune

with peace. Little Mike felt a secret joy so secure that the far-distant hum of an automobile made him laugh to himself. No car could ever lure him away—not even Joshua Volkner's. The full glow of the moon was showing him what was good: the barns, the cows in the fenced-in-yard, the unpainted chalk-block houses, the shops and the little school where Evensong had been held.

"Was Joshua Volkner really a boy in the commune as I am, Sarah mother?"

"What are all these silly questions tonight?" Sarah demanded, winding the knitting around the needles. "That's all past. Who knows the way things go or what can happen to anybody? Didn't a boy in a Canada colony run away during the war because he wanted to be a soldier—?"

"He was killed," Little Mike interrupted.

"Yes, he was killed——"

"God's punishment. Wasn't it God's punishment because war is wrong?"

"Don't always ask questions and always have your own ideas about things. Go to bed where boys like you should be anyhow."

The trees were lovely in the moonlight and the roof of the big barn was trimmed with silver. A bat swirled around the house wall where they sat. It flew so close to Little Mike he could feel the stirring breath of its wings. Sarah sat with face inscrutable, her eyes absently following the erratic flight.

Little Mike's voice was hushed. "I remember what James the Teacher said, 'A bat will never touch you or fly against you. Still it cannot see at all. It has feelings. God put something in its nature that guides it.'"

Sarah reached down to pick up the knitting pail. "Did Joshua Volkner say how long he will stay?"

"He'll go tomorrow because he has business in Yankton."

"After that he goes back to Chicago," Sarah mused.

"He has only two children," Little Mike explained. "His wife has a lot of money. Michael father asked him if she had much money and he said yes. Michael father asked him if that was why he married her and he said no."

Sarah stiffened.

"The Householder told Michael father afterwards that it would be just as good if Joshua Volkner did not stay here too long," Little Mike hurried on. " 'He's living the way he wants to live and we're living the way we want to. America is big enough for all of us.' That's what the Householder said. America is big, Sarah mother. Our river runs a thousand miles upstream and a thousand miles down. But it is best right here where it comes through our land."

He raised his eyes to glance at his mother, for her fingers had covered his hand gently. How his heart leaped when he felt her caress! How jealously the moon shone on her and how beautifully the light sparkled around her. It was almost daylight, it was so bright. And the moonlight brought back Joshua's Volkner's car. When he saw it a sense of sadness for Joshua returned. The worldling had come back and no one was anxious that he stay. His brothers and sisters and his father and mother had long ago given him up. Would they want to see him even today if he went to visit them? They would never cover his hand as Sarah mother covered his. They would never sit together in the shelter of the commune as his mother and he were sitting now.

"Poor Joshua Volkner!"

Sarah, with an exasperated, fluttering motion, got up. "It's high time you went to bed," she ordered. "Bring the cradle and come along."

She went quickly into the house.

Little Mike sat for a moment with his chin on his knees. How plainly he could hear the voices from within!

"Sarah, Joshua Volkner sleeps in the children's room and they sleep with us. Little Mike can find a place on the floor. That's good for him."

"Everything is taken care of, Michael," Sarah assured him. "Rachel and Ruth are staying with Rebecca Mueller. There's plenty of room. After all, Joshua Volkner knows how life is in the colony."

"That I surely do, Sarah Neumann. But, Michael, how much easier life would be for your women if the elders could only be persuaded to put in a few conveniences— running water, electricity——"

"And how much better life would be for women in the world," Michael retorted, "if they just had fewer conveniences and a little more responsibility. Don't start to make comparisons between your world and ours because in such an argument you haven't got a chance. If you pound too hard on an anvil you'll only break your hammer."

Happily Little Mike jumped down from the house bench, picked up the cradle and put it over his head. Now he played that he was in a cage, but a cage that he could discard or press down harder, whichever he willed. Through the smooth round spindles he could see the moon and the commune. He could see Rachel and David Wiese walking together near David's home. Little Mike walked around, too, so that he could see the house benches and the outline of people who sat quietly and the forms of people who moved in the yard. Through his make-believe prison, looking this way and that, wandering here and there, he was possessor of all that he beheld. And as he passed a house he heard a family singing:

"Once more, O God, we near the end of day;
  The darksome night again is hovering o'er us . . ."

He twisted and turned his bare feet playfully in the cool dirt of the commune yard, joining the song, singing half to himself, half to the cradle, making sure that Volkner's automobile could see for itself that he was not one bit afraid of it, not any more than Michael father was afraid of the Angus steer. Then, laughing at the eerie shadows of himself, he went forward humming the song with a happy heart. Brightly before him the lamp was burning in his father's house.

CHAPTER 3

*M*ICHAEL NEUMANN sat in the center of the room on a sturdy, straight-backed chair that he had made in the cabinet shop. He took off his colony-made shoes and dropped them heavily to the unpainted, clean-scrubbed pine floor; then he pulled off his gray wool socks and stuffed them inside. He sat with legs outstretched, hands in his pants pockets, relaxed and at ease, exercising his toes and yawning when he felt like it. His black beard was untrimmed, his eyes had a deceptively dreamy appearance, but he made sure that nothing escaped him. He had watched Sarah enter in her customary efficient manner which no sooner brought her into the room than she was already magically getting things done. She put her knitting pail on the wall shelf, swooped a baby's dress from the back of a chair and picked up Michael's shoes in one uninterrupted motion. Then she went into the bedroom where the fretting voices of the children assailed her. Her voice quieted them quickly and the door was closed.

Michael saw it all and observed that she did not so much as glance at Joshua who sat at the table near the lamp, turning a leather-bound book idly in his hands.

Michael yawned and spoke in a detached way. "That's a book that James the Teacher wrote, all by hand."

49

"I see he still uses the style of the fathers, the capital letters in red and blue, carefully shaded, the beginning of each chapter impressively lettered. But to do it all by hand! A printing press would have done it quick."

"Yes," droned Michael, "and phonographs can sing songs, too. If you want us to be modern maybe you would suggest putting a record machine in our church service."

Joshua laughed. "I meant only that it would have saved time for James the Teacher. And be easier to read."

"Every child in the colony can read it," Michael boasted. "They've got good eyes. Furthermore, things that are important should be memorized."

Little Mike came in with the cradle on his head. As he set it down he grinned at his father, for he sensed a hint of amusement in Michael's eyes.

"Here, you!" Michael ordered. "Tell our guest what James the Teacher's book has to say."

Little Mike brushed his hair from his eyes, stood with hands obediently at his side and in a rapid, eager voice recited: "The book tells about Hutterian life and about Jacob Hutter from whom we take our name. He was killed in Innsbruck, Austria, in 1536, because he did not believe in war nor in the union of church and state. Great were his sufferings and great was his torture, but greater was his faith in his ideals. With joy he gave his life as a testimony to truth as others of us may be called upon to do. The Hutterian Brotherhood perpetuates the one true faith and the tradition of the apostolic church. This means being in the world but not of the world. It means living in a form of Christian communism as we are practicing it today here in America. The first Hutterians were Swiss Brethren——"

"All right, all right," Michael interrupted with a satisfied chuckle. "Our guest knows Hutterian history, too."

His eyes came around to his son and appraised him with a glance that was a warm and tender light searching and satisfied. Little Mike felt it and made believe that the glance meant nothing, but he knew now how his father felt in the cabinet shop when one of the men said, "That's a good table you made there, carpenter," or a woman quietly admitted, "You made me a fine wall shelf, Neumann Michael."

"Yes, I know the history," Joshua confessed. "But Little Mike does take me back to my boyhood. The days we sat under Daniel the Teacher, eh, Michael? The hundreds of things we had to memorize! The martyr hymns we had to learn! The prayers we had to commit, all in rhythm, while we stood with hands folded, palms together, like this, eyes straight ahead——"

"That's just the way we do!" Little Mike exclaimed.

"Quiet!" ordered Michael. "When a man speaks, a child keeps silent."

"We stood there for hours," Joshua went on, stirring up the past. " 'Once more, children, once more; it must be burned into your hearts, not just written on your minds. All together now: I believe in God—the Father Almighty ——' It went like clockwork: Daniel the Teacher beating time, the leather discipline strap in his hand, his head moving with a jerk like this—a big man, full beard, nearly eighty years old, one of the first settlers of Old Portage. 'Together, children, the books of the Old Testament: five books of Moses, Joshua, Judges, Ruth, Samuel, two books ... Now the Psalms: Blessed is the man that walketh not in the council of the ungodly——Joshua Volkner, how long have the Hutterian Brethren observed a community of goods?' 'Since the spring of 1528 in Moravia. Jacob Wiedemann spread a cloak before the people and all laid on it their earthly possessions——' "

" '—unconstrained and with a willing mind,' " completed Little Mike eagerly.

"Yes, yes." Joshua nodded. "That is how it went. That is surely the way it was."

Then, suddenly aware that he stood in the room and that his voice had grown loud and excited, noticing that the bedroom door had opened and that eager childish faces peered out at him, Joshua returned to his chair and sat down.

The children were snatched from the door by an unseen hand and the door closed. Little Mike looked at the solemn face of his father and quietly seated himself on the floor. He drew up his legs and rested his chin on his knees.

Joshua said, "Daniel the Teacher died shortly after I left, didn't he, Michael?"

"Yes. His work was done."

"Then came James Wiese. A new teacher but the old curriculum, the old method."

"If a thing is good, why change it?"

"But tell me, Michael, hasn't James the Teacher changed anything? I have the feeling he's a different man than old Daniel was."

Michael shifted in his chair. "He's a Hutterian," he said shortly. "The only difference is that he reads too much."

"And thinks too much?"

"There's no law here against thinking. You've talked to James the Teacher. What are you driving at?"

"I often wonder just what he thinks about the relative merits of your system over against our system. After all, he was the only one who ever went to school out in the world."

"For one summer." Michael shrugged. "That didn't poison him."

"I went to a school in the world for a while," Joshua explained, "and it taught me that there are many things that the Hutterians can learn without being corrupted."

"That's a trap you can set for us, but we need not walk into it," said Michael suspiciously. "Corrupt us with outside learning and you'll see the end of our way of life. We have our colony school and the children are taught what they should know. Hutterian teachings pure and away. A boy can still learn a trade from his father; a girl learns about raising a family from her mother. James the Teacher and Pastor Kunz can tell us about God, and for history we have the Hutterian tradition. All other education can stop right out at the colony fence. It's over-educated people who are farthest from God and it's over-educated nations who cause all the wars."

Little Mike clamped his arms around his knees and swayed delightedly under the fervor of his father's words. Nothing was ever more thrilling than when the men got together in their visits after churchtime, and now with Joshua Volkner in the commune there would be some mighty speechmaking. He knew, too, that the evening was just beginning, for the door opened and the House-holder sauntered in.

This tall, impassive, shrewd-looking man entered in a most casual manner. "Let it never be supposed that I came over special, Joshua Volkner, because you are here," he seemed to say. "I have more important duties than to engage in conversation with a man of the world." But he made himself comfortable on the unpainted clothes chest and dangled his black hat between his legs. He sat down without a word, but as his shadow passed over the room, Little Mike was assured that here was another mighty champion of the Hutterian cause.

Joshua said, "Good evening, Caleb Wiese," but the Householder merely nodded and stroked his graying beard. "Michael and I were talking about education," Joshua went on. "I contend that it's high time that you introduce a system which will let your people know what is going on in the world. And you ought to give your young people a chance to go on to school if they want to. All you have now is your little school where the children are indoctrinated with Hutterian teachings and your eighth-grade school which you must have to comply with the laws of the state."

"What do you recommend for us?" Michael challenged. "The kind of education that has put the world in the state it's in? The kind of peace that the world doesn't have? Religion that it doesn't practice? Or maybe the kind of money system that everybody is afraid of? Before you recommend any kind of life for us, you better give ours a chance."

"I gave it a chance," Volkner replied confidently. Then he glanced meaningfully from Michael and the Householder to Little Mike as if to say, "There are many things that I could tell you, but if I did you would accuse me of influencing your youth."

Michael read his thoughts. "Go on, speak!" he said

defiantly. "Don't be afraid that any of our children will be lured away by your piping."

"The great potentials going to waste here!" Joshua lamented. "The great potentials in all of you. But never any freedom, never any self-will. Never a chance to grow and improve. Never a chance for self-unfoldment. And if your young men did go beyond the commune, they would have to leave as I did, without money and without help. They would have to run away."

Michael was bewildered. "When a man has everything he wants, why should he run from it?"

"But you don't have everything. Why not admit it? Communism is a false hope, Michael, and when the great test comes, down it must go."

"May I remind you, Mr. Volkner," said the Householder pointedly, "that we have more colonies today than ever before?"

"True," Joshua retorted, "and they are all dying forms of escape. Hutterians came here from Europe in flight. Later many fled to Canada and now they are fleeing to South America, always trying to escape from reality, always tightening the commune fences, afraid that the world will swallow them up."

"To that, my dear sir," Michael mocked, "let me say that there has been only one Joshua Volkner in the history of our community. Only once has anyone failed to see that this way of life is best."

"It's not best, Michael. Twenty years in the world have taught me that."

Little Mike was conscious of feelings rather than thoughts; feelings for the bravery of the man who refused to tremble under his father's words; feelings for the enthusiasm of the stranger who had stood on his feet reciting Hutterian school learning. And now while Joshua was saying that every communal attempt in America had failed and that only the Hutterians still lived co-operatively, Little Jake Linder and Little Dan Mueller edged into the room. Jake, with the fleshy growth on the side of his neck, and red-faced Dan made silent steps as they entered, half-concealed by their fathers, who strode in boldly, black hats in hand. The shaggy-headed boys slid down beside Little Mike, nudging each other at the prospect of exciting happenings. They peered up at Joshua Volkner.

The man was a curiosity with his brown, well-pressed suit and a vest with a gold chain running across from one pocket to another. There he sat with his legs crossed, calmly dangling a shiny brown shoe, hands in his lap, occasionally rubbing his palms together as if to keep them warm. A necktie dotted with small brown flowers was tied closely under his white collar and the tip of a white handkerchief peeped out of his lapel pocket. His neatly trimmed brown hair was brushed carefully into place. James the Teacher had called him suave and urbane. His deep-set hazel eyes were wise and fearless as if they hid a great secret and had seen many wonderful things. Now he raised his hand to stroke his chin, and a gold ring flashed in the lamplight. Would the Hutterian men look like Joshua if they shaved and dressed as he did? How could they ever shave, for beards were in the tradition and Scripture plainly said, "Thou shalt not touch a razor to the corners of the face?" Joshua must have discarded that text along with many others when he went out into the world.

Little Mike, pondering on this, was confused by the fact

that the man looked well and strong and that God evidently
had not punished the worldling, even though he had cast
aside the only true way of life. Well, God had not punished
him yet. But surely He would. If not in this life then in
the life to come. What was it that Pastor Kunz said in
his sermon at Evensong: "The worldly rich have a good
time, but their time is short. This world is but a brief
sojourn and eternity is with God. Who will not do His
will for these few mortal years so that he may have endless glory in the everlasting years to come?" Poor Joshua
Volkner!

While Little Mike turned these thoughts over in his
mind, other men of the commune came into the room.
Here was the Bee Boss who knew all there was to know
about bees and honey. Here was James the Teacher with
a knowing light in his eyes, reading the scene as solemnly
as he read his books. Behind him was Thomas Moessner,
the Town Man, tossing a handful of toasted sunflower
seeds into his mouth as he entered. Little Mike searched
his own pockets for some but did not find any. Dan had
a few and shared them with him. Joshua looked at the boys
as if remembering the traditional commune treat.

The Cattle Boss and Blacksmith Daniel Mueller, Little
Dan's grandfather, came in. Young men and old men
were filling the room. Boys squatted on the floor so closely
together that Little Mike was squeezed in between Jake
and Dan. Men sat shoulder to shoulder on the clothes
chest and the three extra chairs in the room were occupied
by fathers who held young sons on their laps. Men stood
along the walls, dangling their black hats and thumbing
their suspender straps. By an instinctive grouping they all
seemed to flank Michael father, who still sat squarely in

the room, looking at them with his beard against his chest.

"This room wasn't built for a community hall, gentle-men," he quipped. "If more than the thirty of you come in, I'll have to move out."

"Build another room, Carpenter!" The Cattle Boss laughed. "The elders will give you permission."

"Turn up the lamp," Michael told him. "So many beards in here make things dark."

This provoked a round of laughter during which Joshua turned up the lamp, saying, "I can turn it up, Michael, since I'm sitting right beside it."

"I thought maybe you were too used to electricity by this time. Push buttons and switches—that's what makes the world go round, they tell me."

Little Mike shifted his position so he could keep a watch-ful eye on his father and also keep Joshua Volkner in sight as the man sat at the table against the outside wall close to the small-paned window. As for hearing every-thing, there was no difficulty in that. The men all spoke right out, having nothing to conceal.

"Push buttons and switches," Joshua repeated somberly. "Yes, that's not far wrong. And there is something about an old lamp that really makes a path back through the years."

"Well, Joshua," said James the Teacher, "he who is whipped by his own hand should not cry."

"Oh, I'm not crying," Joshua corrected. "I'd be the last to try to hold back progress."

"I wouldn't be surprised," said the Town Man, "if Joshua Volkner wasn't thinking of coming back to the colony. I get my fill of the outside just through my weekly trips to Yankton."

"Are you having that in mind, Joshua Volkner?" asked old Daniel Miller.

"No, I think not, Daniel." Volkner smiled. "This is purely a business trip, purely business."

Michael Neumann took the floor. "I say this to you," he insisted, facing Joshua squarely: "When a man knows the right way to live and doesn't live that way, there's a greater condemnation on him than on one who has never known the right way. The trouble with the world is *possessive* trouble, and that's what you have fallen into. You want to be able to say *my* house, *my* money, *my* gold watch, *my* automobile. That's what causes wars, hatreds and godlessness. You should know that, even if you have been out of the Hutterian way for twenty years."

"But just a moment, Michael!" Joshua smiled. "You are possessive, too, and rightly so."

"I?" Michael flashed. "I own nothing in the world. The chair I sit on, even though I made it, is not mine. The clothes I wear are not mine. Everything is the colony's. And the colony is a picture of what the world should be like. I, possessive? Don't make me laugh!"

Joshua put his thumbs in his leather belt and leaned back in his chair. "You say *my* children, don't you, Michael? And of Sarah you certainly say *my* wife."

"A ridiculous argument," said Michael in distaste.

"The comparison, friend Joshua," observed James the Teacher solemnly, "is unfair. The Scriptures intended man to possess a woman in order to replenish the earth in moral purity. I will put the morality of the Hutterian life above the standards of people anywhere. Yet, honestly speaking, I must confess I never say *my* wife nor have I ever heard Carpenter Michael say *my* wife in speaking of Sarah. We possess in keeping with the Bible and make as little of the matter as we can."

"Come now, James," Volkner chided, "you've been in the world. Why do you insist that your way of life is superior?"

"It is superior," maintained the Teacher, and the room seemed to relax. "There is but one way to judge a system and that is in terms of what it does for the individual."

Joshua's eyes twinkled.

"You see how contented and secure we are here," James the Teacher went on. "Nothing can entice us away. And I, of course, intend to see that nothing does. Give me a child until he is through the little school and he'll know which is the right way. No Joshua Volkners will ever come out of my regime."

"No system is perfect, gentlemen," Joshua announced. "None is completely right. So, now, what we must do is sit down together as we are doing, your system and mine, and say, 'Let's see what we're driving at. Let's see what your system has that I can use and what mine has that will be of benefit to you.' "

"Compromise is for men without convictions," declared the Householder.

"No, Caleb," said the Town Man. "It would be interesting to have Joshua Volkner tell us more. What is there in his world that makes it so attractive? I go to town three times a week and the happiest time for me is when I come back and see the commune gate."

"Now, gentlemen," Joshua told them, "let's be honest. Do you really feel that way, Thomas Moessner, or is that just a phrase you're accustomed to using?"

"Oh, now, you're accusing me of telling lies, are you?"

"Not at all. I'm simply interested in how a Town Man reasons."

Michael Neumann rolled up his shirt sleeves and bared his muscular arms as though a hard job lay ahead. Jake Linder nudged Little Mike. The men in the room nodded understandingly. Michael knew how to handle timber no matter how rough it was. "I would like very much to ask our worldling if, now that he has gained the whole world, he is happy? To put it frankly, Mr. Joshua Volkner, do you really enjoy the world with all its lying, stealing, whoring, scheming, wars and killings and sin? Do you want all of that more than the pure Hutterian way?"

Joshua turned the question over in his mind while thirty men pinned him down with probing glances. Little Mike stared at him, feeling he knew not what, but wondering how anyone could stand against his father's dreaded words. One thing was sure: the stranger was not a person to be hurried into confusion or to be forced to say what he did not really believe.

"We—you Hutterians must always be extreme in your viewpoints," Joshua began. "There must never be any middle ground. It must always be either-or. Since the world is a large place, of course there are all kinds of people. But there are also all kinds of good people."

"Isn't money the measure of everything, though, whether the people are good or bad?" asked the Householder.

"I would not go so far as to make such a general statement. Money is important. It is important in the colonies, too, is it not? How do you intend to expand here in America unless you make money? Why are you so frugal if money is not necessary?"

Tossing his head in disgust, Michael said, "A fox does not

go into a hole unless there are two holes for him to come out of. But I will put a straight question to our worldling. If he had to choose between being a rich man of the world or a poor Hutterian, which would he choose?"

Joshua's reply was firm. "I believe in the complete advantages of life, gentlemen. I believe in freedom—freedom of will and of work. The world offers me these advantages. The commune does not."

"It depends on what you mean by complete advantages," said James the Teacher.

"Personal liberty. The right to come and go unhindered. The right to find what is truth for myself. The right to think and to speak——"

"The right, the right!" shouted Michael. "Lucifer thought he ought to have the right, too, and the Lord had to throw him out of heaven."

"I mean the advantages of education, cultural things, inventions——"

"And I mean spiritual advantages," Michael countered. "I would rather build my house of *those* boards. First of all, *we* are living according to God's will——"

"But you narrow and compress your lives. You will tolerate no progress. You will allow no investigation of the world. Discipline comes first——"

"Discipline should come first," avowed the Cattle Boss. "A wild horse is good for nothing unless he learns who holds the reins."

"The standards by which we live are as different from those of the world as night is from day," Michael declared. "We do not believe in your capitalistic individualism. We do not believe that your education has made you better people. We do not believe in war and we refuse to bear arms.

We will never judge a man by the money he has or doesn't have, but that is the only measure you people know anything about. We know whom we can trust. We know on whom we can count. For seventy-five years we have lived in America as one great family and we are happy. Yes, we are happy even if you, as the exception, ran away so you could taste the bitter joy of the world."

Joshua held back the words that sprang to his lips. His eyes traveled around the group, touching the inexorable bearded faces without evoking a single responsive smile.

As his glance fell upon the aged blacksmith, Joshua said, "I remember when I was a barefoot youngster about Little Mike's age. Jacob Linder found me crying in his shop. I wanted a hoop and a stick, but I wasn't allowed to have one. You remember, Jacob, what you told me that day? 'God's love is a forge that bends the soul through its burning.' God's love is a forge——" He smiled at their silence. Then he sighed. "Well, I guess I am back in the fire!"

The Householder said, "It wasn't that the elders didn't want you to have the hoop and the stick; they knew that you needed discipline."

Michael spoke up. "Let the past be past. Let's talk about the present. You told us when you came that you were just in the neighborhood. Is that true or were you really getting homesick for the old colony?"

"Just in the neighborhood."

"On business?"

"On business."

"The grain business? We hear you're quite a rich manager or director or something in a Chicago concern."

"It's no secret that I'm with the Central States Grain Company," Joshua replied.

"You didn't say anything about buying our wheat when we walked through the field."

Little Mike spoke up impulsively, "That was on a Sunday, Michael father."

"There should be no business on Sunday," Little Jake chimed in.

"All right," said Michael sternly, "if you boys want to handle the conversation maybe the rest of us should go to bed."

"I think that was a good answer, Michael," Joshua asserted. "And after all, maybe someday we will do some business. If it weren't for us who buy and sell, where would you farmers be?"

"We would be right here." Michael chuckled wisely. "Ninety per cent self-sustaining! We could get along without the other ten if need be."

"You know as little about the world, brethren, as the world knows about you," Joshua told them. "When you come to visit me in Chicago——"

"For which you will wait a long time," Michael muttered.

"—when you come to visit me, I'll try not to find fault with what you believe. Here I am being wounded in the house of my friends." Seriously he went on: "I suppose the thing I notice most here, now that I've been in the world, is that you Hutterians never had the courtesies that we try to have."

"So that you can better cut one another's throats," boomed Michael, and the others supported him with comments.

"I mean courtesies and good sportsmanship," Joshua went on; "friendly exchange of ideas——"

"Which gets you nowhere," said Michael.

"But which is the only way in which we'll ever get together. In the world we are learning to give and take, and that's a good sign. We enjoy healthy amusements which hurt no one. When I think of the wonderful inventions and conveniences you could have, I would surely like to throw open the commune gate——"

"When the fox starts preaching," cried the Cattle Boss, "lock up your hens."

"Well, keep the gates closed then—" Joshua sighed— "but let me ask James the Teacher, is it because of discipline of body and soul that Hutterians will not even observe birthdays or anniversaries or make anything of such matters?"

From his position of authority, Michael answered before James the Teacher could frame a reply. "Such things are nonsense!" he contended with a sweep of his hands. "Furthermore, they are world-manufactured. Where does the Bible say we should keep anything but religious festivals?"

"But what's wrong about them? Must life always be lived in the forge? Maybe we in the world carry these things too far, but some of the most wonderful days are the times when we observe birthdays and holidays and special occasions. I remember on the fifteenth anniversary of our marriage——"

The bedroom door opened and Sarah came unobtrusively into the crowded room. The men, intent on listening to Joshua, paid no attention to her. She stood silently as Volkner paused and glanced at her.

"Yes, yes, on the fifteenth anniversary of your marriage?" urged Michael.

"We went to New York," Joshua said quietly.

Sarah's quick gaze searched the room for Little Mike.

"To New York," divined James the Teacher. "And to the theater, I suppose."

"Well, yes," Joshua admitted, "to the theater."

Everyone spoke at once.

"Pleasure! Pleasure is all the world thinks of!"

"Never have I been in a theater and never do I want to go."

"Oh, the Devil is cunning."

"You have gone a long way, Joshua, a long way."

"Then I suppose there were presents that had to be given?"

"Were there?"

"Why, yes," Joshua said awkwardly. "She gave me this ring."

Sarah made herself heard. "Little Mike, go over to Pastor Kunz and see if you can get a lamp. There is none for Joshua Volkner's room."

"Pastor Kunz will be in bed," said Michael.

"No," Sarah answered. "He still has light."

"Get along then, Little Mike," ordered Michael.

There was no excuse, no alternative. The golden ring on Joshua's finger, the excited whispers among the men, the hundred things that seemed ready to happen—all would have to be forfeited. Once in Little Mike's lifetime such a night, and he could not stay. Never before such a gathering in his father's house and he was being sent on a senseless errand.

"Mike, I said go!"

"Yes, Michael father."

He put one hand on the shoulder of Jake Linder and the

other on Dan Mueller and raised himself to his feet. He
adjusted the kerchief bandage on his leg. He hooked up his
shirt. Anything to take time. Anything to hear a little
more of the big talk. It seeemed to him that his mother
hesitated to leave, too. She lingered at the bedroom door.
And all the while the conversation was growing in excitement. He shoved his way through the rows of men and
tarried near the outside door. He looked through the wall
of men for one more glimpse of Joshua. He was glad that
he did, for Volkner just then took a gold object from his
pocket.

"I hope you don't mind if I smoke, gentlemen," he said
good-humoredly.

Bitterly Michael exclaimed, "Since your world allows it,
go ahead! But since you will not find an ash tray, I hope
you have brought your own."

"Here's a saucer on the table." Joshua indicated.

"Use it, then," grunted Michael. "The sins of the world
are no temptation to us. Show the young boys what a hu-
man chimney looks like."

Joshua put a cigarette between his lips and snapped a
flame out of a lighter. Every eye was on the hypnotic fire
and on the unbelievable sight of a onetime Hutterian un-
concernedly blowing a puff of smoke in the midst of the
elders and colony men. Sarah gazed at Joshua, and her hand
lifted heavily as if in warning and surprise. Then the bedroom door closed quickly behind her. It was enough for
Little Mike, too. Out into the moonlit night of the commune he went, wide-eyed at the courage of Joshua Volkner. But with a tinge of sorrow he consigned the stranger
fully and completely to the world of lost and godless men.

CHAPTER 4

~~~~~~

*L*ITTLE MIKE walked through the familiar colony yard to where the dim and yellowish lamplight burned in the room of Pastor Kunz. Through the curtainless windows of other homes he saw women knitting or a mother putting a child to bed. At the Jacob Linder home a group of girls were singing evening songs. The slow, solemn strains filtered through the walls and gave their own answer to Joshua's abdication. New York and the theater, birthdays, a gold watch chain, a flashing ring and the shocking sight of a cigarette—what did they mean? Of what use were they?

The peace of the commune drew Little Mike more and more into the unfalterable belief that only the ways of the fathers were right. He had heard about cities and towns, but who could imagine places of the kind that Volkner talked about where so many people lived together that no one knew his neighbor, and boys did not know the names of those they met on the street. In the commune everyone was known intimately. Little Mike knew all the boys, and their parents and grandparents. He knew every house and every crook and cranny in barn and shop. Now, as he walked, he lifted a carefree, playful hand to a low, squat structure of unpainted boards. He said, "Hello there, house of the Bee Boss, and behind you there, house of the Cattle Boss." He walked close against a large structure and scraped a stick along the chalkstone. "Hello, house of Daniel Mueller." In the flat-roofed second floor, which was made of boards, a light burned dimly. He looked up and waved, laughing. "Hello, house of Daniel J."

Daniel's son was called Daniel J. to distinguish him from his father. When Daniel J. was married, at nineteen, Carpenter Michael Neumann had built the second story. And when red-faced Little Dan, who was the son of Daniel J., got to be nineteen, he would marry, and Michael father would simply build another addition to the house. Not another story—that would be too high—but a few rooms to one side of the house.

That reminded him: when his sister Rachel married—soon now, for the banns had been read—she would move to her husband's home, to the rooms of David Wiese. David was a grandson of Pastor Kunz, and that would make Little Mike related someway to the pastor himself. Everyone in the commune seemed to be related, and that was why there was a *Stammbaum*, a chart that told where everyone belonged in the relationships of the communal system.

Close to the Mueller quarters was an unpainted board building with a slanting, shake-shingled roof and two windows which in the moonlight might have been widely staring eyes. The door in the center looked like a large nose. "Hello there, face house!" It was really the shoe shop. Inside those walls, Shoemaker Graebel had the correct size for every foot in the commune. All one needed to do was to go to him and say, "Shoemaker, I

need a pair of shoes." Shoe Boss Graebel usually managed
to repair the old ones, but if they were really worn out,
he would make a good solid new pair ready to put on. As
Little Mike gazed at the "face house," he wondered how
one got shoes out in the world. They had to be bought,
of course, with money, but who knew the size?

Which reminded him that Elizabeth Mueller, the wife
of Daniel J., had once wanted to buy a pair of factory-
made shoes. She had saved her allowance money, which
was thirty cents a month for the women and fifty for the
men. Everyone saved the allowance money if he accepted
it at all, and Elizabeth Mueller thought she would like
some shoes out of the world. "And if you buy factory-
made shoes," said the pastor, "pretty soon every other
woman will want factory-made shoes and then where will
we be?" So Elizabeth went to Shoemaker Graebel.

Walking past the gray outline of the low chalk-block
eating house and the adjoining community kitchen, he
thought of Joshua Volkner's children out in the world
and how terrible it would be to have to eat with strangers.
Who would know what to eat or when to eat unless there
was a Kitchen Boss and a kitchen crew? Who would say
the table prayers unless there was a boss to decide about
that? He looked at the building where the children ate
and wondered what would happen if no one had a prescribed place to sit or if the boys wanted to sit at the girls'
table or the girls at the boys' and if there was no boss to
say, "This is the way it must be."

Every roof silhouetted against the night was familiar
and whispered to him that he would find nothing like this
anywhere. It disturbed him to think that Joshua Volkner
had given up all of this in favor of the world. It disturbed

him, too, that he did not dislike the man and that he was even somewhat fascinated by the way in which he sat among the colony men unconquered, calmly smoking under the stern and stinging comments of Michael father. The stranger was a stronger man than Little Mike cared to admit, and the source of his strength was a mystery that annoyed Little Mike. Preoccupied by these thoughts, he pushed open the weathered door in the home of Pastor Kunz.

He was greeted by a stern voice. "Children should knock."

Startled into obedience, Little Mike said quickly, "Yes, Pastor Kunz."

He went out faster than he had come in, meekly closed the door and rapped.

"Yes, yes," came the dubious welcome. "After you spit in a man's face, 'excuse me' doesn't make him feel any better."

Little Mike came in, chastened.

Pastor Kunz sat at a small square table with his big Bible open before him, peering at the pages through his thick-lensed spectacles and tracing a line slowly with his wrinkled hand. Without looking up, he asked, "What brings you here like Nicodemus?"

"Sarah mother asks for a lamp."

The pastor bent lower over the Bible until his white beard touched the pages. "Is it so dark at your house that you need another lamp?"

"One for Joshua Volkner."

"Yes, yes. Joshua Volkner. He needs light to be sure. Selma, get Little Mike the lamp."

In a shadowed corner of the room, near the dark and

deeply recessed window, the pastor's wife paused in her spinning and quieted the wheel. She brought her pudgy, rotund body heavily to her feet. Her round, wrinkled face peered from between the folds of her polka-dot head covering with a kindness lurking behind make-believe severity. She took a few steps and then, as if remembering her affliction, took her hickory cane from where it hung on a nail against the gray, plastered wall. Graciously grumbling about her rheumatism, she sighed and said, "At sixty, one is already more than half in the next life." She smiled wistfully at Little Mike. He looked at her and loved her. He loved her for the way she smiled while in apparent suffering. He liked the way the cord of her green apron was tied around her waist, the string cutting deeply into her loose-fitting black dress and into the flesh.

"How long will Joshua Volkner stay?" she asked in a tone that said it did not matter whether anyone answered her or not.

"He should go tomorrow," murmured the pastor into his book. "I do not see him as a good influence."

"I know—" Selma nodded—"but what can be done about it?"

The pastor looked at her over his spectacles. "We cannot help it if a bird flies over our head," he told her, "but it is our fault if he makes a nest in our hair."

Little Mike grinned at this worthy saying, and Selma chuckled as she started for the ladder with its solid, wide rungs. She put aside her cane and grasped the sides of the ladder contemplating the ascent.

"Once when a visitor from the outside dropped in," she remarked, "he said I should have eaten oranges when

I was young; then I wouldn't have the rheumatism. In the first place, how should I know that? In the second place, where would the oranges have come from?"

She put a heavy foot on the first rung, pulled herself up that far and rested.

Pastor Kunz grimaced. "Yes, the same man said I should have eaten carrots and my eyes would be better. The world has an answer for everything." He held the Bible in both hands. "Sometimes I think my eyes are getting better."

Selma went up another step. "Maybe it's second sight coming to you," she said.

The pastor replied impatiently, "Whatever it is, it is God's will. He gives everyone a cross according to his strength."

Selma sighed and went on up.

Little Mike sat on the clothes chest turning the pastor's words over in his mind. It was wonderful to be as wise as Pastor Kunz. Michael father always said, "The pastor is no different from any of us. He owns no more, he can claim no more, his house is no better and his table is no sturdier than mine. But because the heart of the commune life is religion and because we have chosen him to be our spiritual leader, it does make him different to an extent. Just as all wood is good wood, but cedar is best."

Little Mike spoke softly out of his thoughts. "Was Joshua Volkner really a boy here in the commune—just as I am?"

Unhearing, the pastor mumbled Scripture to himself in a low voice. Little Mike watched him, listening to the rhythmic, nasal singsong of the words. Sometimes it sounded like grain being ground in the mill. Sometimes the voice was a chant, pretty as the songs at the services. For the first time Little Mike seemed to understand why the reading of Scripture and the singing were in High German. It was softer than the Tyrolean dialect which was used in the colony in everyday conversation, and it was prettier than the English which nearly everyone could speak.

Pastor Kunz sighed and turned a page.

"Is he a wise man?" asked Little Mike.

"Joshua Volkner?" Pastor Kunz groaned and his frail shoulders contracted as if in pain. "Wise he thinks he is," he replied with his eyes on his book, "but, oh, so ignorant! He can tell you everything that is happening in the world, but himself he does not know. Books he is reading all the time, but the greatest Book remains to him a mystery. He has traveled much, but he has found no home."

Selma's heavy round body appeared on the ladder, filling the trap-door passage. Little Mike went to the ladder and relieved her of the kerosene lamp.

"I must dust it first." She sighed again. "Time was when Joshua Volkner would have done it for himself. You can tell him this was the lamp his parents used for a while. When you are through with it, give it to the House-holder. Shouldn't he, Jacob?"

"Yes, yes," agreed the pastor. "Very likely the House-holder is there now at the visit."

"He is," Little Mike assured him. "Many are there, but Michael father is giving Joshua Volkner hard things to answer."

"Just let your father remember that it takes a strong broom to sweep back the ocean. The world is that ocean and Joshua is a broken dike through which it would come into the colony."

"Don't you want to go over and see what is going on, Jacob?" Selma asked.

The pastor ran a finger through his beard and sat for a long moment thoughtfully twisting the tangled white strands. His thinning gray eyebrows contracted above his spectacles.

"I should go?" he said, sniffing distastefully. "What have I to learn from Joshua Volkner?"

Selma dusted the lamp. "What he can learn from you is what I was thinking of," she told him.

Her words had a sly, kindly lilt and she saw to it that they were lost in a heavy sigh of resignation. She handed the lamp to Little Mike and shuffled without her cane over to her spinning wheel. The low, backless seat groaned with her as she sat down. She smoothed the white wool as gently as if it were lining out of a fleecy cloud. The wheel turned and squeaked under her rhythmic treading. Then the pastor's hands came down on the table with a bang. He got up as if called, shoving his chair back and straightening his short, lean body with effort.

"Selma, my coat!"

Smiling with a touch of achievement, Selma stopped the wheel and got up. "Age and the rheumatism," she complained. "Double trouble."

Pastor Kunz took his blue vest from the back of his chair and put it on over his gray, tieless shirt. Slowly he snapped up the hooks and eyes. Little Mike waited, thrilled at the prospect of having the pastor go with him. Selma came with the short, black jacket and held it for him while he slipped his thin arms into it. Then she scraped over to get his black hat from its peg above the bed. The pastor took it and set it squarely on his head. "I want to see the Householder about a matter anyway," he explained defensively.

Selma nodded happily and went back to her spinning. Pastor Kunz started toward the door, then remembered that he had not closed the Bible. He did so now and laid it reverently in the center of the table. Squinting at Little Mike who stood faithfully holding the lamp, he asked, "Why carry a dark lamp on a dark night?"

"It's bright moonlight, Pastor Kunz."

"A light will help with baby wagons and who knows what in the yard. Selma, a match!"

"Won't lighting it break the chimney?" Little Mike asked.

"A match, Selma!"

The spinning wheel stopped and Selma got up. She shuffled her way to the wall shelf where there were stick matches in a jar. Little Mike set the lamp down and removed the chimney. Selma struck the match on the bottom of the table.

"Leave it turned low," she ordered. "It works up by itself."

"Yes, yes," murmured the pastor; "just like some men. They climb so high they end up in smoke. Well, come along, Little Mike."

They went outside and Mike hesitated, wondering whether Pastor Kunz wanted to walk ahead.

"Go on, go on!" ordered the pastor. "The man with the light leads the way."

Had anyone in the commune ever had such a pleasure? Had any boy ever lighted the path for the boss of bosses? Even the moonlight made way as the charmed circle of light which he carried started up the dirt path; past the blacksmith shop and the cabinet shop—that was the closest way—then on to the board sidewalk which was raised slightly where it went over the soft dirt near the home of Titus Wiese, the Hog Boss; through the yard between the homes where long-tongued baby wagons and holes which the boys had dug made it necessary to thread a cautious course. But Pastor Kunz merely said, "Go on, go on! I've walked this for sixty-eight years." And when a woman looked out of a doorway to inquire about the light passing by, the pastor said, "If you were in bed, Liza Linder, where you should be, nothing would trouble you."

The lamplight mingled with the moonlight and filled the tree branches and the house walls with shapes that might have been the Angus herd. This time they followed him. He could have walked on forever and been happy. What was better than to be near Pastor Kunz? Better even than to hear Joshua Volkner's talk about the world was to hear the sound of the pastor's steps close behind him.

All too soon he heard his father's strong voice dominating the conversation inside the house. A few older boys hovered outside at the open window, listening, pressing their faces against the panes to see what was going on. A row of bearded men leaned against the house, hands in their pockets, black hats on their heads. A whisper passed among them: "It's Pastor Kunz! Sure enough!"

Little Mike went straight to the door and entered with the pastor at his heels. The men in the room made way for him. Little Dan Mueller and Little Jake Linder and the other boys gaped up at him as he marched in. Could they know the pride he felt? Could they hear the inner voice that said, "This is a night you will never forget. See how Michael father looks at you proudly!"

The men squeezed themselves tighter against the walls to make room for Pastor Kunz. Volkner got up from his chair at the table.

Michael Neumann sprang to his feet. "Welcome, Pastor Jacob! Here, I have this chair all warmed for you."

Little Mike marched to the bedroom and his mother opened the door at exactly the right moment. With characteristic haste she took the lamp. Excitedly he whispered, "Pastor Kunz came along."

"You go to bed," Sarah told him.

"To bed? On such a night? Who could sleep?"

"That I agree with," she confessed, and he knew from her voice that she did not blame him for going back among the men.

Jake moved over to make a place for him and Dan pulled him down so hard that he landed on the floor with a thump. No one noticed and no one cared. He brushed his hair out of his eyes, clasped his arms around his legs and hoped it would be a long evening.

Joshua Volkner stood at the table. "It was good of you to come, Pastor Kunz. I would have felt badly leaving in the morning without a chance to talk to you."

Pastor Kunz remained standing although Michael Neumann again offered him the chair. He despised even to remove his hat and remained planted in the center of the room, his blue, birdlike eyes piecing together the scene. His stooped posture thrust his face slightly forward and his eyes bored into the apostate as if dragging every secret sin out of the past.

Then, shaking his head ominously, he said, "Oh, Joshua Volkner, if you were still one of us, how our hearts would burn to have you speak! How many things we would have to ask you and how much we would have to say! But you are gone and there is no path where our thoughts can meet. There is no bridge that reaches across the gulf between us. There is no light in which we both can stand. You have come unto your own, but we cannot receive you. What a pity! I was reading tonight how the Apostle Paul said of his faithless helper, 'Demas hath forsaken me!' Having loved this present world more than the glory of the world to come. Yes, yes, that is it. An old story has been repeated."

Slowly Joshua ground out a cigarette in the saucer, turned it round and round until there was no more fire.

"Remember what I tell you, Mr. Demas," Pastor Kunz admonished. "The path a man chooses to walk in he must take, though the stones bruise his feet until they bleed and the valleys are darker than he can bear."

"Come, Pastor Jacob," said Joshua gently. "Forgive me for what I did so many years ago and let us be friends and brothers again."

The pastor shook his head. "Forgiveness is easy, but one does not put out fire with straw. Let us say we do forgive you. Then what?"

"Why, then the wall between two worlds will be broken down."

"Between the world's people and God's people there

must always be a wall," proclaimed the pastor. "Between the world and God there can be no compromise. You are not running from us. You are running from everything that you know to be good and true. But you will continue to run though your feet bleed and your heart faints. The world has you, for it is the world you want."

"The world is not as you think it is, Pastor Kunz——"

"I know. It is worse."

"Then let's redeem it. But we never will by isolating ourselves and by withdrawing from society. Come, then, show people that you have something they need."

The pastor looked at him coldly and turned to appeal to the crowded room. "Satan's emissary, brethren," he told them. "An ambassador of darkness comes to offer us the kingdoms of the earth. Ah, Joshua Volkner, how men have blinded you! Have you forgotten that there can be no salvation or hope for the world unless one group somewhere upholds the only ideals that can save mankind? I mean nonresistance in a world that says there must always be war; equality where men say there must always be rich and poor."

"Ah, but Pastor Kunz, these principles are constantly being preached in the world——"

"Preached," the pastor broke in, "but are they being lived? No, Mr. Demas, we will keep on as we are and when the world is finally ready to destroy itself, someone will say, 'Maybe those old Hutterians were right after all.'"

"Bravo, Pastor Jacob!" shouted old Daniel Linder. "And it won't be too long before that happens."

"But, gentlemen," Volkner chided good-naturedly, "are you right and is everyone else wrong? Will you condemn people whom you do not know and pronounce a judgment on a system which you refuse to investigate? Shame on you for that! Here you are enjoying the privilege and freedom of a land which you will not defend. You criticize the country but you have never voted in an election. You will not get acquainted with your neighbors and you will not keep up with the times."

"You were in the world and tried to redeem it," exclaimed the pastor contemptuously. "And it has only corrupted you. Why wish the same disaster on us? Walk among the lame and you will soon limp. Good luck to you, Joshua Volkner! It is good luck you must have now that you have thrown God out of your life."

"Come, come, Pastor Kunz! I have not thrown God out of my life at all. Sometimes I think my experiences in the world have helped me find Him."

"A god in your own image, yes!" stormed the pastor. Then he quite unexpectedly changed his tone to a melancholy whisper. His eyes softened and in a chanting voice he said, "It is given to all men once to die. There is no escape from that, Joshua Volkner. You can run from the colony and from the elders, from parents and loved ones and from me. But there is always the last day coming. There is always the judgment. To every man, the inevitable hour. There he is at his destination. He may have deceived many people along the way. Now he reaches the end. There he is, as he is. It is over. He has had his chance and now he stands naked and alone before Almighty God. In that day, Joshua Volkner, I would not be in your place. Remember what I have said."

For a moment no one spoke. The night lay silent in

the room. The frail-looking man in his black hook-and-
eye jacket raised a wrinkled hand to his eyes.

"Yes, yes!" mourned the aged Linder. "And how near
some of us are to that day, how very near!"

Joshua insisted quietly, "But Pastor Kunz, if a man is as
good as he can be in this life, how can God possibly condemn him in the life to come?"

Pastor Kunz looked at him in complete amazement.
"The world has done its worst," he said finally. "Are you
God that you know what God will do?" Emphatically he
appealed to his hearers. "There, brethren, you can see
what happens. You can see how the world drains a man
of truth and reason and leaves him as it has left one of our
own people, one of our own flesh and blood." He raised
a warning finger and his eyes flashed as he included everyone in the room. "Take care that it never happens to any
of you."

"To whom should it happen, Pastor Jacob?" asked
Michael Neumann, springing forward and gripping the
old man's hand.

"Never to any of us," came the assuring voices. "Would
a man run into the fire of his own free will?"

Michael said, "It's a good thing this evening came along,
for it has been a lesson for all of us."

"I agree with you," Joshua admitted with unquestion-
able sincerity. "The world and the Hutterians have never
met as we are meeting tonight. You've been honest with
me, Pastor Kunz, and I shall be honest with you. The
world is what we make it. If we are looking for sin we
find it, and if we are looking for salvation we find that,
too. The world throws a man full force on what he believes. That is the test. No commune elders or commune

pastor to shield him; a man stands by himself and he must prove what he believes and what kind of man he really is. No one can build a fence around his life. No one can find a place to hide."

The men listened attentively. Joshua went on: "Ah, Pastor Kunz, I wish you knew the world, and I wish that you could see America as I have seen it from one shore to the other—the open roads and the land and the people. I have been over it all, and that is the only way anyone can really find out about it. And do you know, once I flew over this colony? From above the earth Old Portage looked like any other farm settlement, like any part of the South Dakota country; nothing exclusive, nothing superior. There it lay and from where we were flying it was almost impossible to see the commune fence. Yes, I had to look very hard from up there. At such a distance all land appears to be one land, all life dissolves into one life, all people into one people, all belief into one belief. When we rise high enough there is only one truth and one creation."

"Just because a man can fly above the earth does not make him the Creator," said the pastor severely. "But that is just another example of the way things are going. The greater man has become in these things, the smaller becomes his God. Man fortifies himself with money so that he no longer needs the care of heaven. Once he prayed for protection; now he trusts in armies. Once his power was in the Lord; now it is in the state. In the olden days he was always seeking divine counsel; today his own mind is good enough for him. Once he prayed for the sick; now he has his own cures for every disease. He used to seek for heaven in the world to come; today he must have it here and now or he feels that he is cheated. Fear and wonder have gone out of the life of man and to see the result, go and walk once more through the world."

"So there is no good in it anywhere?" Joshua asked.

"None!" cried the pastor contemptuously. "He who has God for his friend must ever have the world for his enemy. The Devil has fitted you with his own glasses. Better you were blind, Joshua Volkner, and could still call your soul your own. Good night—and a dark good night it is."

Beckoning impatiently to the Householder, he turned to the door. The men who had stood silent stepped aside and the Town Man whispered, "Good for you, Pastor Kunz, good for you!" They provided a sheltered corridor for him as he stamped from the room with the Householder obediently at his heels. Outside the screen door banged and it was the signal for everyone to begin speaking excitedly. Gesticulating with hands and hats, men murmured to one another on the merit of the pastor's words. They turned their backs deliberately upon Volkner as if to show their prejudice and to remind him that they wanted no part of his worldly kingdom.

But Michael Neumann, rolling down his sleeves as if the hard work was over, asked, "Well, Joshua, have you anything else to say for our betterment?"

"Nothing," said Joshua patiently. "Nothing else."

"You have seen a most remarkable example of communal life," Michael exclaimed proudly. "The things I felt, Pastor Kunz put into words. That, you see, is a wonderful advantage. Here in the commune there is always someone to do the job."

"But does he express your ideas, Michael?" Joshua asked. "Do you really believe as he does?"

"Do I?" Michael cried. "Be assured, Joshua, that we still have a community of spirit as well as a community of goods. Do I believe as Pastor Kunz does? Don't make me laugh! Here we are all of one mind. And that is the way our children are going to be, too. They follow our pattern. My son Mike will think as I think. That is as natural as that he will someday be colony carpenter." His gaze found Little Mike sitting enraptured on the pine floor as if everything that had been said had been recorded in his eyes. "How about it, Little Mike? Do you want to be colony carpenter someday?"

"That is all I ever want, Michael father."

"Good sense runs in the Neumann family," Michael acknowledged. "But, gentlemen, everything has been said on the matter that can be said. We can't change Joshua Volkner's mind if we talk till morning and he can't change ours if he talks till doomsday. I am for sending us all home. Tomorrow is another day."

"Yes," agreed the Cattle Boss, "and there's a truckload of cattle to be taken to town in the morning. We have a stock car ordered to ship them to Omaha."

"Don't tell me you're doing business with the world, John!" Joshua laughed.

"That's as far as it goes," the Cattle Boss retaliated. "Somebody has to see that America gets first-class meat."

There was laughter at this and Joshua joined in.

Michael waved a quieting hand. "One moment!" he cried in sudden thought. "We don't break up a meeting like this without a song. Since Joshua Volkner leaves in the morning, I think he should go with a good taste in his mouth."

"Yes," agreed James the Teacher, "no matter if part of

the meal is burned, let the last mouthful be tasty, and the dinner was good."

Michael Neumann threw back his head dramatically and proclaimed, "We Hutterians have a 'Great Song!'"

"Yes, yes," answered the men. " 'The Great Song' indeed!"

"We have a song that you may not remember, Mr. Demas," said the Town Man.

" 'The Great Song?' " Joshua repeated thoughtfully. "That is one a man does not easily forget."

"Of course not," Michael said, laughing, "for it is difficult to learn. What comes easily one holds too lightly, but when one must spend days and weeks and months to learn a thing, that is different. 'The Great Song' it shall be."

Little Mike sat upright between Jake and Dan. Great was his expectancy as the crowded room leaped into excitement and as the men vowed they would sing all thirty verses. Few were the occasions when "The Great Song" was sung; many were the hours that Hutterian children spent in memorizing its words. It was a "special time" song only. For the church service it was too long. For at-home singing it was not suitable. "The Great Song" needed many voices and the right occasion, an occasion like this, rare as it might be, when a sinful prodigal returned to his father's home.

Michael was already intoning the first line:

"Come, brothers, and let us sing of the true faith."

The chorus of men joined in unison on Michael's second word. Always they would join in on the second or third word. Michael Neumann as the *Ansager* would start every line and that would be their cue to mingle their voices with his.

> "Let us tell you of our history,
> How we were driven from Germany,
> Into Moravia, into Hungary, into Transylvania;
> Let us sing of how we fled from Sabatisch to Levar."

The voices were a mighty wind rising. They were the torrent of the river at springtime. The cramped, crowded room became for Little Mike the center of the universe. He sat intently blending his voice with the voices of the men, singing loudly the words that he knew, humming and groping for lines which were still unfamiliar. Sometimes his heart seemed to stop, he listened so breathlessly. Then the song rushed over him, and the voices and bearded faces and strong fists gripping the rims of black hats made him gasp as if he himself had been running from the world back to the rescuing shelter of the commune.

> "Let us tell you how our brethren were beaten,
> And how no one would offer them refuge;
> How emperors, priests and reformers despised them,
> Hunted and killed them mercilessly, without pity."

Little Mike leaned across Dan Mueller so that he could get a better view of "Mr. Demas." Dan pushed him back into place. It did not matter. He had caught a good look at the onetime Hutterian. He felt he knew what the song was doing to Joshua. It was taking him back through the long years and making him a boy in the commune once more. He was standing in the Hutterian school committing the words, hands over his heart, palms together, eyes straight ahead.

"We petitioned the Russian government
For permission to live in that vast country.
We dared settle in the Molotschna region
Until we were driven from there by the sword,
And robbed and plundered and newly persecuted.
Why? Why? Because we believed and lived the
     only true faith,
Because we would not be shaken from the way of
     God."

Was Joshua Volkner singing? His lips moved, but he seemed only to be repeating the words slowly to himself. He was turning them over and over, as Michael father turned a board before using it for building, this side and that. Joshua sat at the table examining every line.

The song went on to tell how the community of goods was for Hutterians the "highest command of love." The glory of the Hutterian life, its enviable history, its unyielding ideals, its hopes, its martyrs and its people marched through "The Great Song" under the banner of an avenging and all-remembering God. It told of trials yet to be faced and gave assurance that all believers would be molded into one brotherhood possessed of an inner joy surpassing anything yet dreamed of by mankind.

"Die if you must! Go to the stake, the firing squad!
Give your head to the gallows! Only be true;
Only and always be true to God and the fathers."

The voices transported Little Mike to heights he had never known. Good Hutterians everywhere on earth were singing—the women and girls in their homes, Pastor Kunz and Selma, Hutterians in Canada, in England and in

South America, Hutterians in the free land that was America, in the colonies in South Dakota and Montana. On and on went the song and he suddenly realized that he was standing with Jake and Dan, stamping his feet and clapping his hands. Michael father was hammering the air with his fists; the crowded room was marching and the men outside the house were marching, and Hutterian history was marching, from Jacob Hutter in Innsbruck to Little Mike Neumann in Old Portage, South Dakota. Everything was marching and the world was being left farther and farther behind. The song was swelling over the mountains and echoing in the deep valleys. It was singing in the chalk cliffs and stalking through the prairies. It was calling to settlements and cities, and it was spreading over the waters of the Missouri a thousand miles upstream and a thousand down!

Don't you hear it, Joshua Volkner? Don't you see the communes on the march? See the South Dakota communes: Bon Homme, Wolf Creek, Rockport, Rosedale and Old Elm. Michael father sets the word and tone for another line. Why do you sit there with your fingers going back and forth on your gold watch chain? Don't you remember? Doesn't it all come back to you?

Joshua's clean-shaven white face held only a deep, mysterious, saddened smile. Lost and homeless he seemed, deserted and forgotten, left by himself in the world where there were only sorrow and sin and loneliness and war, just as the song described. Rich he might be, thought Little Mike amid the thundering climax of the singing— rich in worldly things—but Pastor Kunz was right: The man had nothing. Nothing at all. Poor Joshua Volkner!

CHAPTER 5

~~~~~~

*T*HE next morning as day was breaking Little Mike was awakened by the determined shove of a heavy homemade boot turning him over on the floor where he had slept. He looked up along the baggy legs of black, patched pants, up along the faded blue hook-and-eye shirt to his father's bearded face canopied by the straight-brimmed black hat. A voice came down to him jestingly: "If you sleep that good on the floor maybe I should stop building beds for the colony."

"I sleep good anywhere, Michael father."

Michael grunted. "Get up and help your mother. The bell has rung for milking. We're all late."

Michael Neumann strode from the room expecting that he needed only speak to be obeyed. Ordinarily Little Mike would have jumped up, but for once he remained on the pallet, stretched himself and locked his hands comfortably behind his head. Morning looked in through the small-paned window and told him not to hurry. "There should be a special morning after a special night. Take your time, Little Mike."

Interpreting the sound of a child's cry, the faraway cackle of the geese, the creak of a laundry cart, the voice of the Cattle Boss calling for helpers to round up the Angus gave him an idea of the time of day. It must be a

90

little after five-thirty. Milking was between five-thirty and six. Breakfast followed whenever the milking was done and the commune bell always sounded a five-minute warning. He heard Blacksmith Linder clear his throat loudly in the yard. Little Mike knew without rising that the blacksmith was washing himself at his house bench next door. He always cleared his throat that way every morning. Someone passed by close to the window, humming the marching tune of "The Great Song" as though the melody still echoed in his heart. It sounded like the Householder. He was very likely on his way to check with the truckman about the cattleload.

When Little Mike thought about this he wondered why he did not jump up at once and hitch a truck ride out into the field. It would be an exciting ride over the bumpy road, and it would be a great sight to see the cattle rounded up and to hear the Cattle Boss call, "*Mo-kaa.*" Jake Linder would be there. So would the other boys. Maybe the Cattle Boss would have to lasso the big steer. But just now none of these things seeemed important. The flush of light at the window told him that it was morning all over Joshua Volkner's world and that the stranger still lay sleeping on the other side of the thin pine wall.

He raised himself up. On the sturdy bed Baby Leah slept peacefully, tucked in between two pillows to keep her from rolling off. The bed against the other wall was empty. Anna and Mary had occupied it during the night, and he contemplated how comfortable it would be to enjoy the deep feather mattress for a while and wait for Joshua to stir.

Instead he got up and walked between the two beds and leaned for a moment on Rachel's wedding chest, looking out at the waking of another Hutterian day. The kitchen women were bestirring themselves and smoke drifted lazily from the kitchen chimney. The geese were coming in and the pet lamb was ambling through the yard with the brown colony dog sniffing at it. There went the Cattle Boss, riding the big black horse bareback. There hurried the women with the red-painted milk stools and the milk pails under their arms. Little Mike pressed his nose against the window.

"Everybody's late! Everybody's late!" cried the Householder as he kicked a long-handled baby cart out of his way. "Come, get a move on!"

He said this to no one in particular, but his tone assured Little Mike that this was again an important day. "The sun and the seasons never rest" was the Householder's motto, and the words seemed to wind up the commune every morning and set it into action, just as it was part of his task to wind up the official colony clock and keep that going, too.

Little Mike put on his black pants and unrolled the faded gray shirt he had used for a pillow. He brushed back his hair and went yawning into the outside room where his mother was working her customary magic. She stood over the washbasin set in its squat, four-legged stand, washing Mary's face with a splashing motion. Ruth had just finished braiding Anna's hair and was tying the polka-dot scarf under her chin.

"Mike," Sarah ordered the moment he appeared, "quick to the kitchen and get some warm water! Here, use the knitting pail!"

"Warm water? Who's sick?"

"Nobody's sick. I want it for Joshua Volkner."

"To wash with?"

"To shave with. Hurry and go."

Thoughts of Mr. Demas sent him with businesslike steps into the commune yard. Was it winter that a man needed warm water? Was Volkner so special that everything in the colony had to be changed for him? Why could he not wash the way the men and boys were busily washing themselves with rapid splashes on the house benches? It did not take anyone long to wash in the morning because no one was dirty so early in the day. Just a splash and then a quick dry on the long flour-sack towels that hung ready at hand. Warm water to shave with? The noisy geese stirred up the dust and shuttled their chattering bills into the dirt made moist by the discarded wash water. They hung around the rain barrels at every colony door and came in ever-increasing numbers until they filled the spaces between the chalk-block homes. Little Mike walked through the midst of them swinging the small tin pail.

"Morning, Mike," called Little Dan Mueller, drying his hands on one end of a towel while his father dried his at the other. "Wait, I'll come along wherever you're going."

Jake Linder waved to him. Paul Wiese had found a piece of rope and was snapping it like a whip. Out of somewhere came the voice of Paul's father: "Stop that, Paul, or you'll put out somebody's eyes." Joey Kunz, pulling a baby brother in a long-tongued wagon, said, "Did you run out of wash water, Mike? Going to the Missouri for some?"

"It's worse than that," said Little Mike and continued on his way.

Michael Neumann came busily out of the cabinet shop heading with his toolbox in the direction of the mill. When he spied Little Mike he stopped long enough to ask, "Where with the pail?"

"To get warm shaving water for Joshua Volkner."

"Shaving water?" Michael sputtered. "Tell him we've seen men with beards before."

The Cattle Boss galloped through the yard on the big black horse. Children ran after him yelling excitedly.

"Don't go in the field before breakfast, children," cried the rider over his shoulder. "Later some of you can go on the truck."

"Hey, Carpenter Michael!" called the Town Man. "Is the worldling up? Is he going today for sure?"

"Ask me something easy," Michael rejoined. "You know how visitors are. They say they're going and then they stay. If they like the outside so much I should think they would want to leave even before breakfast."

"For me," said Thomas Moessner, "I get my fill of the world just with my weekly trips to Yankton."

"Get the elders to appoint a new Town Man if you don't like the assignment."

"Oh, it's all right," the Town Man hastened to say, "It's all right. I only meant—you know——"

The Milk Boss hurried to the cowyard lugging two tall cans. "Everybody's late," he complained. "Even the cows are getting impatient."

Little Mike pulled open the screen door. Fleshy, good-natured Mary Kunz, the Kitchen Boss, stood over the huge iron range and her cheeks were red as paint. She had pulled her blue, polka-dot head scarf over her face for protection, but it was not enough to save her from the heat as she stirred the gruel in the large iron kettle.

"Warm water, if you please," said Mike.

"Warm water? What kind of game are you boys playing already today?"

"For Mr. Volkner," he told her. "To shave with."

She gave a little cry. "He keeps everyone up until past midnight. Now he wants to be served first thing before breakfast."

"The staying up was not his doing," Mike had to say. " 'The Great Song' took the time."

Mary Kunz shook the steam and water from her hands and wiped them on her apron. "And when Neumann Michael leads, every single verse and every line must be sung. In our household the menfolks didn't come home until who knows when."

"How late was it?"

"How late? Do we have watches and clocks all of a sudden?"

"Joshua Volkner has a gold watch and a gold watch chain, too."

"He even has a wrist watch!" Mary Kunz cried. "It all depends on what suit he wears, I hear. He is even supposed to have three suits right in his automobile. But he can wear only one at a time no matter how many he owns."

She chuckled at this until her body shook, took the pail and began removing the lids from a number of kettles, sticking in her finger to find the water that would be just right. Filling the pail, she observed, "Joshua Volkner will have to shave fast if he wants breakfast with the rest of us, or does he want it served him in his room?"

She laughed loudly. "And you," she observed, stirring the gruel with the long wooden spoon, "I suppose today you boys will want to build the big wheel."

"What big wheel?"

"Like Joshua Volkner told our Joey." The spoon turned faster. "A big wheel that carries people. Filling his head with such ideas! If you boys want to build things, build me a bigger woodpile."

The wheel with people stuck in Little Mike's mind. The thought that Joey Kunz was in possession of such startling information was momentous. He withheld his eagerness for more information and went out quickly.

Catching sight of Joey he called, "Come here to me! I'm in a rush."

Joey came with the end of the long tongue of a baby wagon sticking out from between his legs, a piece of wood clamped in his mouth like a horse's bit, and his bare feet imitating a gallop. His shirt was made of a print material like the remnant of an apron hastily utilized, and over his black hair he wore a small, dusty, short-visored cap from beneath which sparkled mischievous black eyes. Arriving at Mike's side he slowed down to fall in with him. The baby, ten feet back in the cramped, boxlike wagon, its tiny white cap tilted down over its face, bounced up and down on a gunny sack as the uneven wheels of the wagon wobbled crazily on their broom-handle axle.

Joey said, "Is it Missouri water you got, Mike?"

"Warm water from your mother in the kitchen. For Joshua Volkner to shave with."

Joey took the bit from his mouth and threw it away. "That I'd like to see!"

"What?"

"Shaving. Over the face with a sharp knife! Whee!"

"I've never seen anybody shave either," Mike said.

Joey seemed to dance a little jig while the wagon and the baby bounced. "Where does he do it?" he asked.

Mike gave him a guarded glance and spoke in a whisper. "You could see it, Joey, through the window, if nobody sees *you*."

"Which window?"

"My room window where I usually sleep with my sisters. Only I didn't last night because Joshua Volkner had the whole room to himself."

"Your room window is not too high," Joey assured himself.

"No, it's low."

Joey said, "I should maybe get Dan Mueller. He'd be glad to see that, too."

"So would Jake Linder. Jake we should have."

"Too many make a scene," Joey figured deeply.

Mike nodded. "Too many do."

"But a person doesn't get so much enjoyment if he is alone. How about you?"

"I?" Mike said, stopping dead in his tracks. "I'll be on the inside, come to think of it." His hand tightened on the water pail. "But what if the breakfast bell comes too soon?"

"To see shaving I would miss breakfast any time."

"I, too, Joey! Look, there goes Sarah mother to the milking. It will give us time enough."

"How long does it take?"

"You know how long it takes to milk as well as I do."

"I mean to shave."

"Who knows that?"

Mike watched his mother hurry to the cowyard, her black apron and long, black dress swinging with her rapid stride. Under her left arm she carried her red milk stool. On her right swung the milk pail.

"Wait, Amelia Mueller, I'll walk with you," she was calling.

Joey pricked up his ears. "I can get Dan easy now," he said. "There goes his mother and your mother together and there Dan stands letting the gander snap at a stick. Hey, there, Dan! The baby I'll turn over to my sister. Baby care is a girl's work anyhow. Thank you, Mike, for the invitation."

"Joey?"

"Yes, Mike?"

"Joey, what about the big wheel?"

Joey's black eyes grew large and he locked his legs together to hold the wagon handle in a manner that afforded him the use of both hands for description.

"It's a wheel that Joshua Volkner showed us in a picture. In it his boy was riding. A Ferris wheel, he called it, five stories high. That is two and a half times higher than Mueller Daniel's house or twice as high as the mill, I figure. The wheel goes around and it carries people, even at night, because it has lights on it and the lights go around with it, too."

Mike turned his eyes to the Mueller home and caught his breath. "Two and a half times? That would be higher than the highest tree."

"And trees don't turn," Joey hastened. "You can sit on a tree and you just sit. You can turn and look in different directions all right, but think of going up and down and around all at once."

"From so high, a person could see across the boundaries of the commune. From so high, a person could look right out into the world."

"In the daytime he could see all over the world from such a height."

"And at night, Joey, think how close you would be to the stars and to God's lantern."

Rachel stood in the doorway. "Mike! Come with that water and hurry up!"

"It's only Rachel," Mike figured. "It's not Michael father."

"I'll get Dan Mueller," Joey whispered, "for two to watch a great thing like Joshua Volkner shaving will be more enjoyment than for one alone. Also it is easier to be scolded together with someone if we should be caught."

Rachel was angry that women had no more say in the commune than they had. "Get into your room!" she scolded. "Mr. Volkner has already asked twice where the hot water was."

Mike started to push open his bedroom door. Then he bethought himself and rapped.

"Come in, come in!" came the welcoming voice. "Since when do we rap in the commune?"

Joshua Volkner stood with one foot on the clothes chest, running a soft wool cloth over his already shiny brown shoe. Then he folded the cloth and put it neatly into his suitcase. "Good morning, Mike," he said cordially. "Your mother said you were bringing this." He took the pail and stuck in a finger. "H'm, it's not too warm. Now if they would just pipe this in here from the kitchen instead of depending on boys' legs . . . Well, thank you, Mike. Thank you very much."

Mike took note of the open window, judged its distance satisfactorily, but saw with concern that there were more people in the yard than he had bargained for. There was Jake's mother pushing a heavily loaded laundry cart, making the tall iron wheel squeak dryly on the uneven ground. There was James the Teacher walking with an open book, using the early morning hour for his memory work. Almost in front of the window was Paul Wiese's older sister carefully braiding her younger sister's hair. The Bee Boss sat on a house bench fixing a smoke box. Children wandered in the yard; a pink-capped little girl embraced the pet lamb; little boys picked up the geese, held them a moment against their bodies, then let them go; young girls carried their baby brothers; older girls collected the long towels and began scrubbing up the house benches.

Joshua looked out, too, and said with a sigh, "Yes, I had almost forgotten mornings in the commune. The three-legged milk stools, painted red now, I see—a touch of the world; the procession of the polka-dot head coverings; forty milkers trudging to the cowyard every morning and every night. The crisp smell of autumn, the scent of wood smoke from the kitchen. Listen, the colony truck! That's a sound that wasn't heard twenty years ago. And I noticed that your mother put a mirror here on the wall for me. Twenty years ago mirrors were *verboten*. The world?" Then he said again reflectively, "The world . . ."

It was awkward being alone with Mr. Demas. The man

looked different from the way he had last night when he sat under the withering words of Pastor Kunz. Last night the men had formed a strong wall behind which Little Mike could sit securely. Now there was nothing to protect him but his own knowledge, nothing to fortify him but his own hatred of the world. Even the room did not seem familiar. Joshua had taken it over. His brown leather suitcase was on the bed, the pillows were tossed one on the other, and the blanket was thrown back so that the soft, deep feather mattress seemed to be up for inspection. On the sleeping bench, in orderly fashion beside the oil lamp, stood a bottle, a brush, a small leather case and also the gold watch and chain and a leather strap, everything in as neat a line as articles on the commune kitchen shelf.

Joshua poured some of the warm water into a basin. "I want to thank you for the use of your room, Mike."

"It's not my room; it's the colony's."

"Yes, of course. Excuse me."

"My sisters sleep in the bed. I sleep on the sleeping bench. That's the sleeping bench where your things are. It's a bench, but it opens for sleeping. Michael father made it. He made nearly all the furniture in the colony. He made the big bed, too."

"I remember that you said last night you wanted to be Colony Carpenter someday. Yes, someday you'll be a cabinetmaker if you follow the tradition. Carpenter Michael they'll call you."

Little Mike wanted to say that he had already helped his father many times, but the quick thrust of a head wearing a dusty, gray-visored cap arrested him. Joey Kunz

was springing up and down at the window like a young
colt. Joshua was busy taking things from the little leather
case. Mike made an excited motion to Joey to stay down
out of sight, but instead Dan Mueller's red face shot up,
then Jake Linder's, so high and daring that Mike could
see the fleshy growth on Jake's neck. Joey Kunz appeared again, and then up came Little Mike's cousin, Matt
Neumann, with ears that stuck almost straight out. Up
and down bobbed the heads. Four pairs of eyes leveled
for a moment over the window sill, alert and furtive as
mice in the granary. They disappeared in one motion as
Joshua turned to dip the brush into the water. He worked
the brush around a few times on a sweet-smelling stick of
soap. Up came the eyes every time Joshua's back was
turned. Down they went whenever he swung round to
the window. Now the brush was growing thick and white
with foam.

"By the way, Little Mike, how did you like 'The Great
Song?'" Joshua asked.

"I still hear it."

"I wouldn't have missed it for all the world," Joshua
agreed. "Do you like music?"

"Singing I like," Mike told him. "Music we don't believe in."

"Yes, yes, of course," Joshua assented.

He stepped to the mirror and painted his cheeks with
the brush, then his chin and his neck until he had a beard
whiter than Pastor Kunz's. The faces at the window crept
up and stared openmouthed. Paul Wiese, whose freckles
covered his face and forehead and ears, had joined the
group and wrestled to make a place for himself at the

crowded sill. The five boys clung there now cheek to cheek in a solid row.

"I thought you must surely like music," Joshua said through his soap beard. "Your father is a good singer."

"He knows more than a hundred tunes," Mike replied, hoping to draw Joshua's attention over to where he stood near the clothes chest. "He knows many hundred songs."

"Yes, Michael Neumann was always good at memorizing."

Joshua now whipped open his shining razor. It came out of its black case like a silver fish out of a dark pool. It was long and cold-looking and had an edge thinner and sharper than any tool in the carpenter shop. Carefully he touched it to his cheek and drew it down almost to his chin. Mike held his breath. He could almost feel the sensation, and the fragrant smell in the room was of a kind never found in the hard, brown chunks of soap which the colony made in its iron kettles. The smell and the sight of the shaving almost transported him away, but the heads at the window were craning over the sill and into the room. Joey Kunz forgot where he was. Hanging wide-eyed over the recessed window ledge, he gasped aloud, "One slip and the blood will squirt!" Joshua turned and caught sight of his audience before they could withdraw from their perch.

"Come on in, boys, come in!" he invited good-naturedly.

But just then a powerful voice rose over the commune yard. "Boys, away from there! Back where you belong."

The faces dropped from the window like apples when the Garden Boss shook the tree. Little Mike felt the words strike the chalk blocks with a thud; the yard lay stunned in silence. But Joshua went in amusement to the window. Pastor Kunz stood on the board sidewalk in front of the home of Titus Wiese, and he looked like Moses come down from the mountain. The boys were running riotously through the yard, scattering the geese and stirring up the dust. Pastor Kunz shook his fist in their direction, black hat squarely on his head, his spectacles mirroring flashes of sunlight, his beard bristling.

Joshua called in a friendly tone, "Good morning, Pastor Kunz."

The pastor squinted at him distastefully as the worldling leaned half-shaven over the sill. "So that is the attraction!" Pastor Kunz exclaimed. "An early morning show for the children, is it? Beware, Joshua Volkner, beware!"

Then he wheeled about and with firm steps walked haughtily away.

Joshua laughed and turned away from the window while Little Mike was filled with wonder and awe at the fearless ways of the man, for Mr. Demas went to the mirror and continued drawing the sharp knife back and forth over his smooth skin. What was the secret something that made him so sure of himself? Why did he not tremble at the pastor's wrath? Why did nothing seem to bother him? He did what he liked. He dressed the way he wanted to. He had no one to tell him that he had to be like other men. There were no boundaries that he could not cross. There were no forbidden things that he could not do.

Greatly disturbed, Little Mike started from the room. Volkner's voice was gentle. "Wait, Little Mike. There's something I want to show you."

Wiping his face with the towel, he went over to his suitcase and took from it a small wooden box no larger than Mike's hand; a box with gold and red pictures on it, pictures of a boy playing on a musical pipe in a meadow where sheep were grazing. Joshua pressed the box and the top sprang open. Inside was something that gleamed brighter than the morning sunlight.

"It's a harmonica," Joshua explained.

He took the sparkling instrument from its soft, velvet-lined case and handed it to Little Mike. It was cool to his hand. It was the brightest and loveliest thing he had ever seen. The edge, which had tiny air compartments, was white as the whitest chalk block.

"That's ivory set in ebony," Joshua said, "and the top does look like silver, doesn't it? It's from a store in Chicago."

Mike could not speak. Helpless and conquered, he feasted his eyes on the harmonica.

"I'll show you how it works," said Joshua. "My boy Robert has one and he knows a number of songs. It's not difficult."

He put the harmonica to his lips and drew soft music from the instrument. Gentler than the sheep bells it sounded. High and low tones, short and sharp as voices, then slow, beckoning melodies that whispered just for the room and not for the commune yard at all.

"Almost as good as singing music," Joshua assured him.

"So, Little Mike, the harmonica is yours. All yours."

He pressed it into Mike's hand and hurriedly proceeded to finish dressing.

Mike wanted to say, "I can't take it. We have nothing like this in the commune. I'll have to give it to the House-holder, for it's a personal possession. He will sell it or do something with it, for if I have one and the other boys don't, that would not be right. Thank you very much for the offer, Joshua Volkner, but you know how it would be."

He said nothing. Something he had never felt stirred his heart. His fingers caressed the cool silver surface. His admiring gaze devoured the box and explored the texture of the lining. When he touched the inside of the box it was as soft as down and the color was pink as the sunset sky. Tenderly looking at the harmonica, he addressed it in a faraway voice, "I could put music into you, too."

"Of course you can," Volkner agreed. "You'll have a great time with it. It will be our secret."

Little Mike looked up with frightened eyes. He could not explain his feeling, but it caused his hand to tighten on the instrument. For the first time someone had given him something for his very own. "So, Little Mike, the harmonica is yours. All yours." He put the instrument into its box. He would tell Joshua Volkner he was sorry but that it was not for him. He would be glad all his life that he gave it back. It was not right that he should keep it. He felt it was not right and he snapped the box shut. The sound was like the closing of the big Bible. It was final. He had made up his mind.

Volkner, standing at the mirror, was tying a red tie

and pulling it tightly against the collar of his white shirt. He was speaking in his casual way. "I sometimes think that if a person could play the harmonica real well, it would be like the music of the big wheel. I was telling the Kunzes about that; the Ferris wheel that Robert and I often ride in the amusement park. It carries people in seats—seats with a bar across so that people can't get out at all, until they are let out by the Ferris wheel boss. Around and around they go. They never really get anywhere, but there they go just the same, round and round and round, and it's great fun. And all the time there's music. There's music just as if someone is playing a big harmonica. Everybody hears it and it makes the riders happy. Even those who are afraid when they're up where the wheel is highest, they hear the music and they say, 'Everything will be all right.' "

There was a sound outside that sent fear through Little Mike's body. He had heard the breakfast bell all his life, but it had never sounded so near, so loud, so accusing. It had never struck at him as it did now. He always sped out of the house and raced Jake Linder and Paul Wiese and Joey Kunz to the community kitchen when the bell rang. Now it was like a hammer pounding. It nailed him to his spot as tightly as if Michael father had driven him down with one of the long spikes.

"Breakfast," exclaimed Joshua, glancing out of the window. "Yes, there are the women returning from the milking. There comes the Milk Boss from the separator shed with the big cans. James the Teacher puts his book away. Everything on schedule. No time wasted. Everything according to the day's plan. Ah, Hutterians, Hutterians! Stubbornly holding to a system that can't survive."

He put on his coat and took a wrist watch from his suitcase. This he slipped quickly over his hand and fastened it.

There was a rap at the door.

"Joshua Volkner?" came Sarah's voice. "Breakfast."

"I'm coming, Sarah Neumann."

"I'll go on ahead," came the quick reply, and Mike heard the outside screen door slam.

"Yes, yes, of course," said Joshua with a sigh. "It wouldn't be right for us to walk together, Sarah. It wouldn't be right for us to go laughing and free across the commune yard. No, you must hurry and I must hurry. The bell has rung. I see the men going, swinging their arms. They do not hold open the screen door for you. No, they let it slam. They will sit at one table and the women at another. And it will not be right to come in after the breakfast prayer. Traditions are starting another Hutterian day." He turned to go. "Well, come along, Little Mike."

He went out, leaving the door open, expecting Little Mike to follow.

Mike stood alone in the center of the world, his hand moist over the precious gift. "All yours . . . all yours," something kept saying.

Joey Kunz galloped past the window and looked in. "Hey, Mike!" he shouted. "Better come. It's your morning to pray."

Mike clung desperately to the box as he walked into the outside room. There in a final moment of confusion, he slipped the harmonica into his pants pocket, flung open the screen door and ran from the house with all his might, ran as if he were running from Pastor Kunz, from the seven stern and bearded elders of the Old Portage Colony, and from Jacob Hutter himself, though he knew that Jacob Hutter had died in Innsbruck more than four hundred years ago.

CHAPTER 6

ITTLE MIKE lay on his back on the sheep hill while the musical clank of the bells could be heard on the white sheep counters. He raised a hand from the cool grass. Then he lifted his head to spy out his surroundings and to assure himself that he was all alone. Cautiously he touched the harmonica to his lips. The sounds he drew softly and guardedly from the instrument nestled in the clumps of grass on which he pillowed his head. He had learned to play notes that sounded like the bells themselves, but best of all was the enchantment of having learned to play one line of the melody of "The Great Song." He played that over and over. He played it to the morning sky and to the graying clouds. He played it to the sheep and to the river running soundlessly below the hill.

Come, brothers, and let us sing of the true faith. . . .

For three days the harmonica had burned in his pocket and every night he had guarded it under his pillow. For three days he had tried to be alone as much as possible so that he could learn to play. Even Joey's talk about building the great wheel held only minor interest. But sometimes he was afraid. Would he ever forget that first

110

morning and how he sat with the boys at the long breakfast table in the children's refectory? He had felt like a
stranger, a worldling himself, as he took his place on the
backless bench. The touch of the harmonica in his pocket
kept enticing him away from his surroundings. When he
prayed at the table, his hands, still trembling from holding
the instrument, were pressed palms together, and he wondered if God would punish him right there during the
prayer or wait awhile. Falteringly he recited, "Thank
you, Father, for these Thy gifts," and when those words
came out uneventfully, he hurried through the rest, "which
we have received from Thy bounty. Amen." He was
through. That much was over.

Paul Wiese had nudged him and whispered, "You sure
slid down the hill fast once you got started. But that's all
right. I'm hungry."

Little Mike had no appetite. The harmonica lay in his
pocket like a heavy weight. He wanted only to get away
and examine it all over again, maybe blow on it just once
more and then return it to Joshua Volkner. But after
breakfast everything happened at once. The colony truck
roared into the field with happy, shouting children clinging to it and inviting him to come along. His father ordered him to get the measurement of the schoolhouse windows so that he might cut the curtain sticks. Then Joshua
Volkner began taking his suitcases to the automobile and
there the important talk with the Householder and Michael
father took place.

Volkner said, "Well, I'd like to pay for my room and
board, gentlemen."

"All you have to do is try it," snapped Michael. "Then

we'll know you have laid aside every bit of Hutterian belief for good and all."

"On the contrary," Volkner answered, "I remember one
of the cardinal tenets is that no sojourner in a commune
shall ever be permitted to pay for his keep. How does it
go—here, Little Mike, you tell me. Surely it's still part of
the training."

When Joshua said that, Little Mike came to attention
and recited: " 'If any man is absent from his home and
lodges with us, let him be taken in and entertained, served
and hospitably treated according to our ability, but never
for money, ever free and without cost. This we do because the saints of old did likewise.' "

"Yes, that's exactly right," Volkner affirmed. "Not a
word has been changed. Thank you, Little Mike, for
refreshing my memory."

"It wouldn't be honest for us to say that we are glad
you came or that we are sorry to see you go," observed
the Householder gravely. "We elders regret that the
world has corrupted your thinking and warped your life.
That you cannot think clearly is easily seen and that
your sense of what is good and useful in life is all confused goes without saying. But as for taking money or
anything from you, thank you, no. Keep your worldly
goods in private and we will keep God's things co-operatively as He has ordered."

"The reason I'd like to pay," Joshua said, "is because
I should like to come back."

"Didn't I tell you?" cried Michael. "I told you when
you came that you were unhappy in the world. Why
else did you come but for homesickness? The world is
wide, but there is no room in it."

"No, no!" Joshua corrected. "I only meant that I'd like to come back for your Rachel's wedding and perhaps bring Mrs. Volkner and the children with me."

"Stop making out that we're a theater," Michael warned.

"So say I," said the Householder. "You've been here now and the thing is done. I know how Pastor Kunz would feel if you started to bring the family."

Then Volkner surprised them by saying that he would go to the pastor and ask him just how he would feel about it. With that he marched straight off to the home of Pastor Kunz. After a while he returned to say that the answer of the Boss of Bosses could be summed up in a proverb: The poor man has God in his heart, the rich man has Him in his purse.

Then Joshua came for the last time to his car, carrying his coat on his arm and his hat in his hand. Only six of the men found time to gather at the car and say farewell to him. The others had said their offhand good-bys when they saw him at breakfast. No one asked him to return; none asked him to extend his stay. Michael Neumann shook hands with him hastily, then thrust both hands deep into his pants pockets. Volkner came to where Little Mike stood with Jake Linder. Mike's heart stood still for fear the man would say something about the harmonica. But Joshua only said, "Good-by, Little Mike, and good luck. If I come for the wedding you'll meet my Robert. He's just your age."

The only woman at the leave-taking was Sarah Neumann. She happened to be pulling a laundry cart through the yard at the moment. Volkner raised his hat to her and called, "*Auf Wiedersehen.*" Her steps quickened and she was soon out of sight behind one of the houses.

Then he took his place behind the wheel. The Town Man stood on the running board and rode along to the boundary where he opened the gate; then the big black car passed through. The men remained standing almost as they were when the car first started; they seemed to be listening and wondering while the sound of the motor grew fainter and fainter and finally faded into the unmeasured acres of the outside world.

Michael broke the silence. "Well, gentlemen, Mr. Demas must work out his own salvation. When a man thinks he is too good for the commune, it shows that he is bad enough for the world."

Poor Joshua Volkner! He drove away before he had a chance to see the cattle truck come rolling out of the meadow with the big steer and the other cattle safely behind the wood bars. That was a sight. The pastor came out to see it and the elders examined the sagging springs of the truck and the Householder sucked at a straw, already seeming to judge the weight and the cattle receipts. Michael father tested the truck bars to make sure they would keep the stock captive on the long trip to Omaha. The women quit work long enough to come near and admire the sleek black coats of the Angus. Then the Cattle Boss climbed into the seat next to the truckman and off they started, with the children running and shouting alongside all the way to the commune gate. There went the big steer proud and stubborn even though he was caught. Defiantly he raised his wonderful strong head and showed off his muscular neck. No more would he hear the call of "*Mo-kaa, Mo-kaa.*"

"Good-by, big fellow, good-by! Out into the world you must go; out into the world to be killed."

The sound of the truck had faded away even as had the sound of Joshua Volkner's automobile, and the commune returned to its routine.

> Come, brothers, and let us sing of the true faith.
> Let us tell you of our history,
> How we were driven from Germany . . .

Here on the sheep hill the harmonica seemed to add new lines by itself. Mike pressed both hands over it tremblingly and huddled as closely in the grass as he could. The harmonica was a thing alive, and warmly its musical heart was throbbing. The taste of the ivory and ebony was sweet as honey. The feel of it was magical. Little Mike whispered affectionately, "I love you so very much, harmonica." He thought of the words in the song that spoke about the hard and barren heath, and he thanked the cloudy heavens for the soft ground on which he lay. No one to harm him here. No one to demand martyrdom of him. No one to say that his people should move on. This was America.

He needed only to move his lips over the harmonica and he was marching at the head of all the American communes . . . he was Colony Carpenter . . . he was riding in the big wheel . . . he was with Joshua Volkner traveling all over the country . . . he was on the sheep hill, satisfied, happy, wanting nothing. He played the harmonica low and subdued, seeking out the notes of "The Great Song." He lay with eyes closed, transporting himself wherever he wished.

A sound intruded that was not the soft, roving sound of the sheep. It was a grating noise and the crackle of grass. Frightened, he opened his eyes. Standing close by, looking down at him were Jake Linder and Paul Wiese. Then along came Joey Kunz pulling a banged-up tin bucket on a long crooked stick.

Mike quickly stuffed the harmonica into the grass under his body. "What do you want? What are you doing here?"

Paul asked, "What have you got? Where did you get it?"

"It makes music," Joey said.

Paul's freckled face was livid with excitement. "We heard it even down the hill."

"It sounded like 'The Great Song,'" Jake suggested. "Only without the words."

Mike said, "It's nothing."

"That is lying, Mike Neumann," Paul accused him. "We know we heard something."

"It's like a willow whistle," Mike told them.

"We dare not make willow whistles," Joey reminded him. Then he asked hopefully, "Or did you make one anyway?"

"Show it to us, Mike," Jake urged. "We won't tell."

Mike looked at Jake earnestly. If there was such a thing as a best friend in the commune, Jake Linder was that one. But Jake was really no different from Joey Kunz. Mike could trust them both. And it was Paul Wiese who gave up his chance to come to the sheep hill today and never even asked why Mike was so anxious to come. Three friends were here, Mike told himself, and he ought by rights to tell them all about the harmonica, especially since they almost knew already.

Paul Wiese kicked the grass impatiently. "Keep your

willow whistle. All I'm looking for is Paul father. Is he
here?"

Mike shook his head.

"Oh, I know he isn't right *here*," Paul argued, "or you
wouldn't be playing music. Paul father is an elder."

As he said this he gave Mike a glance of special warning. It was enough to cause Mike's hand to seek for the
harmonica and cover it. He sat up.

"All right," he said, "I'll tell you what it is. I'll even
show you."

"We won't tell," promised Joey, excitedly tossing aside
his long stick and flopping down beside Mike.

Jake and Paul sat down, too, plucking expectantly at
the grass. Which, Mike wondered, was the greater sin: to
hold a secret or to possess something for oneself alone?
If I show the harmonica to them, he thought, it will be
like sharing it. Sharing is what we're supposed to do.
James the Teacher taught us that. "He who has a coat will
give it to his brother who is naked." Sharing is like giving.

Aloud he said, "It's this," and held out the harmonica
in his open hand for all to see.

Quick as a goose stabbing at a chunk of bread, Paul
Wiese snatched the instrument. "What is it?" he cried.

"Not something to be rough with!" Mike exclaimed,
wresting it from Paul's hand.

"You fight about it," Paul accused him in a tone that
was already reporting Mike's action to his father. "That's
what comes of personal possession."

"No, it's not, Paul," said Mike in an awed voice. "I only
mean that this is something to be careful with. It makes
music only if you're kind to it."

"How does it play?" asked Jake gently.

"He's stingy with it." Paul accused.

"Where did you get it?" Joey wanted to know.

"I got it from Joshua Volkner——" Mike began.

"Him?" Paul shouted.

"Oh, I'm going to tell Michael father all about it," Mike assured him. "I'll tell him just as soon as I learn to play it a little more."

"Well, let's hear it," said Jake.

Mike turned the harmonica over in his hand. "Look around and see if it's all right, Joey."

Joey sprang to his feet, glanced around with a whirling motion and flopped down in the grass. "Nobody but the sheep," he reported.

Mike put the harmonica to his lips.

Paul spoke up. "Why do you close your eyes? Doesn't it work without closing them?"

Jake said, "If he wants to close his eyes, freckle-face, let him. Just be quiet."

"Yes," urged Joey, tossing a handful of grass jubilantly into the air, "make believe it's churchtime."

Softly Mike drew from the harmonica the marching melody of "The Great Song." He had thrilled when he played it to himself; now he was filled to overpowering with the melody. Behind his closed lids he saw scenes that moved and changed and stirred at the sound of the music. He was in a beautiful meadow. He wandered among big wheels turning. He heard angels singing. It must be angels that played the harmonica, for the three lines were ended and still the music did not stop. The fourth and fifth lines of "The Great Song" came out of the harmonica. He believed he could have played on and on had he just been used to the wonder of it. The music painted the words for him in its beautiful melody. Against the sun-red curtain of his closed eyes the words unfolded:

> Let us tell you how our brethren were beaten,
> And how no one would offer them refuge;
> How emperors, priests and reformers despised them,
> Hunted and killed them mercilessly, without pity. . . .

He stopped and opened astonished eyes. His listeners sat as quiet and motionless as bundles tossed into the grass. The restless, reassuring tinkle of the sheep bells drifted over him as a gentle echo, and he held out the harmonica to Paul Wiese. Paul took it tenderly.

Jake's voice faltered. "I have never heard anything so pretty in my life. It's nicer even than the wild bird we had in the cage."

"The wild bird didn't sing at all in the cage," Mike recalled, as if he had been thinking of the same thing.

"No, but before it did. It sang before we ever caught it."

"The harmonica sings if it is in a cage or not," Mike explained. "It is even better than a bird."

Paul put the harmonica between his teeth, puffed out his cheeks and blew.

Joey said, "All you get out of it is spit."

Paul had to agree. "It spits if I close my eyes or not. Can you do it with your eyes open, Mike?"

"I can, but it sounds better when they're closed."

"It is much music from such a little thing," Paul observed. "It isn't any bigger than a currycomb."

Joey said, "How could you get it in your mouth if it was bigger? It's the mouth that plays it."

"It's not the mouth at all," Jake said thoughtfully. "Paul's mouth is as big as Mike's and you see how he drips. It's not the mouth only; it's something you must have inside. This is something you must have in the head."

Paul blew a loud discordant blast and Mike silenced him. "Do you want the whole colony to hear you?"

Jake took the harmonica. "Nobody blows it except Mike."

"Listen to the Householder," Paul laughed. "Have you taken this up with the elders, Mr. Householder?"

Jake's dark eyes were serious. "I wouldn't even tell the elders about this."

"You mean really not tell them?" Mike asked with a catch in his voice.

Jake held the instrument between both hands.

"You mean never to tell them, Jake?" Joey's eyes danced in expectation and wonder.

"You mean it to be a secret?" Paul asked hesitantly.

The group sat half hopefully, half fearfully. Then Jake, assuming the voice and manners of the Householder, twisted a finger in a make-believe beard. "As Householder, I appoint you, Neumann Mike, Harmonica Boss."

Joey Kunz rolled laughing in the grass. Paul slapped his knees excitedly at the impersonation.

Mike said, "Yes, Jake, but that needs the endorsement of the seven elders."

"Well, well!" replied Jake in the same voice. "Kunz Joseph, will you stop rolling long enough to tell me if you are in favor?"

Joey sprang to his feet and proclaimed, "I am in favor, Householder. I am for making Neumann Mike Harmonica *Ansager*."

"Come, come!" said Jake. "Do you want him to lead the singing with the harmonica? Isn't that going too far? Elder Wiese Paul, what do you think?"

"We need more elders," Paul shouted. "I'll run down and get some more boys."

Mike sprang up and held him back. "Wait, Paul! I am tired of being scared, whether you are or not."

"We can get Dan Mueller and your cousin Matt——"

"Scared of what, Mike?" Jake asked.

"I don't know. I have been scared ever since I took the harmonica. If Joshua Volkner had given it to everybody, that would be different. But he gave it to me. He said it was mine. That makes it like something in the world where people own things personal. That isn't all. Has there ever been a musical instrument in the colony? Instruments are of the devil. James the Teacher told us that many times. That makes me scared, too. I just wanted to play it a little because it is so pretty, but I don't want to play it much and not at all in secret. To have a secret is as bad as having a possession. Tonight I'll tell Michael father and tomorrow whatever he says, I'll do."

Jake plucked at the grass. "You had the harmonica only a few days," he marveled, "and already you can play 'The Great Song!'"

"That comes easy."

"All right. It is more than Paul or Joey or I could do. I think, Mike, you were supposed to have the harmonica, and you were supposed to play it, or else God would never have let Joshua Volkner give it to you in the first place."

Mike devoured him with a glance. "You think so, Jake? You really think so?"

"God sees everything, doesn't He? God even makes you blow on the harmonica the right way. I'm older than all of you. I am eleven, but I would just like to stay here in the grass and listen to you make music all my life. That would be enough for me."

With this pronouncement Jake stretched himself full-length on the sheep hill, locked his hands behind his head and gazed up at the sky. Mike looked down at him. He saw how Jake always had to lie with his head slightly to the side because of the lump on his neck. He figured that anyone who carried such a cross as Jake did ought to know something about God's ways and God's plans. The harmonica had never felt so completely right as it did now. Jake's words were true. If God did not want him to have the instrument, He would never have given it to him, and He would certainly not have put it into his heart to play the way he did. If it were something bad, it would be different. If it were painting pictures, it would be breaking the commandment about graven images. If it were making a sling to throw pebbles, it would be wrong because it might kill something. But to make sweet music—— Jake was right. To lie in the grass and hear the harmonica was all a person should ever want.

Suddenly Joey Kunz leaped into the air. "If Mike makes the music, I can make the wheel!"

"What wheel?" asked Paul.

"The big wheel! It won't be five stories high, but it

will go round. Didn't I make this old pail turn on the stick? Look, here in the open end I forced in a board and cut a hole in for the axle. I cut a hole in the pail bottom, too. When I pull the pail it turns and the stones inside give it a good rattly sound. I'll build the big wheel and it will have seats—if not for people, then for something just as good."

"Then let's get the elders quick!" Paul exclaimed.

"Let's get them quicker than it takes to ride the truck," Joey agreed and, with the long stick between his legs, he and Paul started down the sheep hill.

"Paul! Joey! Come back!"

Mike's cry was lost in the rattle of stones in the tin pail; and the sound of bare feet running, scattering the sheep, thumped an accompaniment.

"Jake, what will they do?"

Jake lay as before, only that he had closed his eyes. "Jacob father told me once I had no music in me," he confided quietly. "He said it must be because of the bump on my neck. Do you think if I didn't have the bump I would have music?"

"Does the bump hurt much?" Mike asked.

"It hurts sometimes. It's a cross."

"Like Sarah Kunz's rheumatism?"

Jake nodded sadly.

"Why does God give anybody a cross, Jake?"

"Why does He let weeds grow or why does He let flies come or let the rust get on the wheat?"

"I don't know."

"Jacob father says it is to make us work and keep us humble."

"Pretty things would make me work—not crosses. Since I have the harmonica I would do anything no matter how hard it is. I have even been thinking I would build up the woodpile for the Kitchen Boss."

"That we'll have to do anyhow when the Wood Boss tells us."

"It's the feeling I meant, Jake. Since I have the harmonica it is just as if I had wings."

"Play the song again, Mike, just for us."

"I should see if the sheep are all right."

"The sheep are all right. Play the song."

Mike played and when the inspiration of the music carried him almost halfway through "The Great Song," Jake said, "You play it better than any boy in the whole world. No matter how big the world is."

"Joshua Volkner's boy has one, too," Mike remembered.

"But can he play it?"

"I don't know. But if he comes here, as maybe he will come for Rachel's wedding——"

Jake shook his head. "No, we want nothing to do with him. Everything that Joshua Volkner does is wrong. All the men say that. But one thing that wasn't wrong was to leave pretty music with us. As for the way his boy plays the harmonica, you could beat him even with your eyes open."

A strong voice broke over them. "There's a black sheep down at the potato patch and the whites are with him."

Paul Wiese, the Sheep Boss, stood above them, hat pulled low over his eyes, his thick lips set in his short-cropped beard. "Get up, Jake Linder. Go back where you belong. When two of you boys get together, nothing is done."

Jake and Mike stood accused before him, but Mike succeeded in slipping the harmonica into his pocket. The stern green eyes of the elder saw the motion, but for some reason he said nothing. He did not seem anxious to condescend to any further talk with the boys who had done their work badly. "Go on home," he ordered. "Better the sheep watch you than you them."

He started down the hill toward the potato patch, his short, stout body moving through the grass with arms swinging.

"Elder Wiese," Mike called, "your Paul wanted you for something."

"I know, I know," Wiese called back. "I got the message. There is a meeting of the elders tonight."

"Jake, do you hear? A meeting of the elders!"

Jake shrugged. "They have many meetings."

They started down the hill.

"Do you think it could be about the harmonica, Jake?"

"Nobody knows about that."

"Nobody, unless Joey or Paul——"

"They just heard about it. The meeting was called early."

"Or unless God told it to somebody," Mike whispered.

"Could that happen, do you think?" Jake asked.

Troubled at Jake's tone, Mike felt his fears deepen. "Sure, that could happen. Sure, it could." And he broke into a run. "I am going to tell Michael father right away. I must tell him everything."

"Wait, Mike! Wait!"

But Mike was speeding toward the path that led to the commune and to the cabinet shop. The cluster of buildings rushed to meet him. The big barn and the shops were on him before he realized it. But he did not stop. Guilt ran with him and he was saying half aloud, "I know it was wrong, Michael father. I know now what you mean by owning things personal like people do in the world. I am ready to give it up and confess everything." But another voice within him said, "Think how pretty it was! Jake lay in the grass and it made him feel good all over. Think of all you see with your closed eyes. Think of the good taste. Pretty music it is, Mike, like God's music. Where does it come from if not from Him? Who showed you how to play it unless He did? Wait, Mike! Wait!"

He was walking now, slowly. He was near the house of the Town Man which stood close to the riverbank. He could catch a glimpse of the cabinet shop through the openings between the houses. Abruptly he found himself turning into the long, narrow path that ran to the river flat. This trail led past the mill, into the meadow and through the wheat field if he wished to pursue it that far. He did not know how far he would go. Here where he walked, the river flowed. The river, with its incessant humming sound, understood. It did not stop to ask what he was doing or where he was going or whether the harmonica in his pocket had a right to be there. The river just went on out into the world singing. How free it was! How wonderfully free!

Here was the spot where Jake and he had once made a sailing raft. The fathers said it was best to destroy it because it might float them out of the commune grounds. Farther on was the balanced rock, a flat stone the height of a man, leaning out over the water. Here was the gravel pile, thick with flat, round stones for skipping. The river never complained about the skipping stones. It swallowed them up with a gulp and kept right on its way. It turned the mill wheel and stirred up the foam as white as the lather on Joshua Volkner's face. The water laughed and played to its heart's content under the mill wheel. When the Mill Boss pulled the big lever and all the machinery was quiet, the water was quiet, too, and went on its way. Nothing in the commune was quite so free as the river and just now it seemed to Little Mike that there was some connection between the Missouri and God.

Hopefully he raised pleading eyes to the sky. Anxiously he hoped for some special sign that would make the whole of life a little less mysterious. The river did not even bother to ask for anything like that. It did its work and it was free and God seemed always to guard it though it flowed a thousand miles up and a thousand miles down into the sinful world.

CHAPTER 7

~~~~~~

*T*HAT evening, long after the church service had ended, Little Mike worked with his father in the cabinet shop. A wedding chest was ready for the finishing touches, and it was Mike's job to rub oil into the smoothly sanded boards. Michael Neumann worked at his bench in the lantern light, his black hat pushed back on his head, his mouth full of nails. He was building three new beehives for the Bee Boss. Working at this hour was not unusual, but for Little Mike the moments were endless with the terror of the unknown. The elders were gathered in the school building and their meeting was overly long.

Rub . . . rub . . .

He had many matters weighing on his mind. Shortly before suppertime Joey Kunz and Paul Wiese had summoned him to the willow clearing in the river flat. Here Jake Linder was waiting and with him were Matt Neumann and Dan Mueller. They were waiting to see the harmonica and hear it played. All vowed to keep the secret, and after they heard Mike's music they pledged themselves to be secret elders who officially endorsed Neumann Mike as Harmonica *Ansager*.

Joey Kunz had some crooked nails and string and a discarded barrel hoop out of which he tried to fashion a

Ferris wheel, one that would turn while Mike made music. He hammered strips of wood crosswise on the hoop and then drove a nail through the place where the strips intersected. This nail was then suspended between two stakes driven into the soft ground and the wheel could be spun around. But when he tried to make seats for "the people" that was more difficult. With string and rusty brads he fixed small strips to the outside edge of the hoop.

Jake asked the question that was in everyone's mind, "How are the people going to stay on?"

Joey made believe he knew, but he did not. No matter how hard he tried he could not figure that out. Pebbles representing people dropped right to the ground as soon as the wheel turned. He could tie them on or stick them on with shoemaker pitch, but as Paul Wiese said, "The blood will rush to their heads and probably kill them twice around."

Dan Mueller concluded it could not be done. Joshua Volkner had probably lied. Jake suggested that in figuring out these things people in the world might be smarter than Hutterians. Matt Neumann tried to put the seats on the inside of the hoop.

"Then," said Joey, "everybody will sure be killed. They'll roll around in the hoop like the stones inside my pail wagon." There was no finding the answer. Joey studied the wheel from the ground, from above, from behind. He arranged a seat this way and that. It was no use. Out came the pebbles at every turn. "There has never been anything in the making line that I couldn't make," he concluded, "but I can't do this."

It was then that Mike said, "What nobody can figure

out, Michael father can, and whatever can be made with wood he can make."

"Please, Mike, please," pleaded Joey, "get him to tell you how, and I can make it."

"Sure," boasted Mike, "Michael father will tell me quick."

But now as Little Mike rubbed the oil tirelessly into the chest top, and as the moments passed and the hours went by, he found it ever more difficult to come round to the big question. His father, so near that he could reach out and touch him, was as far away as the world. "Where did you get the idea for the Ferris wheel in the first place? Who gave you boys permission to use the material? Who said you should have playthings? What is your part in this business? Did you take this up with Pastor Kunz?" These and other questions Little Mike asked himself in his father's stead and he had no answers.

Rub . . . rub . . .

There was a sound at the door. A strong hand swung it open wide and Blacksmith Jacob Linder strode in with his head down to keep from striking it against the doorframe. He closed the door with a bang that sounded in Little Mike's heart. Linder's huge bulk filled the room. Everything became smaller wherever this elder went. His shoulders were broad and his head was massive, and his gray, crinkly beard stuck out from the sides of his face. As Little Mike looked at Jacob Linder now he remembered that here was one man who had a specially made bed to fit his giant size. He was blacksmith because he was the strongest man in the commune, and he was an elder because the men who elected the elders believed he would handle colony problems as competently as he handled the heavy duties of his trade.

"Carpenter," he said, "I came to pick up the tools you want sharpened so I can do them before breakfast."

"Good," said Michael. "I'm glad for that. I thought maybe the meeting had sent you right home. You had a long session."

"Long and important." Jacob nodded as if to say that weighty matters had been discussed from churchtime until nearly eleven. "But it can't be too late. Here is Little Mike rubbing down boards, and I saw Little Jake, my Jacob's boy, sitting outside on the school steps when we came out."

Little Mike dipped his rag into the saucer of oil. He could not trust himself to betray the interest he felt. Anxiously he rubbed back and forth on the smooth chest top. Jake had promised that he would sit on the steps and try to hear what the elders said. Mike's plan was to help his father, hoping that when the meeting was over one of the elders would drop in just as Elder Linder now had done. The elders were always anxious to talk about what had happened, though they made believe they were not. Come on, Elder Linder, Little Mike was saying to himself with each frantic rub, tell me the worst. I still have the harmonica, but if you want it, all right. If you must have it, well and good. Just tell me, tell me.

Michael Neumann took some cutting tools from where they hung on the wall properly in place. Running his finger over their sharp edges, he said impassively, "The Cattle Boss told me they got four hundred dollars for the big steer. Was that a good lot?"

He mentioned this by way of inquiring whether the elders had discussed cattle receipts.

Jacob Linder seated himself on a pile of boards with his feet squarely on the floor. He took off his black hat and laid it beside him. He brushed his white hair back over his ears. When he locked his fingers around his knee they seemed like braided ropes.

He nodded. "Prices are good. I am glad for it. But not for the same reason that Joshua Volkner might be."

Rub . . . rub . . . rub . . .

Was it Joshua Volkner and the harmonica they talked about? Had the all-seeing elders already caught on to the secret?

Michael Neumann said, "Let Mr. Demas rest in peace, Blacksmith. He is the world and we are the community. Which way each goes we'll leave to the Lord. We live our life and he lives his."

Little Mike glanced with wonder at his father. Brave he was to speak this way to Jacob Linder. But the blacksmith said, "Yes, and live our life we must, though the road be hard at times."

He paused and Little Mike noticed how sorrowfully his eyes were set in his wrinkled face. The door opened and Jacob J. Linder, the blacksmith's son, came in. With him was Rudolph Kunz, the Bee Boss. By the magic that governed the colony, these men seeemed to know just where and when to come to learn the news of the evening. Elsewhere in commune homes the other elders would have their audiences. They would spread the doings and progress of the meeting in characteristic, casual manner, quietly reporting what had taken place. Jacob J. and the Bee Boss sat down without a greeting.

Michael Neumann spoke impatiently. "Well, well, what happened? What's this talk about the road being hard? We have a good life. We have plenty to eat. We have work that we like. We have everything, in fact."

"God was good to give us a good price for the cattle," said Elder Linder. "We'll need the money. There will soon be another colony here in South Dakota."

"A new colony?" Michael Neumann burst out while the others echoed his interest. Little Mike dropped the oiled rag into its saucer.

"Today the Town Man brought a letter to Pastor Kunz," the elder explained. "It was from our brethren in Canada. You'll all hear the letter read tomorrow after churchtime. It's full of the trouble that our people are having in the Alberta Province. There, as you know, a law has been passsed restricting our brethren in future land purchases."

"Such a law was introduced in Manitoba, too," the Bee Boss announced.

"More than that," Elder Linder continued, "there are evidences of ill will against our Hutterian system."

"Persecution," proclaimed Michael, "must be expected. Were we ever promised an easy life?"

"Persecution is spreading," the elder went on. "The world is coming too close with its demands for conformity. What can be done? Escape. Flee. Do as the Scripture enjoins. Where people will not have you, shake the dust of that place from your feet. Many of the colonies will do just that. Some have gone to Paraguay already. But some will come here if we can help them."

"Let them come, Jacob father," exclaimed Jacob J. "Here there is always room."

"If our brethren can live on honey," said the Bee Boss jokingly, "they won't starve here."

"Where does Joshua Volkner come in?" Michael wanted to know, but before Elder Linder could reply the door opened and Sarah Neumann entered, her knitting pail on her arm, the needles automatically working under her hands.

"When are you coming home, Michael?" she asked. "Are you working all night?"

"Quiet, woman!" Michael ordered. "Go on with the talk, Jacob."

Sarah moved into the shadows where Little Mike sat, watching and listening. Here she stood knitting, while her eyes roved the faces of the men.

"The colony that wants to return here is the one that has in it most of Joshua Volkner's people," the elder explained.

"How things work out!" Michael marveled. "So they want to come back! Didn't we tell them to stay in this country?"

"Of course we did!" affirmed Rudolph Kunz. "But they thought there would be better farmland and better commune tracts in Canada."

"Well," Michael explained, "Joshua's running away made them want to leave, too, though I could never understand that. His sin was not their sin. Now after twenty years the world into which he ran is pushing them so they must run. But they're running the right way. Let them come. We can build them a new colony. Only some of you must learn to drive a nail. And get those stockings done that you are knitting, Sarah. There will be big doings here one of these days!"

Elder Linder chuckled. "You're ahead of the times, Carpenter. First we must buy a tract of land and that may require more money than we can scrape together."

"Yes, yes!" Michael said impatiently. "That is why I am not an elder. An elder has to be conservative, Mr. Blacksmith. But I tell you this: when the brethren come, I'll have the buildings up and ready."

"Cattle I'll see to," promised Jacob J. Linder.

"Bees I'll have," vowed the Bee Boss. "No colony can live without bees."

"Who knows?" ventured Sarah. "Maybe Joshua Volkner himself will help if he knows what is going on."

"Nail me down!" shrieked Michael. "That shows what would happen if women ran things around here. Knit, woman, and be silent!"

Elder Linder put on his black hat. He raised himself up, his head almost touching the ceiling. He walked over to the workbench and picked up the tools. "I wish that all of you," he said, "might have heard Pastor Jacob after he read the letter from our Canadian brethren."

Jacob J. asked, "What did he say, Jacob father?"

"He told us that we should be thankful that we are in America. America will never pass such laws against our people. America knows that we have much to give the country, not only in spiritual life but in improving the land. America leaves us alone and free. The pastor re-

minded us that we were persecuted during the First World
War. Our cattle were driven from the fields and some of
us were thrown from our wagons. Two of our young
men died in prison during that time. But it was not so
during World War II. Then our rights were respected.
Then we learned how America can treat its people. 'I
will write to our brethren in Canada,' Pastor Jacob said,
'and say, "Come, we will build a place for you in God's
land. Come, we will provide for you until you can provide for yourself. Come home, brethren, to the only land
where we can live unmolested and unharmed. If we have
two coats we will give you one. Where we have two
sheep, one will be yours. Half of all that we have shall be
yours until you can pay it back to us again. We will help
you build your community and we will sing the old songs
with you in a free land." ' "

Jacob J. Linder exclaimed, "Ah, Jacob father, that must
have been a meeting!"

Elder Linder gathered up the tools. "Yes, but standing
here doesn't get us up before daybreak. I'll have the cutting tools sharp for you before breakfast, Carpenter."

"Sharp I want them," Michael insisted. "Sharper than
Joshua Volkner's razor which, I understand, held quite a
fascination for a certain young boy." But his manner said,
Have no fear, Little Mike. This is not the night to scold.
This is the night to thank God that we are free and happy
and able to help those who with us follow the true faith.

"Good night, Carpenter."

"Good night, Blacksmith," said Michael. "Good night,
Jacob J. And good night, Bee Boss. Your new hives will
be ready when you need them."

"Thank you, Michael. And let me remind you, gentlemen, there are, as you know, only two perfect communal systems in the world: bees and the Hutterians."

"And God watches over each of them with equal care," concluded Elder Linder.

He swung open the door, bent low and trudged out, followed by Jacob J. and the Bee Boss.

The door closed. Little Mike jumped to his feet. "Isn't it wonderful, Michael father?"

"It's wonderful how you get out of work, yes," Michael reproved the boy in make-believe disgust. "And you there, Sarah, why are you hanging around like a screech owl?"

"I came to get some kindling," Sarah said.

"Little Mike can bring it," Michael told her. "Go to bed. It's late."

"I don't know how late it is," Sarah said wearily. "But all of a sudden I feel tired as midnight. Come, then, Little Mike, bring the kindling."

"I must finish the wedding chest, Sarah mother. Michael father always says, 'It's a poor carpenter who lets the oil go to sleep on the wood.' "

He sprang to his work and started rubbing vigorously.

Michael looked pleased. "You'll make a good cabinet man, Little Mike."

Sarah rolled up the sock she was knitting and stuck the needles through. "He's better cut out for outside work, like with the bees or the cattle."

Michael shrugged. Then with suddenness he said, "Produce me some more boys, Sarah Neumann, and I'll let you help me choose their careers."

"You just be patient," Sarah countered. "The Neumann family isn't finished yet by a long way."

"Is that so?" Michael inquired, tilting his hat back and

looking at her calculatingly. "Thank you for the information."

Sarah laughed softly, tucked her knitting into the honey pail and departed.

"It must be midnight," Michael complained with a yawn. "That's the time women start to talk foolish." But as he banged his tools into place on the wall, Little Mike heard him hum snatches of a hymn. Then he seized the stub of a broom and began sweeping off the workbench.

"No, Michael father, you said never to make dust when you oil the wood."

"H'm, that's right. Well, come, let's get this oiling done so a man can sweep his shop and go to bed."

Two pairs of hands gave the chest a thorough going-over until it shone almost as bright as the silver harmonica in Little Mike's pocket. A good gloss, Carpenter Michael argued, was not ornamentation or false beauty; it was merely bringing out the natural hidden texture which God had put into the wood and for which God demanded rubbing. As they worked, Little Mike asked without looking up, "Michael father, did you ever see a wheel go around—with people—a Ferris wheel with people?"

"That you should have asked Mr. Demas."

"He told us."

"Yes, I hear he even had pictures of it. Well, then, you know."

The rubbing continued.

"He only said it carried people, Michael father. He didn't say how it carried people."

"And he didn't say it was an amusement of the Devil either, did he?"

"No, Michael father."

"Well, it is. And Joshua is one of the men the Devil likes to take for a ride. He is sitting on the wheel going around and around and up and down. What a picture of the world! There's a sermon for you, Pastor Jacob."

"How do the people keep from falling off?"

"They don't." Michael chuckled as the image impressed itself on him. "Joshua himself will fall off the big wheel and break his neck. And who will pick him up? That is the question. Who in the world cares about him? But the wheel goes on."

"But on the Ferris wheel they don't fall off, unless Joshua Volkner told a lie."

Michael straightened to relieve a kink in his back. "Oh, I see. You want to build a Ferris wheel and you don't know how to make the seats. There's a new commune to be built but you want to make playthings."

"Joey Kunz——"

"Oh, Joey Kunz! Yes, he will make a wheel to reach to the sky, I suppose. He is always building—in his mind. He even saw the picture of the Ferris wheel and still he doesn't know how to make it. There's a great carpenter for you."

Little Mike took courage from his father's jesting mood. "Joey made a Ferris Wheel out of a barrel hoop, but when he made the seats, the people always fell in the mud. The pebbles for the people fell in the mud. None of us could figure it out. Not even Jake Linder. Then we said, 'The only person who can figure it out is Carpenter Michael Neumann.' That's what we said and then Joey said——"

"And I say, 'Finish the chest top so we can go to bed.' "

"Yes, Michael father."

Rub . . . rub . . . A person should never think that the fathers or the elders would understand. How wise he had been not to say anything about the harmonica! What would that have led to? The fathers had never been boys. They had always been old men with beards. All they thought about was discipline. They wanted life to be as hard as it could be. Playthings would make the days full of fun and wonder. But playthings were not allowed. Work is what the men wanted. Only work. Rub . . . rub . . . He would go home soon and bury his head in his soft pillow and shed tears which he would never let his father see. He would put the harmonica under his pillow and that would be a great comfort. The beautiful instrument understood his feelings better than his father did.

"That's good enough, Mike. Put the oil back in the bottle and the rags in the stove."

He obeyed.

His father spread a canvas cloth protectingly over the chest, then seized the broom and swept the workbench clean. "Get the kindling ready for your mother, Mike."

Little Mike picked up the sticks and shavings from the floor and stuffed them into a gunny sack while his father swept.

"Hold the shingle so I can sweep this on," his father told him.

Obediently Little Mike took the thin, wide shingle that was the dustpan and held it while his father swept the dirt onto it. Then he put the dirt into the squat, rusted stove in the center of the shop.

"You want the towel, Michael father?"

"No," said Michael shortly, wiping his hands on his pants. "Wipe your face. You have more oil on it than on the chest top."

Slowly Little Mike wiped his cheeks. They were wet with oil. He wiped them dry, hung the hand towel back on its nail and walked over to pick up the kindling sack. Then he noticed that his father stood at the workbench and that he had before him two small baby-wagon wheels held together by a wooden axle. Little Mike came over. The lantern was set to spread its light over the scene, but it shone even brighter in Mike's heart. The expert, strong hands of his father pressed the wheels together on the axle so that they were about four inches apart.

Little Mike's voice was a whisper of wonder. "You need *two* wheels to make the Ferris wheel, Michael father?"

Michael whispered back in a tone of friendly mocking. "Yes, two wheels you need to make one wheel. Isn't that what Joey Kunz, the great colony inventor, used?"

"No, he just used one. He just tacked the seats on to the hoop."

"Then he just made a mistake," breathed Michael in a voice of utmost secrecy. "Then he is not such a great inventor after all, is he?"

Little Mike shook his head. "No, Michael father, no one anywhere is so great an inventor as you."

Michael hummed a hymn under his breath. Now he held a small strip across the two wheels and broke it off, then tacked it onto the wheels so that it looked like the rung of a ladder. He tacked on six of these strips and the contrivance took the form of a miniature mill wheel.

"But they will still fall off if you put people on there, Michael father."

"We don't put them on there. We make chairs for them like this, out of two pieces of wood. Chairs with backs so that the world's people will be comfortable. Then we hang the chairs from the crosspieces with wires. We put a little loop in the wire so that it turns and the chairs are always even. See, like this. Here's a nail. This is Joshua Volkner. You see what a big head he has? We put the nail in the seat. I hold the wheel and you turn. There, the nail stays in. Joshua Volkner has a free ride."

"Let's make some more seats, Michael father, and put one on each crosspiece."

"All right, we will make four. One for Mrs. Volkner. One for Robert Volkner. And one for Elaine Volkner. The whole family gets a free ride."

The golden moments in which he watched his father work transported Little Mike to such a dizzy height that he himself might have been riding the wheel five stories high over the commune. How quickly his father could make the seats and loop the wire! How deftly he hung the chairs in their places! And when the four tiny seats dangled from the sure-enough Ferris wheel, Little Mike held the axle and his father spun the wheel round and round and accompanied the turning with the humming of a song. Four nails had a glorious ride. Four "passengers" were spinning in the cabinet shop. In his delight Little Mike thought of the harmonica. He would take it out of his pocket and play while his father spun the wheel. He would let the harmonica sing "The Great Song" so his father could hear. But something within him warned, *Don't, Mike, don't.*

Michael Neumann turned the wheel slower and his eyes grew thoughtful. "Those seats," he said, "are like life here in the colony. Always balanced. Always straight. Always even. The world turns but it cannot dump us out. We're in the right seat."

So saying he took the wheel from Little Mike's hands and began tearing off the miniature chairs with his customary vigor. He tore off the crosspieces and began forcing the wheels back into their original places.

"So now you know how it works. Here, throw them in the stove."

Little Mike gathered up the seats reluctantly and carried them to the stove. He deposited the broken pieces upon the shavings and the dirt inside. Reverently he closed the stove door and turned the handle.

His father grabbed the kindling sack and blew out the lantern. He called to Little Mike, who still stood near the stove, gave him his hand in the dark and led him from the shop.

"I'm glad you knew how to make it, Michael father. I knew you would. Did you ever see one really, or did you just know, like you knew about the river?"

"I think I saw one once," Michael said distantly as he marched Mike over the commune grounds. "I saw one once when I went with the Town Man to Omaha. There was a wheel there at a circus or something. I saw it. When it went round it played music."

"Yes, yes, I know it plays music, Michael father."

"Well, then you know everything. Be careful you don't get so smart that they call you Mike the Teacher."

Michael Neumann swung open the door of his home. Little Mike hurried in close at his heels and went happily to the children's room. In the darkness his sisters stirred in their sleep. Soon he heard his father speaking to his mother about the elders' meeting and the new colony and the work that needed to be done. In a little while Michael father was murmuring his prayers.

Little Mike took off his pants and pulled the harmonica from his pocket. Clasping it jealously, he crawled into his sleeping bench. The bench had a soft feather pallet, and the small pillow was stuffed with down. Through it he could feel the harmonica where it lay warm and concealed. Into his ears it played its sweet melody. In the darkness the big wheel turned. And lying there wide-eyed in the night, he asked himself why he had not shown his father the instrument, especially since he knew that Michael father loved him so very much.

CHAPTER 8

~~~~~~

*E*ARLY the next morning before milkingtime, Little Mike stole into the cabinet
shop. He closed the door, then peered stealthily through
the window. Assuring himself that his father was on his
way to Blacksmith Linder's to pick up the tools, he walked
quickly to the stove. The door handle was warm. The
fire pot glowed with smoldering ashes. They were gone!
The Ferris wheel seats had burned along with the dirt and
shavings and the tiny pieces which he had laid into the
stove with such care. Had his father guessed he might
come and try to reclaim them? Or had God put it into
the heart of Michael father to light a fire so early that
morning? Nothing happened just by chance. The eye
of God never slept and its watchfulness had doubled since
he had come into possession of the harmonica. How far
could a boy go before something happened? How much
joy would God allow before His voice thundered through
the commune like the voice of Pastor Kunz?

Anxiously Little Mike closed the stove door and went
into the yard. Joey Kunz came running, pulling his tin-
pail wagon with the end of the long handle between his
legs. "Hey, Mike, ready for the big day?"

"Yeah, but, Joey, why doesn't your wagon rattle this
morning?"

145

"Joseph father made me take out the stones because of the noise. Mike, what about the wheel seats?" Joey asked anxiously. "Did your father know?"

"Sure he knew."

"Did he tell you?"

"Sure he told me."

"Can it be done?"

"It can be done easy."

"Well, then," Joey cried, "it is a big day. I can build anything by directions. I can even build things without directions, unless it's something from outside the commune like this wheel is. Why is it, Mike, that it's usually the things which are against the rules that are so full of excitement?"

Mike could not say. He wandered aimlessly from the cabinet shop and across the meadow road to the yard space between the "face house" and the barn. Joey followed, begging for the wheel information. Mike's meandering steps led him in the direction of the schoolhouse.

"Where are you going?" Joey wanted to know. "What's the matter with you?"

"Joey, there were even four seats made and they burned in the fire."

"Well, the information didn't burn in the fire, did it?"

"No, that is in my head."

"Then don't burn your head," Joey cautioned. "But out with it quick before you forget."

Dan Mueller and Matt Neumann came running from the cowyard where the Milk Boss was fastening the cows into the wooden stanchions.

"The wheel!" Dan gasped.

"The seat information!" Matt urged.

"Mike's father knew," Joey reported. "He's a smart one at building, too."

The words filled Little Mike with pride. What did it matter if the seats were gone? He stood again with his father at the workbench. He heard the whisper: "You need two wheels to make one wheel."

"All right, come along!" Little Mike ordered and led them to the school steps.

Dan picked up a small flat stone, spit on it and polished it on his shirt. "This can be the first rider," he said.

Joey tossed his pail wagon aside. "I've got string and nails and even some strips of wood," he said, emptying his pockets on the steps. "Go ahead, Mike. All we need are the wise words."

"All you do," Mike explained, "is hang the seats onto the bars with wire so they can swing free when the wheel turns."

"On what bar? How can they swing free?"

"You need two wheels, Joey."

"Two wheels?"

"They are really one because they turn at the same time. The bars across hold them together. The seats hang down from the bars on wires that have loops and this lets the seats always hang straight."

"I know!" squealed Joey, and he excitedly searched the ground, found two small supple branches and hastily bent them into hoops. "Tie them up, Matt," he instructed.

All hands went to work, for Joey had the idea and Mike had the answers. Soon Matt and Dan held two identical hoops side by side and Joey fastened crosspieces on them "to make the two wheels one." Then Joey proved that he knew how to hang the seats so they would swing free. The wheel was crude. It would not even carry Dan's polished stone, but the idea had been grasped. The wisdom of the commune had solved the mystery. It was decided that immediately after breakfast the hunt would go on for the right kind of hoops and the necessary material. The harmonica elders would be summoned and the willow clearing on the other side of the *Vogelpfad* would be the place for the building. It was the bright dawning of another day.

Proudly the geese strutted across the main yard and invaded the spaces between the houses and sheds. Resolutely the men strode through the colony grounds. At the separator shed the Milk Boss called his orders. Little Mike saw his father walk in full swing to the cabinet shop, carrying the tools. And when Matt exclaimed, "This calls for a song!" it was a benediction that dismissed the last lurking fear that God might be only the elders' God and never understand the hearts of little boys.

"Yes," Dan agreed, "a harmonica song would wake me up for the whole day."

"Have you got it with you, Mike?" Joey asked.

"Sure I've got it," Mike boasted. "I could walk right into the church and play 'The Great Song.' "

"Not in the church," said Dan. "I know a better place. The wolf cave!"

"Good!" Joey agreed. "But first let's stick these things under the school steps."

Quickly the Ferris wheel model was stuffed out of

sight and a moment later the boys were off on a trot to the river.

Along the river westward from the old mill the bank rose suddenly and then gradually dipped to the river flats. On this long, loaf-shaped promontory the grass grew coarse and thick. An old stump clung tenaciously to the edge of the grassy overhang, and its gnarled roots dangled down toward the river. This provided a hazardous ladder on which the boys could crawl down almost to the water's edge. One of the exposed roots led down into a large hollowed-out place in the side of the bank. This was the wolf cave, though the Farm Boss said he had never seen anything in it wilder than a woodchuck.

Joey flung himself to the grass, stuck his face over the brink, grabbed hold of the stump root, swung himself over the precarious edge and clambered down the six feet to the cave. "Next comes the Harmonica Boss!" he called out.

As each boy crawled down the perpendicular wall, he sent a drift of soft dirt riverward. The four boys filled the cave to dangerous capacity, for the edge of the passage was eroded and brittle.

"I must have room," Mike said. "The harmonica isn't made to be played in such shoving."

"Well, don't push me out!" Dan cried. "I don't want to roll into the Missouri."

"I'm going back up," Joey decided, shoving his way to the entrance. "I'll be the watchman. If somebody comes, down comes my head; if it's nothing bad, I'll just dangle my feet."

"Good!" Mike agreed. "You go up and listen. If the notes are too loud, call down."

"This is a good music hide-out," Matt observed as the stump root shook under Joey's ascent and dirt rolled down. "It'll be fine for our seven elders."

Dan spit through his teeth. "You couldn't get seven in here without the sausage squeezer," he figured. "Here, Mike, you stretch out in the front and Matt and I will curl up behind you. Where's the harmonica?"

"Right here in my pocket," Mike assured them, but as he reached for it something told him it was not there. The frightening premonition sent his hand clutching frantically at his empty pocket. "The harmonica!" he cried, looking wildly about. "The harmonica!" In desperate fear he searched his pockets while the voices of Matt and Dan were his own thoughts assailing him:

"Lost? Where did you have it last?"

"Did it fall into the Missouri?"

"Did you drop it somewhere?"

"Think, Mike, think! Where is it?"

Merrily Joey called down, "Play, *Ansager*, play! You're the Harmonica Boss."

"Joey," Dan shouted, "the harmonica is *gone!*"

Joey hung down over the edge of the grassy bank, defying danger to bring his eyes as close to the wolf cave as possible. Below him Mike grabbed hold of the stump root and crawled almost out of the cave, head downward, scanning the brown water of the Missouri.

"Mike," Joey cried, "do you think that our river could have taken it?"

Matt and Dan pulled Mike back.

"Don't fall in," Matt warned.

"Maybe it's right here in the cave," Dan suggested, beginning a hurried search.

"When was the last time you know you had it?" Joey called down. "When did you have your hands right on it so you knew it was there?"

Mike could not answer. He brushed the stinging tears from his eyes and worked his hands imploringly in the loose dirt of the cave floor.

"When we find it," Dan said, "you better put a chain on it, like Joshua Volkner had on his watch."

Mike heard the words in distress. To put a chain on the instrument would be like putting the wild bird in the cage. A chain like the one on Volkner's watch would make worldly something that was beautiful and free. It was so free that it was gone. But only for a little while. God would surely give it back. God would feel what he felt in his heart and help him find it again.

Joey shouted that he would search in the grass. Of course, that was where the harmonica would be. Up on the high bank. When he crawled over, it must have slipped out of his pocket and it would probably be somewhere in the grass. Mike seized the stump root and climbed up. Pulling himself over the brink, he saw Joey down on his knees pawing through the thick growth.

"Not a sign," Joey said. "It would shine, wouldn't it? But it's not up here. I even rolled and it isn't here. If it was it would have stuck me in the ribs."

Dan and Matt came up and joined the thorough search.

"All we have to do," Dan suggested, "is go back over every inch of the way we came. Things don't just walk away."

"That's right," agreed Matt. "The harmonica didn't have legs."

Their words were no consolation. Dan and Matt and Joey did not understand. They did not know how the eye of God had been watching. Why could not things just disappear if God wanted them to? Nor did his friends understand what the harmonica really was. They did not know how the music was made deep in the heart of the lovely shining thing.

"I was going to ask you to play the morning song," Matt said.

"Which morning song?" asked Dan.

" 'The Day that God has Made.' That's one of the best."

"Mike could have played it like nothing."

Far below, the Missouri flowed on unheedingly. Up on the bank excited hands raked through the grass. Joey was rolling, trying to discover the harmonica's hiding place.

"It must be in the river," Mike said fatefully. "That's where it must have gone. I'm going down."

But now the commanding tones of the colony bell struck the chalk cliffs with authority and bounced back to the grassy ledge.

"Breakfast," Dan announced.

"Let me stay here," Mike said in anguish, wrestling against the summons of the bell.

"I would as soon stay too," Matt said moanfully.

Joey picked up the handle of his pail wagon. "What you would as soon do and what you must do are different," he reasoned. "Anyway it's my morning to pray."

"That's right," said Matt. "That means we can't be late."

Joey stood with the long handle between his legs. "Mike," he said, remembering suddenly, "what will this do to the big wheel? Why should we build it if we have no music? There's no use for people just to go up and around if there's no music for enjoyment."

"This spoils everything," said Dan, spitting.

"All I will do today," Mike vowed, "is look. I will look everywhere."

"Will the wetness hurt it much, Mike," Matt asked, "if our river did get it?"

"The sun will dry it again," Mike assured him, his hope returning as he spoke, "and there's no song that it will not play when we get it back again."

But as he walked to the eating house, never lifting his eyes from the ground, his heart sank with every step. If he could just turn and run back to the Missouri, crawl down the stump root and begin to hunt through the rippling water . . .

Mary Kunz, the Kitchen Boss, stood in the doorway and called, "Hurry up, you four! What is it this morning? Everybody is in and you come as if you were heading for the graveyard. Hurry up with you."

They walked into the drab, rectangular room. Little Mike saw the long, familiar table near the west wall where the girls sat shoulder to shoulder on the backless benches. He noticed his sisters Mary and Anna sitting among the rest with eager, happy faces. They could lose nothing because they owned nothing. They could never understand his loss. There they sat, and Hulda Mueller, the Table Boss, stood at the north wall and looked sternly down the rows. She saw to it that the twenty-four girls sat in perfect discipline, their head scarfs properly adjusted, their hands folded ready for prayer.

As he went to the boys' table along the east wall, he was an onlooker rather than a part of the activity. The thirty boys, ranging from four to twelve years of age, were waiting restlessly for Joey to take his place and speak the prayer. Their confidence and security disturbed him. How well did he really know them? Just now the commune was a little world he had walked into from somewhere outside. He was a stranger. To whom could he go and confess his sense of guilt and pain? Who would understand? Joey and Dan and Matt were climbing over the benches and squeezing into their places. Hulda Mueller came to the head of the table. He heard her say, "Well, Mike Neumann, do you want to be carried across the room and set down? Look at your hands. They're as dirty as if this was the end of the day instead of the beginning. Quick with you—into your place!"

His sister Rachel came in from the kitchen with a large pitcher of milk. She carried it to the heavy, pine serving table near the door and began filling glasses. Every morning as long as he could remember, he had come into this room and things were always the same; always there was the Table Boss and the milk server and the Kitchen Boss bringing the food in the steaming dishes. He spied Jake Linder, who moved over to make way for him. Jake looked at him, and in a glance read his concern. Mike crawled in next to him.

Jake asked gently, "Did you lose it, Mike?"

Mike nodded. He showed no surprise at Jake's omniscience. It did not seem strange to him that the mystery and magic of the commune should play their part in his moment of distress. He sighed and it was almost a sob. Jake nudged him as if to say that he should not let the others see.

Joey rapped on his plate with his knife. At the girls' table, heads were bowed over folded hands. Automatically the boys also assumed reverent attitudes. Little Mike closed his eyes and pressed his hands together in front of his heart. He had been taught that during these moments he should think of God; he should remember that in the adult refectory at the other end of the building, the older people were praying in exactly the same manner, the men at one table, the women at another, with a man always rapping for prayer.

But when Joey tapped on his plate and said the customary "We pray," Mike's thoughts darted swiftly from former teachings and covered in one agonizing flight every move he had made since he had risen early that morning. Every remembrance stabbed him with the possibility that even now the harmonica might be somewhere on the floor of the cabinet shop, on the schoolhouse steps or on the meadow road. If he did not find it, one of the men would, and if that happened . . .

Joey was praying: "Bless, O Lord, these thy gifts, us to feed and Thee to praise!"

This was the prescribed prayer, but this morning there

was an awkward pause before the final "Amen." Joey was
not through. His moment of hesitancy was more im-
pressive than had been his words. Mike half opened his
eyes. Joey's face was serious and set. Earnestly of his
own accord he added, "And please help us, God, in You
know what. Amen."

Mike's eyes flashed open. All along the table startled
faces showed surprise. Joey's head sank in shame and
fear, lower and lower, as if he wished he could vanish
completely. At the girls' table eyes peeped anxiously from
under head scarfs.

Then came the voice of Hulda Mueller raised in shocked
surprise. "Where does that new idea come from?"

Dan Mueller burst out in laughter that spluttered over his
plate. It put the spark to both tables and loud laughter sent
everyone swaying as if they all were suddenly riding on the
hay wagon.

Paul Wiese slapped Joey on the back and shouted,
"What is the 'You know what,' Mr. Prayer Boss?"

Spasms of laughter rocked the room while the Table
Boss scolded angrily and Rachel Neumann clapped her
hands for order.

Joey still sat with his head down.

Mike's voice was rebellious. "Why can't he pray the
way he wants to?"

"Because he's not Pastor Kunz!" shouted one of the
boys.

Paul Wiese jumped from the bench and said, "This is as
good as if you had played the harmonica, Mike, right out
in front of everybody."

Joey's head came up with a snap. "Shut up, you fool!
What are you saying?"

Paul scrambled from the bench and pointed his finger at Joey with terrible meaning. "You know what happens to anyone who says that!"

"Boys! Paul Wiese, sit down!" ordered the Table Boss.

Mike's heart pounded. He knew what it meant for a boy to use that word; he knew why it had sent the laughter scattering and why the scared and staring eyes were turned on Joey. Even Paul's words about the harmonica were forgotten. Everyone knew that Pastor Kunz had made it clear that God's Word warned: "Whosoever shall say 'Thou fool' shall be in danger of hellfire."

"Start to eat, children," ordered Hulda Mueller.

The clamorous voices dissolved into whispers that ran up and down the benches:

"What did Paul say?"

"What's a harmonica?"

"Hey, Mike, what you got? Let's see it."

"Boys, what is it with you?" Rachel Neumann demanded as she served the milk. "Eat or leave the table. Mike, start with your eggs."

"It's all right, Joey," Mike whispered.

"All right?" Paul mocked. "He will be brought up in front of the elders and maybe the whole congregation."

If this ominous prediction came to pass, Joey would have to explain just what he meant by the prayer. The secret of the harmonica would be known everywhere in the commune. Was this heaven's way of handling the affair, a step at a time until everything would be laid bare before the people?

Jake Linder leaned over to Paul and asked suddenly, "But, Paul, what did he say?"

Paul retorted, "Say? You heard it. He said, 'You fool!'"

Soberly Jake looked at him. Then he smiled. "Well, Paul Wiese, there you've said it yourself! Now I shall tell Pastor Kunz on you."

Hilarious laughter broke over the table as it dawned on Paul that he had indeed spoken the forbidden word. Joey Kunz bounced up and down on the bench chanting, "If I go to the elders, Paul goes, too. Did Jake ever outsmart you!"

Hulda Mueller came over and shook Joey by the shoulders. "Eat, Joey Kunz, or get out! Eat, Paul Wiese! What's happening to our rules and regulations?"

Her voice was loud and threatening and order was restored. Mike felt Jake's presence as a protector. "What would I do without you, Jake?" he whispered.

Paul had a final word: "If it hadn't been for you, Mike Neumann, this wouldn't have happened. You started it all with a sin and a secret and a personal possession."

Mike looked at him with eyes that were pleading. "You don't have to think of that any more, Paul," he murmured. "It is gone. The beautiful instrument is no more."

"What do you mean?" Paul began ruthlessly. "I suppose you hid it somewhere."

Jake said, "Just like I might hide the sore on my neck. Since when don't you believe anybody, Paul Wiese? Or did you maybe find the instrument yourself?"

Paul sobered. "No, Jake," he said in a changed voice. "I didn't see it. Is it lost, Mike? Is it really gone? Then I'll help you hunt for it."

Mike looked at him. Gradually the scene became real. The sounds around him were reassuring. If he could hold the feeling that Jake and Paul and Joey and the others were

friendly, that was best. Mike had seen the hurt in Paul's
eyes. Joey's prayer had been sincere. It was well that he
was among those whom he could trust, and not out in the
world where he knew no one and where no one would
understand. Jake was saying, "You and I will find the
harmonica, Mike."

They would search the grounds together. He would
rather have Jake with him than anyone. Jake would know
that God had something to do with all this. Only the
Great Eye knew where the harmonica was at this very
moment. Only God could lead him to it. How easy it
would be for God to bend down and whisper, "I'll find
it for you, Mike. Come, I'll show you just where it is."
Had anyone ever heard God's voice? Had the elders and
Pastor Kunz really ever heard anything plain and clear?
All the beautiful stories in the Bible would be much more
real if only something would happen to him now. He
remembered how he had learned and recited: "A voice
came to the boy Samuel. . . . Abraham looked out of his
tent and there stood three angels. . . . Elijah walked with
God. . . . the Lord appeared to David. . . ." These things
had happened long ago. He had been taught to believe
them. He knew the stories by heart. If they were true,
why couldn't they happen now? Mike bowed his head
over his plate and prayed to himself, "O eye of God,
watch over it carefully until I find it again."

He tried to eat, but the morning's events would not
let him. He recalled how he had stood at the window of
the cabinet shop and spied on his father. He remembered
the stove and wondered if it was possible that he might
have laid the instrument on the fire grate. He could not

recollect having felt it in his pocket after he came from the building. Could he unconsciously have put it into the stove like a sacrifice?

Joey rapped loudly on his plate. The boys were through eating and that meant that the girls should be through, too.

Joey said, "We pray."

Heads were bowed. The silence was deep and expectant. The Table Boss and Rachel stood in benevolent attitudes, hopeful that the children would need no more discipline for the morning.

Joey the innovator, was praying again. "We thank thee, Lord, for these thy gifts, which we have received from thy bounty. Amen."

It was the prayer according to the rules. With the "Amen" in his throat, Joey clambered out of the bench. Quickly the boys followed. In a moment they were outside plaguing Mike with excited questions. Joey and Jake sprang to his aid. Adroitly Jake reminded them of the colony rule which forbade loitering around the eating house. In a moment Mike was free and speeding straight to the cabinet shop.

Breakfast was not yet over for the colony men, and the shop was his to search through unhindered. He flung open the stove door and sifted through the cold ashes with his hands. There was no hint of the sacrifice here; this iron altar held only the dubious remains of the Ferris wheel seats and the suddenly sad remembrance of last evening. He wiped his hands on his shirt and turned to go when his eyes caught sight of a bright and shining object on the floor. His heart stopped, but it was only a chisel blade which lay near the window. Had it been there when he was in the room earlier in the morning? He put it on the workbench and started out. As he stood in the half-open door, he saw the men come from breakfast.

The strong, bearded figures strode into the yard putting their black hats on as they filed through the door: the Householder with his serious face, Blacksmith Linder swinging his strong arms, James the Teacher walking reflectively, the Miller, the Bee Boss, the Shoemaker, the Hog Boss, the Farm Boss, the Town Man. Freedom of life was in their step, and theirs was the confidence that God had given them authority for all they did. They had nothing to hide. They owned nothing; they had lost nothing; they coveted nothing. They were possessors together of the chalk-block houses they had built, rulers of the barns and the shops and the mill, partners with God.

Mike could not escape now, for the sharp eye of his father had spied him.

Michael Neumann approached the door. "What were you doing in the shop?" he demanded. "You know you boys aren't allowed in here unless I'm on hand."

Little Mike watched him rebelliously as he laid aside his black jacket, rolled up his sleeves and stuck a pencil behind his ear.

"Go quick and measure the broken window in the chicken house," he ordered.

Michael Neumann put on his carpenter's apron and filled the pockets with nails out of a barrel. Never doubting that Mike would obey him, he took a folding rule and began marking some boards for a beehive.

Instinctively Mike started to go. He had never hesitated to do his father's will, but now there was only one voice he could obey, and that told him to search everywhere, to retrace every move he had made, and it called him now to the schoolhouse steps.

Abruptly he closed the door of the shop and dashed into the yard, across the gate road and on to the school. He flung himself to his knees and began burrowing through the sticks and branches with which Joey had demonstrated the building of the wheel. Then he crawled about, plucking at the grass.

Dan and Joey came on a trot.

"Any sign of it, Mike?" Joey asked.

"Not a sign."

"Did you look good back of the steps?" Dan inquired.

Joey dropped to the ground and wriggled his body through the small gap under the steps. "I'll find it if it's here," he vowed, "unless a rat chewed it up. There do come rats under here sometimes."

Dan said, "Jake went to search the river."

"Did he?" Mike cried hopefully.

"He went to the tool shed and got himself a rake." Dan's voice fell to a whisper, "Without permission he took it. That's why he wouldn't let us go with him, because if he gets caught only he will be disciplined."

"Where did Jake go to start his river-raking, Joey?" Mike asked.

"He went down the stump root for sure," Joey reported, squirming in the narrow gap. "But pull me out by the feet. I've got my belly stuck."

Dan spit through his teeth. "I'll get you out. Make your belly small."

Dan rescued the unsuccessful searcher and Mike told them to comb the schoolyard while he helped Jake at the river.

He sped across the road, darting between the cowyard and the carpenter shop. There was no window in the shop on the east side and his father would not see him. Sometime he would have to face Michael father, but not now. Sometime—— Guilt and fear drove him past the big barn and the sheds. When he reached the thick, coarse turf on the high bank, he slowed his steps. He wanted to look in the grass once more, but first he must see that Jake was safe at the precarious bank where the river ran close to the sloping dirt wall. He reached the brink and looked down. He saw no one.

"Jake!"

Upstream quite close at hand the clattering rumble of the mill was starting. The big wheel was turning. The brown river was being put to work.

"Jake!"

He waited in panic for a sound from his friend. He scanned the river for a sign. Then he swung himself over the bank. The stump root quivered as he let the weight of his body drop. He hung for a moment between the brim of the bank and the wolf cave. Excitedly he let himself down. Half crawling, half sliding, he lowered himself to the water's edge. His bare feet touched the water and he let go of the root. The water was up to his knees and he steadied himself for a moment against the bank. Cautiously he felt his way along the uneven river bottom. A short yard from the wall he looked down. Ahead of him the murky water was impenetrable.

"Jake!"

Shuddering at the feeling that Jake had drowned, he already imagined that he would find the body around the sharp bend where the river eddied. Here where he stood the bank jutted out into a deep channel. The current ran swiftly. He inched forward, standing uncertainly, his feet slipping more and more into the stream. He could cling to the bank and maneuver his way around the bend or he could go back. That would mean climbing the stump root to the high bank and following a path down to the eddy. The quickest way would be to swim. That would mean going downstream about thirty feet. He spread his arms and let himself slide into the channel.

When the shock of the water struck him, he remembered the colony rule against swimming anywhere but in the water hole at the edge of the meadow. He recalled his father's comment that he did not swim the right way. He swam like the colony dog. His clothing was dragging him down. The current was pulling him steadily away from the bank. Dazed and frightened, he tried to touch bottom. His face dipped under the water. He screamed in panic. Then he fought the water as frantically as if he were wresting his life from the entwining fingers of the elders' God. The channel ran swiftly. The bend had been crossed. He was drifting weak and helpless, clumsily keeping himself afloat. A voice came to him. Jake's voice. Blindly he caught sight of his friend standing knee-deep in the water where the hill dissolved into the muddy flats.

"Help me!" he gasped.

"I'll get you!" Jake cried and rushed forward, rake in

hand, until the water almost touched the growth on his neck.

Holding the rake above the current of the river and struggling unsteadily to keep his balance, Jake dropped the handle in Mike's path. "Grab it!" he shouted.

The water pulled Mike forward, but his hands clutched the rescue stick. Jake clung to the prongs and stumbled to shore, pulling the river's half-drowned victim to the mud flats. He helped him to a spot where the earth was cracked and dry. Mike lay trembling with cold and fright, gasping for breath.

"What were you doing out there?" Jake wanted to know.

"I was afraid . . . for you. . . . Didn't you hear me call?"

"No."

"Did you find it?"

"No. I raked from the wolf cave to here. And that's nearly fifty rake lengths. But I only raked close to the bank. When we get dry we'll try it farther out. A rake is the thing to find it with. Take off your clothes and wring them out," Jake advised, as he began to undress. "Do you think the harmonica is in the river?"

"It must be. Unless God would take it. He could, couldn't He, Jake?"

"What would He want with it? If He wants a harmonica He could make one quick."

"But if He wanted this one——"

They squeezed the water out of their clothes.

"Maybe to punish me He took it," Mike went on.

"That could be a reason," Jake said thoughtfully. "But why does He always punish with sad things?"

"Like the growth on your neck," Mike added hopelessly.

"Yes, like that."

"But if He gives it back—the harmonica—everything will be good. I think I could play the morning song easy." Mike shook out his shirt and spread it on the dry ground.

"Well, just now it's good you didn't drown," Jake told him.

"Do you think I almost drowned because I ran away from Michael father?"

"Did you ever think about that really?"

"What?"

"Running away."

Breathlessly Mike looked at him. "You mean—like Joshua Volkner?"

Jake nodded.

"Did you ever, Jake?"

Jake shook his head. "It's different with me," he said, trembling with cold. "Jacob father told me that. 'Here in the commune,' he said, 'nothing makes any difference. Everybody is alike no matter how he looks or who he is or what is wrong with him.' But who would want me out in the world?"

Thoughtfully Mike put on his wet clothes. "Thank you for pulling me out, Jake," he said. "Only you look so cold. Are you all right?"

"I'm all right."

"I'm going up to the high bank," Mike said, "and look through the grass until I dry out."

"You do that," Jake agreed, picking up the rake. "I'll look some more in the Missouri. If the harmonica floated down, here's where it would have come."

"Jake," Mike proposed haltingly, "when the elders see trouble, they pray. They pray for the sick and for the crops and even for the cattle. Do you think that if we prayed for the harmonica—?"

Jake shook his head. "I've never learned any prayers that would fit in the harmonica business," he sighed. "If you want to pray, go ahead. I will keep on raking."

Mike's body ached and his soggy pants and shirt clung to him uncomfortably, but he clambered up the narrow path with a heart full of hope. Soon he was down on his knees on the high bank, folding back the grass inch by inch, combing his fingers through the thick tufts, searching until his arms hurt and his knees were stained and burning. Over and over he told himself that the instrument was near and repeatedly he felt the surge of confidence, a foretaste of that holy moment when he would once more hold it in his hands. The eye of God never winked. The voice of God never spoke. The hand of God never reached out to join him in his seeking. No footprints of God were seen and heaven gave not the slightest hint where the harmonica was hidden.

But as Little Mike remembered how beautiful it had been just yesterday when the sheep hill was made sacred with his playing, he could not imagine that the instrument was gone forever. The wolf cave would have been made holy with the music, too, just as every spot would have been hallowed wherever the music was heard: the big barn and the sheds, the shops and the houses and yards, all tinted with glory because of the music. When he thought of this he raised his eyes pleadingly and made up his own prayer: "Great God whom the fathers trusted and believed, Great God who made heaven and earth, give me back the pretty instrument! In the name of Jesus Christ our Lord. Amen."

He stood in the spell of his words. His hands moved to touch his pocket. He had the sure feeling that God would work a miracle. Now, when he put his hand to his pocket, the harmonica would be there. He would find it safe and unharmed. He could already hear himself calling, "Jake! Michael father! Pastor Kunz! Come and see! It was gone and no one could find it. We hunted everywhere and Jake dragged our river. Then I begged God to give it back, I begged and prayed for it so hard——" In fear and hope, he slid his hand into the clammy wet pocket and lowered his eyes in pain.

Hopelessly he started toward the commune yard, walking back over the way he had come with Dan and Joey and Matt before breakfast. When he reached the first shed, he could see Pastor Kunz hurrying out of his house. Mike stopped. The pastor walked with unusual haste, and he was calling to the Householder who stood at a shed near the barn with the Cattle Boss: "Caleb, who is that coming into the lane?"

"Where, Pastor Kunz?" the Householder called back. "I see nothing."

"See nothing? Surely you can see the dust."

"To be sure there's a wisp of dust!" exclaimed the Householder. "But to think that you can see that, way out there over the hedges! That is God-given sight, Pastor."

"Only sheep or an automobile makes such dust rise," called the pastor impatiently, "and the sheep are where they should be."

."Then it's an automobile, Pastor. Sure it is. There it comes straight down our road to the inside gate."

Mike raced behind the big barn, heading for the wheat field. Breathlessly he dropped to his knees at the fringe of the field where the meadow road separated the acres from the hogyard. Here, shielded from view, he fixed his eyes on the inner commune gate. A big black automobile stopped outside the gate and a man stepped from the car. Mike could almost see the glistening gold chain on his vest and the sparkle of a ring on his finger as he calmly unfastened the chain and swung open the commune gate. Then while he stood holding the gate open, the car moved through. A boy was at the wheel. A boy no older than Mike himself drove the big car into the main yard. Then Joshua Volkner closed the gate and took his place behind the wheel.

Defiantly the car made its way into the commune. Mike sprang out of the wheat and ran to the separator house where he watched from behind a wall. He saw Joshua drive the automobile on into the schoolyard. The colony dog barked. The straggling geese hissed. Everywhere the return of Joshua Volkner was announced as clearly as the ringing of the colony bell. The unusual howling of the dog brought Michael Neumann to the door of his shop. For a moment Pastor Kunz and the Householder hesitated to approach. Then the Householder started toward the car as if remembering what Hutterian tradition said about entertaining strangers. The women peeped out of the laundry house and Mary Kunz stood in the kitchen doorway wiping out the oatmeal kettle. Everywhere in the commune yard children stopped their play and moved shyly toward the visitors. In the vegetable garden Sarah Neumann, along with the other women, paused at the commotion and stood upright. She shaded her eyes and watched Joshua Volkner get out of the car. Michael Neumann walked over to extend a hand.

Little Mike made no effort to conceal himself now. No one was thinking of him. No one would have time for anything except the visitors. The colony would say that the Volkners would not interrupt the day's program, but they would. Life was never quite the same when strangers came inside the gate. Now nothing would be said about Joey's prayer or about Paul's anger at being called a fool. Even Michael father would almost forget that Mike had slammed the door and run away. Yes, he had been saved for the time being. He could go wherever he wished and he could spend many hours in the search along with Jake. His clothes were drying and no one would need to know about his plunge into the Missouri.

But something held him to his spot near the separator shed. He leaned against the rough unpainted boards with his hands doubled inside the wet matted folds of his empty pockets. Joshua Volkner and his two children stood in the yard. Joshua's wife was not with them. The sight of Robert Volkner with his necktie and pretty clothes and his laughter sent sharp pangs of longing through Little Mike. Now Joshua was introducing his children to the few men who had come to welcome him. He reached into the car and brought out a large white sackful of candy with which he tempted the boys and girls.

Everything was joy and freedom for the Volkners as if they never had to think what any elder or pastor might like or not like or whether the Great Eye of God watched or did not watch. Those things did not seem to matter. It was life that they were interested in, and life was kind. Sorrowfully and with an ache in his throat, Little Mike said half aloud, "If it is wrong to have only a harmonica and I am punished so hard for that, why is it that Joshua Volkner is not punished all the time? And if his way of life is wrong and ours is right, why am I not free to go in and out of the gate as he does?"

Now the children were running everywhere in the yard having their own gay time with the candy and even sharing some of the good things with the geese and the lamb and the colony dog. As Little Mike's eyes followed them in their merry, unrestrained joy, he saw Pastor Kunz walking with well-timed steps to his house bench where Selma Kunz sat slowly treading the spinning wheel and smoothing out the wool.

CHAPTER 9

*M*ICHAEL NEUMANN walked from the cabinet shop to the schoolhouse in a line as straight as if he had drawn it with his carpenter's pencil. The pockets of his apron bulged with nails. He carried a hammer and an assortment of small wooden blocks.

The afternoon was rainy and chill. Michael called to the Farm Boss, "Get the wheat in or it'll be caught in a freeze."

"Do you forget we've got a combine now?" the Farm Boss called back.

"If the combine works, well and good," Michael replied. "It's not new, you know."

Little Mike ran from the shop, his arms loaded with thin strips of wood. Slipping in behind his father as Michael swung open the schoolhouse door, Mike saw Sarah mother at the table where the pastor always sat at churchtime. Before her was a heap of white curtain material on which she was busily working.

"Where's the job?" Michael demanded. "And why didn't you tell me I needed a stepladder?"

"Here's a chair that's just the size," said Sarah, getting up.

Michael seized the chair and planted it near a window. "Woman's work," he grumbled. "Curtains in the school.

172

Next curtains in the houses. Then curtains in the barns and pretty soon Carpenter Michael Neumann will be called Colony Curtain Hanger. Hey, Mike, quick with those rods and we'll get this done!"

"Were there eight or ten, Michael father?"

Michael was already on the chair. "Count the windows," he said.

"Ten," Little Mike reported. "That's what I brought, I think."

"You think!" said Michael, nailing a wooden bracket into place above the window. "What were you thinking this morning when I told you to measure the broken window in the chicken house? What were you thinking when I saw you down on your hands and knees near the schoolhouse steps, pecking around like a goose? Don't get the idea that just because there are visitors here, I don't know what's going on."

Pound . . . pound . . .

Michael's hammer set two wooden brackets in a line across the top of the window. He stood on the chair with his mouth full of nails. Imperiously he leaned back as far as he dared and surveyed the brackets for their relationship to an imaginary line.

Sarah looked up. "Have you got two in place already?" she asked, surprised.

"Naturally," said Michael, spitting the nails into his hand. "Should it take me all afternoon? I don't get paid by the hour, Mrs. Neumann."

"Just do a good job," pleaded Sarah.

"Hand me up a rod, Mike," Michael ordered.

Little Mike obediently gave him one of the rods and

watched as his father laid it into the grooves of the wooden brackets.

"There, you see," Michael exclaimed exultantly, "it fits like a mitten."

"It looks to me like that one is lower," Sarah told him. "That right one."

"Maybe you should be Carpenter Boss," Michael answered. "From where I see them they're as straight as a path to a privy."

Little Mike laughed. His father pushed his hat back on his head and viewed his work haughtily.

"Well," Sarah sighed, "give me the rod and I'll put the curtain on. It will probably wiggle when it's hung."

"It will not wiggle," Michael insisted. "Anyhow when the curtain is on it, who will see whether the rod fits in the brackets or not? That, my good wife, is a lesson. That's how things are done in the world. One thing hides another thing, but as long as the thing that is seen fools the eye, everybody is satisfied."

Sarah was unimpressed with this reasoning, and as she took the rod from him, she said, "What has our curtain hanging to do with the world, I'd like to know?"

"Everything," Michael told her. "We certainly all know it's world influence that is suddenly putting curtains up on windows which have always been without curtains."

Sarah said, "You know that isn't so. There was enough complaining that the sun always hit us in the eyes every Sunday morning."

Michael said, "That was the complaint, yes, that put it over with the elders."

Sarah made believe she did not hear. She started putting the rod through the hem of the curtain while Michael moved his chair to the next window.

"But they will be nice, Michael father," said Little Mike.

"Nice," Michael grumbled. "All of a sudden everything must be nice. The curtains must be nice. The window rods must be nice. World influence. The nicest things are the natural things. Natural grain in the wood, natural color in the wood the way the good Lord put it there."

Pound . . . pound . . . pound . . .

Michael father did not understand. With him everything was work and getting things done. What if the brackets weren't just straight? What if they weren't polished or painted? Michael father did not get any pleasure out of seeing pretty things like the curtains. Would he have thought the harmonica pretty?

Michael, moving the chair to the next window, was struck by a question. "You know, Sarah," he said, "there is something very strange about Joshua Volkner and this family of his."

Sarah did not look at him. "What do you mean?" she asked.

"I thought his wife was coming. But only the children came. What kind of business is that?"

"Well, she didn't want to come, and that's the way women do in the world. Don't think women everywhere are the way women are here in the colony."

"Well!" Michael exclaimed in amazement. "Do you hear what I hear, Little Mike? We are getting a schoolhouse lesson on what women in the world are like. Where in heaven's name do you get your information, Sarah?"

Sarah shrugged. "Everybody knows that women in the world have the say. That surely is no secret."

"I guess not!" Michael exclaimed. "But in four hundred years of Hutterian history no woman has ever had the idea that maybe *she* might get to be that way."

"Who said anything like that?" Sarah wanted to know. "I would surely go with you if you went somewhere."

"Where am I going?" Michael cried.

"I said if you were going somewhere."

"The only place I'm going," said Michael, "is to the Jordan Ranch when we buy that. And I go there to work to get it ready for the new Canadian colony. And you stay here. A woman's place is at home."

"And that's just where Mrs. Joshua Volkner probably is," Sarah concluded.

"Get to work!" Michael ordered. "Mike, what are you doing standing there? Help your mother get those curtains on. What's the matter with you? Always thinking, thinking! That's what gets people into trouble."

Pound . . . pound . . . pound . . .

Under Michael father's ambitious hammer the brackets went promptly into place.

"Right to the fraction," Michael said as he completed another window. "I tell you, Sarah, if you had to get work like this done out in the world, you would have to wait a long time. Here in the commune all you have to do is get a boss to say it should be done and it is done."

"Look!" Little Mike exclaimed, holding up one of the curtains. "Color stitching."

Sarah snatched the curtain from his hand. "Just the date cross-stitched in."

Michael looked down. "I wouldn't say that was necessary."

"It's pretty, Michael father," Little Mike told him. "Look! Red and green."

"It's useless and expensive and it took time," Michael observed.

"Rachel and I did it so that you didn't even notice the time it took," said Sarah. "Here, now this one is ready to hang."

"My work is the nailing and I'm just about through," he informed her.

"Well, put this up, please! You're standing right there."

Michael took the curtain and laid it across the brackets. Then he stepped down and stood back to examine the innovation. Sarah saw his face grow stern and thoughtful.

"They will tie back like this," she hastened to say, tucking the curtains back with her hands.

"If they're intended to keep out the sun as you made the elders believe," Michael said, "then they'd better hang so they can keep the sun out."

"But today there is no sun so who can tell how to hang them?"

"And the red and green color stitching?" he reflected heavily. "If the elders and the pastor allow this, then the commune gate is open wider than I think it is. Don't be too sure these are being put up for time and eternity. I'll look at them from the outside."

He strode out into the yard.

"Come, Mike," said Sarah anxiously, "you hold back one and I the other. And hold it far back for now."

Together they held back the curtains so that Michael could see the effect. He stood in the yard with his hands on his hips, his hat pushed back. He tilted his head this way and that. He pointed with his hand.

"Over more with your side, Mike," said Sarah.

Together they looked out.

"Do you think he likes them, Sarah mother? Do you think the elders will let them stay?"

"Of course they will. Who can help but like them?"

Michael entered in a hurry to get the rest of the brackets in place. "They look like something hanging from a clothesline," he commented, "and they'll catch the dust, but if the rest of the colony can stand them I guess I can."

Pound . . . pound . . . pound . . .

Little Mike helped his mother thread the curtains over the rods. The long cross strips were rough. Michael had not been too careful in the sanding and the material often caught on the fine slivers.

Between the sounds of Michael's hammer, the door opened. Little Mike turned and Michael father, from his place on the chair, said, "Well, what's this?"

"I'm Bob Volkner," said the boy standing just inside the schoolroom.

"Yes," said Michael, "that I can see from here."

Little Mike could see that, too. No Hutterian boy would ever wear a brown-striped shirt and a red bow tie and neat-fitting pants. Robert's shoes were brown and so shiny that they looked as if their wearer had just walked through wet grass. Flung carelessly over his right shoulder was a light leather jacket. Little Mike absorbed all of this in one quick glance and noticed the neatly combed hair that looked freshly cut and fragrant. He realized that the newcomer was looking at him with eyes that were friendly.

"Are you Mike Neumann?" he asked.

Little Mike started to reply, but his father was saying, "We're both Mike, so maybe you'd better make some designation."

Robert caught a note of good humor in Michael's tone. "I mean Little Mike," he said. "Can he come out with me?"

"Don't you boys in the world ever have to work?" Michael asked, pounding in a nail.

"Sure we do. I work all the time. Know something? I'm a ticket boy in the grain pit."

"What do you do?" Michael quipped. "Put tickets on the grain so that the cityfolks can tell which is wheat and which is rye?"

"Nothing like that," Robert explained. "There's no grain in the grain pit. That's just where they buy and sell grain, that's all. I carry the tickets from the phone men to the buyers."

Michael moved his chair to the last window.

"You see," Robert went on, "I work only during summer vacation. Course I'm not working now because I'm up here with Dad. Vacation's just about over anyway. . . ." He tossed his jacket aside and sat down on top of a school desk. "I sure make good money——"

"Don't sit on that or I'll have a broken desk top to fix," Michael told him.

"—about three dollars a day with tips counted in," Robert went on, moving himself from the desk top to the seat. "That's the way Dad got started. Ticket boy. Worked his way up. I buy just about all my own stuff that way. Bought this wrist watch. No, Dad gave me that. Bought this knife on this chain, though. Ever see one like it? Look, all you do is press this snap, and out comes the blade. Press the snap—in she goes."

Michael looked down at the demonstration, hammer in hand. Sarah peered at it over her work. Little Mike stood in wonder, suppressing his desire to speak. It was thrilling to see the tiny sharp blade leap out and then leap back. It was fascinating to catch a glimpse of Robert's wrist watch peeping out from under the cuff of his spotlessly clean shirt. But his sorrow was very real when he remembered that he, too, had recently possessed a personal belonging and a thing of beauty. These are all very pretty, Robert Volkner, his heart was saying, but just wait until I find my harmonica. Then you will see something. Of course, you have one, too, but is it as lovely as mine? Does it have the songs in it that mine has?

"What's a knife like that good for?" Michael asked.

"Good for? Lots of things. I'm always using it."

"In my work," Michael shrugged, "it would last about two minutes. It's not even strong enough to peel potatoes."

"Bet y' I can carve my initials right in the top of this desk," Robert threatened, grabbing the knife in his fist.

"You wait a minute!" Michael shouted.

"I was just kidding." Robert laughed, and he snapped the knife back into its sheath.

"Kidding, I guess," Michael scolded. "Looks to me like you need a little discipline, that's what it looks like to me."

"Say, Mr. Neumann," Robert said, "d'you mind if Mike goes along?"

Michael made believe he did not hear.

"Along where?" asked Little Mike.

"Yankton," said Robert.

"Yankton!" echoed Sarah. "You hear that, Michael?"

"I hear the world," said Michael in a voice that was doomful. Then he leveled his eye against the brackets. "Such talk is ridiculous."

But Little Mike was saying, "In your automobile?"

"Would you like to?" Robert asked.

"That's not the question," Michael said sharply. "Don't you have anything better to do than to run around and burn up gasoline?"

"But," Robert insisted, "we've got to get my grandmother."

"Grandmother?" said Sarah. "You mean your mother?"

"No. Grandmother—Dad's mom."

"You better get your relationship straightened out," Michael told him. "Your father's mother happens to be in a Canadian colony."

"Okay," said Robert, "so she is. And she's coming here. She's coming down from the Upper Prairie Colony and we're meeting her in Yankton."

Michael turned to Sarah in bewilderment. "Do you suppose that could be?" he asked in an undertone.

"She's coming for the wedding," Robert was saying. "Dad spoke to the minister up there on the phone. Come on along, Mike!"

"You say she is coming to see Rachel get married?" Sarah marveled.

"Well, of course, she's coming to see Dad," Robert explained. "He's written to her lots of times and telephoned her and now she's coming."

"That I have to see," Michael blustered. "Our women don't waste their time riding on railroads."

"Oh, well," Sarah said, seeking to conceal her eagerness, "you know, Michael, the Canadian colonies have always been more progressive. It can well be that Martha Volkner will come."

"Nonsense!" Michael told her, taking out his disgust on the last nail in the last window bracket. "Don't give me the impression that the colonies are getting modernized."

"Upper Prairie has running water," Sarah submitted. "And electric lights."

"That doesn't mean that Grandmother Volkner is coming. Anyhow since when does a man have to take what a child says for truth?" He jumped down from the chair.

"It's the truth all right, Mr. Neumann," Robert told him. "You just ask Dad."

But Michael had started for the door. There he was almost run down by Rachel and three girls bursting into the room.

"Watch your manners," Michael scolded.

"Sarah mother," Rachel cried happily, "did you hear the news? Martha Volkner will be here for the wedding!"

"She's coming on the train!"

"The Householder thinks she got permission——"

"—because she belongs to the colony that will move down here when we buy the Jordan Ranch."

Michael went out slamming the door.

"Let's scram," Robert whispered to Mike, and while

the girls were lost in comments on the curtains and the prospect of the coming of the Canadian visitor, the boys slipped out into the yard.

"Why can't you come with us to town, Mike?" Robert asked.

"Because we just don't go, that's all." Mike shrugged.

"But why don't you?"

"Rules."

"But why the rules?"

"I don't know," Mike faltered. "If I go that means Jake and Dan should go, too——"

"We'll take them."

"—and Paul and Matt and Joey and all the rest."

"We'll take as many as we can this time and some other time we'll take the others. Come on, I've got comic books. A whole stack of 'em."

They were crossing the commune road, walking along the way where Mike could not go without anxiously searching the ground. Under the spell of this seeking and Robert's enthusiasm about getting permission to make the trip, Mike heard himself say, "I could play the harmonica all the way to Yankton."

"You got a harmonica?"

Mike shook his head. "No, I haven't. Not now."

"Dad gave me one. I didn't bring it along. Never could play much on the thing. If you've got one, bring it along. We'll sit in the back and Sis can sit up front with Dad."

Sorrowfully Mike turned in the direction of the meadow. He did not want to walk to the high bank, for that would mean looking for the instrument all the way, and it did not seem right to have a stranger along when he did that. But when he thought about it he had to admit that Robert did not seem like an outsider. It was pleasant being with him. He had a frankness that invited trust.

Robert was swinging his leather jacket in his hand. "I ought to ditch this thing," he said. "It's chilly, but you're even barefooted. I go barefooted when we go to the beach. Wish you could see the lake, Mike. Lake Michigan. If they'll let you go to Yankton, maybe they'll let you go to Chicago with me. D'you think they would? I'd take you down to the grain pit. Did you ever see a ball game? Dad and I go lotsa times. Y' know what? We've got a television set at home. If we didn't want to go to the game we could sit right in our living room and see it anyhow. I've got a radio. Just a cheap one. Bought it myself to carry around with me. Tell y' somethin' else. We could go to the amusement park and have a swell time. They've got all kinds of stuff there. Roller coasters, merry-go-rounds, crack-the-whips, Ferris wheels——"

The wheat along the edge of the meadow shared Mike's thoughts. Longingly it looked down at the meadow road. It was caught. Its roots were holding it. Someday soon the reapers would come, but the wheat stems would still be left there; the roots would be left, too, and the bare, sharp, headless stems would be standing.

"Let's walk through, Mike. Mind?"

There was no rule against that. Nobody had ever said, "Don't walk through the wheat field," because no one made a practice of that.

"Doesn't it hurt your feet, Mike?"

"No."

"Y' go barefoot all the time?"

"Most of the time. Pretty soon I'll put on shoes. When it gets cold."

"Dad said that shoes are made right here in the colony. That's handy. Dad said in the olden days, long ago, they sometimes made the shoes straight so they could be worn on either foot. Hey, is that the mill? Let's take a look around. Will they mind?"

Neither the Mill Boss nor his helper gave the boys a second glance. The miller's beard and bushy eyebrows were white with flour dust. His strong arms hugged the flour sacks as he lifted them from the chute and set them down for his helper to sew them shut with the long needle. The dull thunder of the giant hoppers and the rattle of the old machinery shook the building. Mike led his companion across the rickety flooring with its open hatches to the worn and slippery stairs. Together they climbed to the tiny window that looked down on the big wheel turning and stirring up the water of the Missouri. Mike took the end of his shirt and wiped the thick dust from the four small panes. Amid the noise and rumble he pointed out the deep holes of the river and drew attention to the chalk quarries on the other bank. The morsels of knowledge which he had gathered from his father and colony talk became storehouses of wisdom.

"The chalk is so soft it can be cut with a saw, but afterward it gets very hard. There's where the men set the fish nets in the fall. Over there Michael father has the power saw for cutting wood. That runs with gasoline. If the sun was shining you could see things plain. All that's in Nebraska. We're in South Dakota, but just over the river is another state."

Robert was impressed. The attic window and the heavy beams, the low, dull roar and the pulsing rafters gave him a sense of adventure.

"It's a storybook place," he told Mike and, forgetting about his clean clothes, he followed the colony boy through a precarious passage in the loft that led past the heavy, moving leather belts.

When they got back to the mill road, Robert brushed himself and tore off his necktie. "The heck with it!" he said, stuffing it into his pocket. "Mom's not along and Dad won't care. Know what? I've got a good notion to take off my shoes."

"Take them off," Mike told him. "We can go through the *Vogelpfad*. That's smooth."

"Okay," Robert agreed and started to untie his shoes. "My zipper jacket!" he exclaimed. "I left it at the mill."

"I'll get it," Mike told him.

He went back and found it hanging on a post. He picked it up and looked at it. The lining was a soft shade of red. The jacket was brown with texture soft and smooth, and down the front was a metal strip that looked like a series of closely fastened hooks and eyes. " 'My zipper jacket,' " Mike repeated, caressing it and walking slowly back.

"Put it on, Mike," Robert called. He was rolling up his pants legs and looking every moment more like a boy of the colony. "Put it on and zip 'er up."

Mike slipped an arm into the sleeve. The touch of the soft material, the richness of possession, the ecstacy of becoming for a moment a worldling in fact rushed into his mind. He put it on.

"Here, I'll zip it up for you."

The hooks and eyes were not Hutterian. The zipper closed the jacket as swiftly as the closing of a trap. Mike was caught, caught in the magnificent attire of a boy of the world. The jacket closed up securely all the way to his chin and the excitement took his breath away.

"Gee whiz, this path is hard on my feet," said Robert.

Mike scarcely heard. He was turning up the collar of the jacket as he started toward the *Vogelpfad*. Here the birds were singing, as they always did, but under the kingly vestment his heart was singing even more. He was Daniel clothed with a princely gown; he was the prodigal and the best robe had been put on him; he was Elisha upon whom had fallen Elijah's dazzling mantle.

Now he was leading Robert up the soft carpet of grass that led to the high bank. How snug and warm he felt! How conscious he was of a happiness that he had not known since the last time he held the harmonica in his hands! Even Pastor Kunz in his Sunday vest could not have felt the joy of leadership which he felt now. Robert was talking about the fun they would have when he took Mike through the crowded streets and how different that would be. Had he never seen a movie? Had he never been to a theater? Robert would take him to a carnival where he could hear a calliope and listen to the carnival music. In his secret soul Mike was content with the dazzlement of the moment. Though the air he breathed was commune air, there was a strange, enticing scent about it that he had never felt before.

As they climbed to the top of the high bank, a figure peered out of the grass. Joey sprang into the air to see who was coming. "Mike!" he shrieked. "Jake, look at Mike!"

Jake sat up. "It's Mike's face," he exclaimed, "and Mike's legs all right!"

"It's Mike," said Robert. "All zipped up."

"It's Robert Volkner's jacket," Mike explained.

Joey was at Mike's side eagerly inspecting the jacket. "It's soft as a goose's back," he said. "How's it fasten?"

"Look," said Mike. "It zips."

He pulled the zipper slowly and as the jacket opened, Joey's eyes popped. "Do it again, Mike!" he cried.

Robert said, "Didn't you ever see it? Lookit, I got one here, too."

Robert opened and shut the zipper on his pants.

Joey screamed with delight. "Let me do it," he pleaded.

"Okay," said Robert.

Joey pulled the zipper down and up and then rolled in the damp grass in glee. "Is that ever handy, Mike!" he cried in a fit of pleasure. "That we all ought to have."

Robert caught sight of something lying in the grass. "What's this?" he asked, walking over to it. "A catfish?"

"We grubbed him up with the rake," Joey explained.

"Were you raking the river again, Jake?" Mike asked. "Did you find anything?"

Jake shook his head. "Nothing."

"Only the catfish," said Joey. "There it is, still wriggling."

"Must be a two-pounder," Robert observed.

While he and Joey bent over it, Jake said, "I guess we must give up now, Mike, as far as the river goes. I went over every inch as far as I could."

Mike took off the zipper jacket. As he laid it on the grass, he wished with all his soul that he had come to help Jake instead of enjoying himself with Robert Volkner's company. The burden of the instrument returned to him. The knowledge that Jake had worked untiringly accused and shamed him.

"I'll look from now on, Jake," he said. "You go with Robert Volkner. Of course, you can't go where he wants us to go—to Yankton."

"To Yankton?" Jake replied eagerly. "In the automobile? No, that we can't do."

"Look here!" Joey hollered. "Look what's happening."

Robert had pulled the gold chain from his pocket and was kneeling over the fish. "I told Joey I could kill Mr. Catfish with a straw," he said. "Want to see how?"

Joey insisted he did, and Robert put the tip of the knife blade against the center of the flat, gray head. He punctured the skin.

"Now we take a straw," he demonstrated, "and push it down into the hole. See how easy it goes? It strikes the spine and——Look! The straw is in almost all the way. The wriggling stops. There, you see? The fish is dead."

The boys bent over the terrible mystery. Solemnly Mike looked at the fish lying motionless in the grass. There was some frightful learning behind the skill that killed the catfish. There was "world-learning" in that. Robert Volkner seemed to sense what Mike was thinking. Soberly he put his knife away. Mike, looking down, spoke almost to himself. "In the Bible is a story of how Peter needed money to pay his taxes. In the first fish he caught, there was the tax money in its mouth. Jake, how wonderful it would have been if there had been something in this fish's mouth for me!"

"I know what you mean!" Joey cried, and he told Mike with a glance that all the day needed was just that, the harmonica in the mouth of the catfish. Joey seized the fish and pried open the jaws. "Just gills," he reported.

"Things don't happen like they did in Bible times," said Jake.

"Maybe we shouldn't have killed it," Robert confessed. "Especially when we aren't going to eat it."

"The pigs will eat it," said Joey, jumping up. "Here, inside my shirt he goes and I'll toss him over the pig fence."

To the delight of all, Joey slapped the wet and slimy catfish against his body and pulled his shirt over it. "Follow the catfish belly!" he cried. "I'm the Hog Boss!"

Robert laughed aloud as Joey swaggered off, shoulders back, stomach out, prancing off in the direction of the sheds.

Robert snapped his fingers. "I promised Dad I'd clean up the car before we went to town. Want to help me?"

"You go with him, Jake," Mike told him. "I'll come later."

"Okay," said Robert. "I'll leave my shoes and the jacket. We'll be back."

Mike watched them until they were well on their way past the big barn. Joey joined them there. Mike was alone and for this he was grateful. Something told him that he would find the harmonica if he looked for it alone with no one to help or hope for him. To be alone was almost impossible in the communal system, and now that he was by himself on the high hill it was like unlocking his heart and examining all thoughts and plans without fear of intrusion. For once there were no curtainless windows through which anyone could watch. There were no voices, no sound of a step, no clang of the commune bell, just the indescribable and wondrously hopeful feeling breaking through the pain of the lost instrument. His pocket was empty. He had nothing: no watch, no gold chain, no necktie. But just now he felt that the Great Eye could not look down on him without tenderness. *The rake, Little Mike, the rake!*

He fell upon the worn gray handle, sprang to his feet and began hacking at the long, tangled growth. The matted grass clogged the prongs. He cleaned them hastily. Gathering the loose grass together, he piled it close to the overhanging edge. System he would have. He would rake through every inch from the brink to the graveled barnyard if need be. He would stack the loose grass together in orderly heaps. The harmonica was not in the river, not in the stove, nor underneath the schoolhouse steps, nor anywhere along the way. It must be here. Somewhere close to him on the high bank it was hiding and beckoning to be found. *Rake, Little Mike, rake!*

The hopeful moments passed into tremulous suspense. The raking went on feverishly. Questioning of heaven's concern tormented him. In the ebb and flow of faith and fear, he combed and searched the ground while memory verses haunted him. "The kingdom of heaven is like a treasure hid in a field; when a man has found it, he hides it and for joy therefor goes and sells all that he has and buys that field." "And what woman having ten pieces of silver, if she lose one piece does not light a candle and sweep the house and will not stop seeking until she finds it. When she has found it, she calls her friends and her neighbors saying, Rejoice with me; I have found that which was lost."

Who would have believed there were so many small stones under the grass? Here a piece of wood, a strip just right for the Ferris wheel seat; a piece of wire, good for hanging it from the cross bar; here dried feathers, quail feathers, dried bones where a hawk had been, tiny flowers moldy and damp, pieces of straw long enough and stiff enough to kill a netful of catfish, a rusty washer, old and brittle, a grub worm and grass. *Rake, Little Mike!* . . . *Rake!* And James the Teacher said, "All together now, children, 'God rules in the kingdom of men and gives it to whomsoever He wills. Remember Nebuchadnezzar. He thought he had great possessions, and he prided himself upon them. But he was driven from the sight of men and did eat grass with the oxen and his hair was wet with the dew of heaven.' "

Did Nebuchadnezzar ever look up out of his suffering and hear music? Did he ever stand with the dew of heaven on his brow and hear singing? Suddenly the air was filled with melodies around Little Mike. It was the sound of many harmonicas, a calliope, carnival music. He stood transfigured on the high bank with the heaped-up grass around him, and in one earth-shattering moment he interpreted the music as a heavenly sign. Marveling, he looked to the sky. Now a chorus of many voices mingled with the instruments.

"Listen!" he breathed, and his heart stood still.

The melody floated between heaven and earth. The sweetness was indescribable. This was the proof for everything he had learned and memorized and believed. The music soared and sang and covered the high bank with beauty and enchantment. Here was the miracle. Surely a voice would say, "Come, Little Mike, come along! I will lead you to where the harmonica is waiting."

There was a voice. Quite close. It said, "Mike, look! Here is where the sweet sound is coming from."

Jake stood on the slope of the high bank. Beside him was Robert Volkner casually holding a small leather box.

Robert turned a knob. The music stopped and a man's voice spoke. Then there was laughter in the box.

"It's a radio," Jake explained. "You remember how the Town Man told us he heard one often. . . ."

Mike let the rake fall to the ground.

Robert said, "There, that's Chicago. Popular music. Mom doesn't like it, but Sis does. Now I'll get Denver."

"The music and voices go all over the whole country," Jake informed. "Everyone who has a box like this can hear everything no matter where he is."

"There, that's Denver. That's a news report."

"Think of that, Mike. It would be as if we sang 'The Great Song' and the colonies in Canada and England and even in Paraguay would hear our singing just as if they would be sitting with us and singing along. This is a great thing. This is greater than—— Mike! Where are you go- ing? Why are you walking away?"

"Gee whiz!" Robert cried, picking up his jacket and his shoes. "I'm the one who has to beat it. Do you hear that? Sis is honking the car horn."

Snap went the cover of the box. Gone were the voices and the music. Gone was the miracle. In the commune yard the silence was broken by the incessant blaring of the horn. Mike walked sadly toward the river flats.

Jake caught up with him. "Mike," he pleaded, "tell me you found it."

"No."

"Then we must look some more. The rake is the way to do it."

"The rake is good," Mike admitted in a choking voice. He thrust his hands into his pockets to brace himself against the disillusionment he felt.

"Let's go back and hunt," Jake urged. "The harmonica won't find itself."

"No, it will not find itself, but I am for going to the sheep hill. Why, I don't know."

They walked together. Jake opened the collar of his shirt. "You know," he said, "I like Robert Volkner. He didn't say even a word about the bump on my neck."

"That was good of him."

"It was good of him to let us hear the radio. No one else heard it, Mike, not even Joey or anyone, because Joshua Volkner told him not to play it. To think of what the little box can do! Who can explain that? Not even Jacob father or your father can make a box like that."

Mike walked on, never lifting his eyes from the ground. Finally he said, "The music was like the angels' song. The singing that came from the box was the loveliest I ever heard. And all Robert had to do was turn a little knob. What do you think, Jake? How can the world be such an awful place and still have things so wonderful?"

"That," said Jake thoughtfully, "is a big question."

CHAPTER 10

~~~~~~

*C*HURCHTIME was over. The men filed out the schoolhouse, deepening the dusk of the commune with their black attire. The children sprang down the wooden steps without speaking. Then came the women with their hands rolled in their dark-colored aprons. No one spoke, remembering a tradition that called for silence until twenty paces from the place of prayer. Even David Wiese and Rachel Neumann did not walk together. It was always a matter of each one going alone so that the words of the sermon could be reviewed. After all were out, Pastor Kunz closed the door, tucked the large Bible under his arm and moved with peremptory step in the direction of his home.

Soon the house benches were occupied by motionless figures, silhouetted against the unlighted homes. Children played in the sandy yard. Three Chore Men walked to the barns to make their final inspection for the night. Everywhere eyes watched the commune gate; everywhere there was a sense of listening for the sound of a car which might turn off the highway and into the commune road. The whine of a horse in the stables, the faint melodious note of a sheep bell, the cackling of the geese, the flutter of the wind, the closing of a door were sounds consulting together about the uncommon waiting as darkness descended.

A lamp was lighted in the Neumann home. Sarah turned up the wick. Michael, who was slouched comfortably on the house bench outside, turned his head. "Why do you light up already?" he called. "Do you think Joshua Volkner will bring his mother here first thing? I know they went to Yankton to meet the train, but I still have to be shown that she's coming at all."

"Who is thinking of the Volkners?" came the reply. "Rachel is having the girls come over in a few minutes."

"The girls? Why?"

"Why?" Sarah echoed. "Isn't it a custom before the big day?"

"What big day?"

He heard Sarah groan in disgust and noted the sound of chairs being pushed across the floor in preparation for the girls' visit. "What big day?" he repeated.

Little Mike, who sat on the ground in the dark area at the edge of the bench, said, "The wedding of Sister Rachel and David Wiese, Michael father."

Sarah came out of the house with her knitting pail and dropped to the bench. Straining her eyes over the yarn, she vented her exasperation on the needles. "What big day?" she mimicked.

Michael chuckled. "What am I supposed to do—pass out the cigars?"

"Cigars don't go with weddings," she told him. "They go with babies."

"Well, Mrs. Neumann," he quipped, "have you got some outside information about how things are done in the world?"

"Anybody knows that." Sarah shrugged.

"Did you know that, Little Mike?" Michael wanted to know.

"Know what, Michael father?"

"Know what?" Michael said in make-believe scorn. "What's the matter with you? When a man speaks, listen!"

"Yes, Michael father."

Michael dangled his hat between his knees. Then he called to a cluster of children playing on the dark ground of the commune, "Anna, put Mary to bed. It's time you go, too. Stay out there and you'll get run over with an automobile, the way things are going around here. That black car always reminds me of a behemoth, ready to swallow everybody up."

The children obeyed. Sarah continued her knitting. "Yes," she said casually, "the Volkner automobile should come soon. But Joshua will park it at the schoolhouse."

Michael did not hear. "Just for amusement's sake," he said reflectively, "let's follow this matter through. How do you know that cigar giving is for babies' coming?"

Sarah moved impatiently. "Who knows where we find out lots of things? Maybe the birds bring us the information."

Michael looked out into the dark. Seriously he said, "It's not only this information. It's many kinds. And it's not only you. It's me, too. I sometimes get things in my mind and I can't for the life of me remember how or where I got them. Things of the world, I mean, and information about the world. And it's getting more that way all the time. How do such things get through the gate? How do they get through the fence and in to us? That's what I'd like to know. Take the matter of the Ferris wheel seats. . . ."

And as Little Mike listened with sudden interest, his father went on, "I said that I saw such a wheel in Omaha one time. But the more I thought about it the more I wondered if I ever had seen one. So this morning I asked the Town Man, 'Did we see a wheel like that when we were in Omaha?' 'Never,' he said. 'I never saw one and neither did you.' Of course he may be wrong. But the more I think of it, the more I don't believe I did see a wheel there. All right, where *did* I see one? Where did I learn about it? How do these things happen?"

"Foolish talk," said Sarah, but her voice was warm, and Little Mike knew that she was as happy to hear his father speak as he was. He wriggled closer to the house bench until his body snuggled against it and the wall. Here in the dark he sat securely, and when Michael laid his hat on the bench, Little Mike took the hat and put it on. It covered his ears and his eyes and made him feel completely concealed from everyone and everything. Beneath it he guarded the thoughts of his great loss. Now he could contemplate his misfortune without fear of being found out and he could sorrow without being asked the reason. He could also contemplate the words his father had spoken. How did the voice of the world come in?

He heard happy, excited cries and hurrying steps in the commune yard. Rachel and Ruth and a group of girls were on their way to the house to admire the things in Rachel's marriage chest. They gathered around the house bench, all talking at once.

"Thank you for lighting the lamp, Sarah mother,"

Rachel said. "There are twelve of us here already. Now don't let David come near."

"Then don't make so much noise," Michael advised. "When the hen cackles everybody knows where she has her nest."

"We would all cackle, Neumann Michael," said Rebecca Mueller, "if it was our wedding day tomorrow."

"Nobody is stopping you," Michael answered. "Consult the *Stammbaum* and get busy."

"Hurry and tell the boys to grow up." Rachel laughed roguishly. "We were just saying that marriageable-agers are scarce."

"I suppose," Michael observed wryly, "that's why the good Lord sees fit to bring a Canadian colony down here pretty soon."

"An idea, girls!" exclaimed Rebecca Mueller, who was two years older than Rachel. "That's where I will find me one."

"Is the colony really coming?" Ruth asked.

"Of course it's coming," Michael assured her.

"But will it be close enough to our colony for us to meet the boys?" came the question.

"Didn't you hear?" exclaimed Rachel. "The elders are going to arrange for the new colony to settle on the Jordan Ranch. That's only six miles away."

Ruth exclaimed, "But to go six miles we must get permission, Michael father!"

"For that we'll get permission unless the elders want us all to be old maids."

"Old maids! That's something one doesn't see in a Hutterian colony."

"I think we should be allowed to travel——"

"Travel?" Michael's voice broke in. "Just don't serve that kind of wine at tomorrow's wedding!"

"We mean travel to the other colonies so that we may look around a little."

"Look around for marriageables?"

"Yes. The rules should be less strict so that we can do that."

"Please, Neumann Michael," pleaded Rebecca Mueller, "when you go to fix the buildings at the Jordan Ranch, let me go along and bring the lunch to the workers. Then, when a nice Canadian boy sees me——"

"He goes straight back to Alberta," grunted Michael.

"Oh, no," Rebecca insisted amid the laughter. "They all want to be Americans and what better way is there to be an American than to marry one?"

"Just be a good Hutterian," said Michael. "America needs us as bad as we need America. Don't forget that we are the only ones in the whole country living the true Christian communal life. That's a responsibility. First be a citizen of the Kingdom of Heaven. The rest is secondary."

"Let's go in, girls," said Rachel. "Here come the others. Come in! All come in!"

"Say, Rebecca," a girl said laughing, "what you should have is an automobile. Then you could visit all the Canadian colonies quick."

"What I should have is an airplane. Then I could just look down and see how the men suit me."

Little Mike heard his father sigh. The sound seemed louder than the voices of the girls as they hurried into the room. It was as sad as the night was for Little Mike. In it there was no make-believe, no desire for any special effect, no request for pity. It was an expression of honest pain.

Now Michael was saying, "Another generation, another problem. I tell you, Sarah, it's good Rachel is getting someone like David Wiese. He knows what is the right way, and when the children start coming, she will stop looking out at the world."

"Rachel never looked at the world," Sarah reminded him, "any more than any of us did."

Michael did not hear. "For that matter," he was saying, "I guess all young people go through a time when they want more liberty than is good for them. They wonder how wise the fathers were in making rules and regulations."

Sarah's voice was faraway: "Yes, there are such times."

"But," Michael went on, "the danger passes. Age brings wisdom. There comes a time when we're glad we are not Joshua Volkners roaming in the world homeless, godless and forsaken. But," he added in a troubled voice, "even though we go through times of doubt and come to our senses, the next generation finds it a little harder and the next a little harder still. Every Hutterian generation moves closer to the world, it seems to me. It's good Joshua is not under the bench to hear me say that. He thinks we ought to tear down the fences and make short work of it. That's because he has lost the spirit and serves the flesh. Thank God that for every one like him there are a few thousand like me, and for every one like his Robert there are a few thousand like Little Mike. Isn't that right, Little Mike?"

"Churchtime was over long ago," Sarah said as the knitting needles suddenly flew. "Must we have the sermon all over again?"

Michael clamped his hands on his knees. "I just wanted to ask," he demanded with spirit, "if anybody in the Neumann household had any idea how things get into a person's mind. That was what I started talking about before these man hunters came along. How did the Ferris wheel get into me if I never saw one? Old Daniel the Teacher told us once that if a boy was kept away from everybody and everything, he would still learn to swear. Figure that one out for me. Where does that come from? That's the question, and when we have answered it, then we know how the world gets into the commune."

Little Mike snatched the hat from his head with an impulse and sprang to his feet. "I can tell you that, Michael father."

"All right, Pastor Neumann, you tell us," Michael ordered.

"I heard things come through the gate and over the fences today," Little Mike said excitedly. "I heard music and people talking and they weren't in the commune at all. They were in Chicago and Denver and in other cities all over the whole country, but they were on the high bank as plain as we hear Rachel and the girls. Plainer even. All because Robert Volkner had a little box that he opened. He opened it and it caught the music and the voices out of the air and brought them to us so that Jake and I could hear them. You see, Michael father, the fence could not stop them and the gate did not hold them back even if it was closed and our river just let them come through——"

"As the Red Sea stood aside and let the Israelites come through," Michael said harshly.

"Like that!" Little Mike continued breathlessly. "Nothing could stop the voices and the music. They were beautiful, but they were sad sometimes, too. And Jake said that Robert told him there were always voices and music all around us, right in the commune—night or day, it doesn't matter. Even in the houses with the doors and the windows closed, there the voices and the music come in. Even in the vegetable cellar which is under the ground, there they are. They're in the schoolhouse at churchtime. While Pastor Kunz is speaking and while we're praying on our knees, they come in. We can always hear the world. All we need is the box. And I said to Jake that maybe we didn't need even the box. Maybe if we just listened real hard sometimes when things are very quiet——"

"Mike!"

His father's word struck him like a stinging blow. Little Mike was plunged headlong out of the rapture to which he had climbed. He stood in the darkness stunned and trembling. Blindly he looked at the two figures darkly outlined on the bench. His mother sat with her hands folded in her lap. His father fiercely gripped the edge of the bench, eyes groping to study the face of his son. Then Michael Neumann lifted a hand from the house bench and held it out. Firmly he said, "Come here, Little Mike, come here to me."

Little Mike moved forward. He did not give his father his hand. He let him take hold of his bare arm, and the strong fingers pierced into the flesh. He felt himself drawn to the bench, and his father's arm suddenly went around him gently, and his father's bearded face touched his cheek.

"Let me tell you something, my son," Michael whispered, and his voice was hushed and compassionate. "Never open the box. Then all the voices in the world can never touch you. But open your heart and you will hear something that even Robert Volkner's wonderful instrument has never heard."

So saying, he drew Little Mike close to him. All that had been pain was warmth and healing. The hurt was gone. Little Mike felt that there could never be any other world than this, no other security, no other home.

"A radio," Sarah exclaimed distastefully. "That would be the last thing I would want drumming in my ears."

"Did you ever hear one, Michael father?" Little Mike asked.

"Of course," said Michael in a thoughtful voice. "Of course I did. Many times."

"Where, I'd like to know?" Sarah asked with a gentle ring of doubt in her voice.

"I heard one in Omaha that time," Michael said uncertainly.

Then he released Little Mike. Sarah's needles paused. Faraway a light flashed over the hedges. It moved through the distant acres, cutting a silver furrow in the commune road. It came quickly and insolently to the commune gate. Then it crawled into the main yard, blinding anyone who sought to meet its searching glare. It was a behemoth taking all that it saw with its eyes and piercing through every snare with its nose. It was a behemoth and it lay under the trees in the covert of the reed and fens, then closed its eyes and let night hide it with its shadow.

Little Mike followed his father and mother to the car

as the families came from their homes to greet Martha Volkner. The rule against going close to the car was disregarded; children crowded around it while the men and women kissed and embraced the Canadian visitor.

"I'll bring your luggage, Mother," Joshua told her.

"Luggage!" said the old woman with a cry. "The paper sack, that is all. What should a person bring when she comes home? Yes, yes, it is home. I don't need that lantern, Wiese Caleb."

"Here comes Pastor Kunz!" was the excited announcement.

"Welcome, welcome, Mother Israel," said the pastor, striding forward and shaking her hand with both of his. "And how did you leave the good brethren in Canada?"

"Look me over," said Martha. "Maybe they're still hanging to my skirts. How are they, Pastor Jacob? How is anyone who stands looking across to the Promised Land?"

"Are you the one they sent to spy it out?" Michael asked with spirit. "Then tell them it's flowing with milk and honey."

Pastor Kunz warned that the Promised Land meant work, and Martha Volkner replied that the people in her colony were ready for it two hundred strong.

In the light of the Householder's lantern, Little Mike had a chance to see the mother of Joshua Volkner. She was a strong, plump woman with glossy pink cheeks that were tucked into the folds of her polka-dot head scarf. Her eyes were sharp and bold, like two brown birds ready for flight. Over the shoulders of her full black dress she wore a wide dark knitted scarf that hung almost to her knees. Her apron was deep-blue and reached to the tip of her heavy homemade shoes. She brushed aside the exclamations of enthusiastic welcome.

As the children clung to her, she picked one up and said, "You're one of Daniel Mueller's. Yes, that anyone can see. And you, there, you belong to the Kunz household."

"Good!" said the pastor. "But when the sheep get out of the fold and feed in other pastures, then what?"

He turned heavily and looked in Joshua's direction where Robert and Elaine stood at their father's side.

"To a mother," said Martha Volkner steadfastly, "a child is known no matter in which world he makes his home."

"Known he might be," exclaimed Pastor Kunz, "but out of the household is out of the life."

"Tonight, Pastor Kunz," Joshua said cordially, "we are all one family."

There was a stirring in the circle of welcomers; an opening formed and Selma Kunz came shuffling through with the aid of her cane. "Yes, yes," she murmured as Martha greeted her with an affectionate cry. "Rheumatism and all comes to say, 'Welcome home, Martha Volkner, welcome home.'"

"Rheumatism or not, you look wonderful to me, Selma Kunz," said the other as she embraced the pastor's wife. "You are good enough to go back to Canada with me for a visit."

"You just come back here," Selma implored. "We have enough for everybody."

"First we three go to the wedding meeting," Sarah Neumann invited, slipping an arm into Martha's and offering her hand to Selma Kunz.

Sarah ushered them out of the crowd as hurriedly as she dared while the children clustered around and accompanied them across the commune yard.

Little Mike ran ahead, followed by Jake Linder and Robert Volkner.

"You know something?" Robert said as they hastened toward the Neumann home. "She's a great guy."

Little Mike stopped and looked at Jake blankly; then he turned to Robert. "Did she like the car ride?"

"She didn't say."

"Did you show her the radio?"

"She wasn't interested."

They dashed into the house where Rachel stood in her engagement dress, showing it off to the group of girls. The room was noisy and gay. The table which usually stood in the center of the room was shoved aside and in its place was the marriage chest. The top was up and on it were draped some linen pieces. So engrossed were the girls in their animated comments that they paid no attention to the boys, who sat down, three on a chair. In a moment a crowd of women pressed into the room close on the heels of Sarah Neumann and her companions. The children were ordered to stay outside.

Grandmother Volkner stopped the girls' excited chatter. "Talk, talk, talk!" she greeted them. "I heard you girls long before I saw you. That's not in keeping with the rules as I learned them."

Sarah was making Selma Kunz comfortable in a chair and already drawing up another chair with her foot so that Martha Volkner would have a place.

"Rachel," Sarah ordered, "come and greet Martha Volkner."

Rachel flew into the elderly woman's arms.

"All right, all right!" Martha murmured. "Everybody gets married. Don't think you're the only one who has had a wedding meeting."

"But no one has had anything so exciting," said Rachel happily. "You came all the way from Canada."

"Let me look at you," said Grandmother Volkner setting Rachel off at arm's length. "I see the proper head scarf all right, but what is this you're wearing?"

"That's the engagement dress." Rachel was thrilled. "I'll describe it for you. It's silk print, but because the light is so bad with the lamp you maybe can't see the green and white figures. The background is brown. Isn't the apron beautiful?"

"That must all come to a dear price," Martha Volkner observed as her hands caressed the material. "But then," she said shortly, "I hear that in America you need only plant money and there is always a good crop."

"Oh, no, Grandmother Volkner," Rachel hastened to say. "This was all bought with my allowance money according to the rule."

"Allowance money?" said Martha suspiciously. "That is still thirty cents a month, isn't it? This material looks like allowance for fifty years."

"It's really very cheap, but it looks expensive."

Little Mike got up and stood on the chair. This was against the regulations, but who was to say anything since there were no men in the room to give the orders? And he wanted to look over the shoulders of the women so that he might see Martha Volkner as she sat down in the chair which Sarah mother had drawn up for her.

There was a movement in the crowded doorway. Joshua Volkner came in carrying a long cardboard box. At his side was his daughter Elaine. "Where's the bride-to-be?" he asked. "Here, Rachel, this is for you."

There was an awkward pause in the midst of a sudden silence. Rachel glanced beseechingly at her mother, then with sudden disregard for everything but her own feelings, she took the box from Joshua's hand. Impulsively she untied the large red ribbon and opened the gift. Her nervous hands touched the bouquet of red roses rapturously. "Thank you, Joshua Volkner, thank you," she said as she pressed the roses to her breast.

"How beautiful!" Sarah began. "But——"

"Flowers!" said Martha Volkner in a tone of dismay. "That is not a custom with us, Joshua."

"But what harm, Mother?" Joshua asked while the room filled with exclamations. "If they bring Rachel some happiness——"

"They'll go beautifully with your dress," Elaine observed.

"They'll go even nicer with the wedding dress," said Rachel, scarcely daring to speak.

"I can see tomorrow already." Rebecca was dreaming. "Pastor Kunz is saying, 'David Wiese and Rachel Neumann, you will come forward and stand in front of me.' Rachel carrying the lovely roses and David Wiese in his new black suit——"

"Don't say any more!" Rachel exclaimed. "I get scared enough already with all that is happening."

"Sit close to the front in church, then you'll not have so far to walk," a girl suggested.

Rachel laughed nervously.

Elaine asked, "What's the wedding dress like?"

The girls became louder and more talkative.

"It must be two-piece."

"The blouse must be lined."

"That's the custom."

"Is it silk, too?"

"Is it blue, Rachel?"

"Is it bright blue or just blue?"

"Talk, talk, talk!" interrupted Martha Volkner in a voice of disgust. She silenced everyone, but as they looked at her they saw that she was smiling. Little Mike saw Joshua Volkner smile, too, and look at his mother with affection.

"The prettiest wedding I ever saw was Michael Neumann's and Sarah's," Martha Volkner reminisced. "There was no fuss and no noise and no old woman from Canada to tell them how it ought to be done. They were married without any specially made clothes and without anything from the outside world."

"Things change in twenty years," said Sarah with a wave of dismissal. "Let the young people do things in their own way. Come, Rachel, show Martha Volkner your apron!"

Rachel dipped into the marriage chest and brought out the apron. Grandmother Volkner touched it yearningly. The deep blue and the texture fascinated her but she said haughtily, "Where did it come from?"

"Yankton," said Rachel. "Isn't it beautiful? And see, here is my name cross-stitched in brown and white."

Grandmother Volkner said, "How dear was it?"

"Two dollars for the goods."

"After the wedding what is it good for?"

"For Sunday wear and even for working when the working is not too dirty."

"You young ones have all the answers. If you could go through life with your tongues, you would all live to be Methuselahs." The girls laughed happily but Grandmother shook a warning finger. "Just laugh," she warned. "We old ones have forgotten more than you young ones will ever know."

"Where did you get your husband?" asked Rebecca Mueller. "Were there enough men in the colony to go around?"

"Don't think so much about a husband," Sarah scolded in playful exasperation, "and one will come along."

Amid the comments of agreement and laughter among the women Martha Volkner said, "I was Rachel's age when one day another family came from Germany. There was Adrian Volkner."

"How old was he?" asked one of the girls.

"Twenty maybe. What does it matter? The pastor came to me and said, 'There is a nice man for you.'"

"You let the pastor pick out your husband?" cried Rebecca.

"Why not?" Martha retorted. "The pastor was old and wise, and I was young and foolish. He knew best."

"What was your wedding day like?" Rachel inquired. "Was it very happy?"

"It was in spring," Martha said. "Adrian was helper to the Farm Boss. On our wedding day, instead of a big dinner, everyone in the community fasted. In those days we had to save food for seed. Everything was planned in terms of what was best for the community. That was our life. You know the orchard where you pick apples? Adrian planted the first trees. You remember, don't you, Selma Kunz, how he once brought the apple blossoms into the church and decorated the table? They were pretty, too, and fragrant. But the pastor preached a sermon on waste and vanity. Well, that was right. Adrian said it was right. There was the time that——" She stopped distastefully. "Talk, talk, talk!" she said.

"It's pretty talk, Grandmother," Elaine told her.

Martha Volkner looked at her warmly, then withdrew her gaze and addressed herself to Rachel. "Tell me, Rachel Neumann, how many petticoats are you wearing under that dress?"

"Two."

"Two! Where are the other two?"

"Nobody wears four any more."

"In the world they don't wear any," Rebecca Mueller spoke up. "Do they, Elaine Volkner?"

"I sometimes do, but that's with a party dress. When I'm dressed like now I just wear——"

"Well, Elaine," Joshua interrupted, amused, "you weren't asked to elaborate on what the world is wearing."

"What don't they wear in the world?" Grandmother Volkner wanted to know. "What I saw on my trip I would never have believed. Sometimes I couldn't tell who was a man and who was a woman. They both smoked. They both wore long pants. They both drove automobiles. There was no difference that I could see."

"It's even worse than that, Mother," Joshua told her lightly. "In the world women control most of the money and most of them control most of us men. So you see things are really in a bad way."

"Well," Martha Volkner observed, "you know where things are better."

"In the colonies?" Joshua asked.

"Certainly in the colonies," said a voice at the door, and Michael Neumann forced his way into the room. "Where would you find more happiness or peace than right here? I heard you brought flowers, Joshua. Yes, I see them. Flowers die like the things of the world. The commune is something that lives on. Why shouldn't it? It is the life that God designed for his true followers."

Little Mike still stood with Robert on the chair. Together they watched the indomitable figure of Michael Neumann take over the room. Prophetically he stood near Martha Volkner's chair and rehearsed the wonders of commune life. The girls hesitated to move for fear of interrupting him. The knitting needles in the hands of the women clicked softly. Word by word Michael transformed the room into a stronghold of Hutterian faith.

"Wait till the brethren come from Canada," Michael was saying. "We'll show the world how Hutterian ideals can be transplanted without loss of the fruit. Come to see us then, Joshua Volkner. Come and visit your own relatives when they are safely settled on the Jordan Ranch."

"The Jordan Ranch?" Joshua asked with a start. "What do you mean?"

Michael answered with a sweep of his arms, "We're planning to buy the Jordan Ranch for our brethren. The elders decided that at their meeting. It's close to us. Six miles. That shows how God provides for his people."

"But the Jordan Ranch, Michael," Joshua said with a

look of pain in his eyes. "Didn't you know that was sold?"

"Sold? When? Who bought it?"

"You didn't know?" Joshua asked incredulously. Then, as Michael studied him, he added, "That goes to show what can happen where radios are forbidden and newspapers are scarce."

"Who bought it" Michael demanded.

"The Central States Grain Company," Joshua told him.

"Who is the Central States Grain Company?" Then Michael's eyes filled with alarm. "You mean your concern? You mean the big business you're in? You bought the Jordan Ranch from under our noses?"

"I wasn't aware of that," Joshua said. "We certainly had no idea that your colony would ever want it. We took it over six months ago. It was heavily mortgaged."

"Well," conceded Michael with a fling of his arms, "what does it matter? Now we will buy it from you. And maybe even for a better price than we could have got it before."

Joshua shook his head. "I'm afraid," he said, "the Jordan Ranch is out of the question. We're converting that into an experimental farm and our plans have gone so far——"

"You mean you would stand in our way? Even where your own people are concerned?"

"It isn't that," Joshua explained. "In fact, if it were mine, it would be different. But it's not mine, you see. It belongs to the corporation, and I am just one of the members."

"I thought you owned it," Michael said accusingly.

"Hardly. This is not a case of private ownership at all,

and that's why I don't have too much to say. This is a corporation and many people have interests in it. No one man has the control. There are stockholders and directors and advisers——"

"That sounds like a complicated worldly business," Michael told him wryly.

"Not much more complicated than a colony system, Michael. In a way it is like a communal enterprise, except that people share according to their investment and most men get their positions according to their ability. But that's something like colony life, too. I suppose you get out of it what you put into it and a man becomes a carpenter—shall we say?—because. he's the best man for that job. So it is in a business like ours. But this is the difference, Michael. We've found our work within the American way itself. We have no fences. We have not isolated ourselves. We know what the system of the world is like and we admit that there are many things in it which should be changed and improved. That's part of our job, and if at times the changes are slow or do not seem effective, we at least feel that we're trying. We know that our future is in our hands and we must make it the best we can. Since the world can never go back, we must fit the good life into the system and not try to fit an outmoded system to life."

The room lay hushed as Joshua finished, not because of what he had said—few understood that—but because his voice was as sincere as that of Pastor Kunz in the midst of a sermon. The women waited with their knitting idle in their hands. Rachel and the girls seemed to have forgotten about the wedding. Martha Volkner sat with folded hands and looked up at Joshua, her lips moving without speaking.

Little Mike gazed at his father. For once Michael Neumann had nothing to say. His arms dropped, his eyes were perplexed as if he was trying desperately to understand how Joshua had admitted him by a new door into "the world." He seemed to be saying, "You see, Joshua, when you compare something with colony life, that I can understand. That I know backward and forward." But where were right and wrong in this picture? How could the world's interests have got in ahead of God's people? Michael had felt a deadly thrust come through the impenetrable commune faith that had always sustained him. He felt the eyes of everyone on him and the room was waiting for him to speak. He looked at Joshua defiantly.

"We mean to get the Jordan Ranch," he vowed. "It's made exactly for our requirements. But if things are as you say, the sooner the elders know about it the better."

He swung around, the women made room for him, and he went out.

Little Mike jumped down from the chair. Trailed by Robert Volkner and Jake Linder, he made his way to the door. Men were gathered near the house. Others stood in little groups in the commune yard. But a hurrying shadow in the distance was Michael Neumann walking straight to the home of Pastor Kunz.

CHAPTER 11

"CHURCHTIME! Churchtime!" Little Mike ran from door to door with the announcement.

"Churchtime, Bee Boss! Churchtime, Town Man! Churchtime, Farm Boss!"

The commune bell was never permitted to disturb the Sabbath silence. Sunday milking and Sunday meals were answered by force of habit at their proper hours. But the call to worship was heralded by a youthful crier whom the pastor appointed. His was the special dispensation to open the doors and summon the faithful to the house of God. On this sun-bright September morning this honor was Little Mike's.

"Churchtime, Householder!"

He ran quickly from the home of the Householder to the next humble house near by. He opened the door.

"Churchtime!" he called. Then he stood chagrined in the sudden realization that he had mistakenly rushed in on Pastor Kunz. He clung to the doorknob.

"Has the whole commune gone mad?" the pastor demanded. "Last night nobody slept and now you think you must wake the pastor so he can hear his own sermon. What is it with you, Mike Neumann?"

"I didn't think, Pastor Kunz."

217

"That is why they put rings in a bull's nose," said the pastor. He raised a warning finger. "I have my eye on you, Little Mike, and on all of you boys. Don't think that just because Robert Volkner comes here with big ideas that you are at liberty to do things without thinking."

Selma Kunz put on a freshly laundered dark-red apron over her black dress. Pulling the band tightly against her body, she observed, "It's the wedding excitement that does it, Jacob."

"It's boyish foolishness," grumbled the pastor.

Mike turned to go.

"Let me look at you," said Selma Kunz, restraining him with a lenient voice. "Let me see how the Laundry Boss did your nice white Sunday shirt."

Little Mike turned to her for inspection as she shuffled over uncertainly without her cane.

"Your face shines like a saucer," Selma observed affectionately and smoothed his hair back with her hand. "The shirt is good. Look, Jacob, this was made out of sugar sacks, bleached white with that new something the Town Man brought."

"Lye water and sunshine have always been good enough for any bleaching," mumbled the pastor.

"This is handier," she had to say. "All you do is open the bottle, pour a little in the rinse water and——"

"All right," agreed the pastor petulantly, slipping an arm into his black vest. "It is a good shirt, so let it be."

"It's as nice as the one that Joshua Volkner wears," Selma murmured.

"Good needs no comparison," argued the pastor. "Good is good and let that stand."

He turned quizzically to her, drawing Little Mike into his observation. "It seems to me," he said suspiciously, "that the talk of late goes altogether too much to Joshua Volkner. And what is Joshua Volkner trying to do? He wants to keep us from getting the Jordan Ranch as a home for his own father and mother. That's his trick and very likely he will drive a hard bargain now that he has outsmarted us."

"Can't the new colony come, Pastor Kunz," Little Mike ventured, "if Joshua Volkner will not sell the Jordan Ranch?"

"Where would they go? Land is no longer plentiful and we need big tracts. We need buildings and fields. Room to live is what we need. A worse thing he could not have done. Compare yourself to the Volkners if you want to, but for me I will live so that the Volkners will compare themselves to me. First you want to compare your shirt to his. Next you will want to wear a necktie."

"Not me, Pastor," Little Mike assured. "That would choke me. Even to wear shoes as I'm doing today is more hurtful than going barefoot."

"You just wear shoes today, Little Mike. Today is something special," said Selma Kunz in a motherly tone. "But if you wore stockings the shoes would feel better. Well, you look good. Your pants are nice and your shirt is nice——"

"And the curtains in the schoolhouse are nice and the wedding will be nice," mocked the pastor. "Brush off my hat for me so I can be on my way to church."

"It is all brushed and ready, Jacob," Selma told him as she went to get the hat for him from its peg on the wall. "It is in good Sunday condition," she observed. "Even Joshua Volkner's is not made of better material."

"Deliver us, blessed Lord," groaned the pastor, "from the vanity of women."

He snatched the hat disgustedly from Selma's hand. Then he looked at it. "This hat," he said appraisingly, "is better than new. And it is twenty years old at least."

He put it on. Little Mike and Selma looked at him admiringly. He squinted at them. "Go on with you!" he commanded, shooing them away. "Get behind me, you two satans!"

But his eyes were twinkling and Little Mike ran happily from the room. The world was bright. Though his work of announcing was done, he wanted to go through the yard calling "Churchtime!" to the barns and cattle. In the reassuring knowledge that the pastor was not without gentleness, he almost forgot about his lost possession.

But starting in the direction of the schoolhouse, he found that he could not cross the path which led to the high bank without searching the ground. A light rain during the night had washed the path clean. He walked to where the grass began and then turned to gauge the time he could spend before the service started.

Pastor Kunz, who was always among the first to take his place at churchtime, was just going into the school. The Householder came from his home. His wife followed behind him and then came their five children in single file. Martha Volkner emerged from the Daniel Mueller quarters with children swarming around her. Silently she stood looking at the commune as a new day revealed it to her. In these half-remembered surroundings she seemed to feel the pulse of her old home beat in her heart on this holy morning. From the colony dwellings the worshipers now came and filled the yard. The men walked slower and more thoughtfully than on week days. Their black pants were pressed, their hook-and-eye jackets clean. The sunlight touched their white, tieless shirts.

Little Mike watched the men and found in each of them the same searchless expression of security and somber faith. Their minds and their ways were established. The women came singly, their long skirts almost sweeping the ground, their colorful Sabbath aprons brightening the surroundings. The Sunday head scarves were especially tidy and smooth, and Little Mike remembered that in each of these the woman's name was neatly cross-stitched with colored thread. The Sabbath quiet sobered the people's steps as they moved solemnly to the schoolhouse. Very young children in long dresses and little pink caps clung anxiously to the hands of older sisters who led them carefully through the yard. With a lingering glance in the direction of the Neumann home David Wiese made his way across the yard. Michael Neumann caught up with him and together they walked to the worship.

Joshua Volkner came from the teacherage, Joshua in his handsome dark suit and colorful necktie against the gleaming white shirt. For a moment he stood at the doorway, surveying the commune. Then he held open the door for his daughter. Elaine came out pulling on a pink glove that just matched the flowers in her hat. She took hold of Joshua's hand and as they started across the yard, Robert came out of the teacherage winding his wrist watch. Together the three started to the service, talking animatedly without regard for rules.

In them the outside world came to life, and Little Mike

dared to imagine himself dressed in Robert's clothes. For a moment he was wearing the brown suit with long pants, the soft brown shoes and stockings and the colored bow tie which seemed not to choke him at all; Little Mike with a wrist watch on his arm and his hair wet with something fragrant, walking carefree to church. He imagined himself sauntering boldly down the center aisle and pictured in his mind the blue-covered heads turning, bearded faces looking up, and the boys gaping at him with excited whispers: "Look at Mike! He's been in the world. A gold chain on his leather belt. A necktie. Hey, what time is it by your watch, Mike?" Straight down the aisle the way he always went. "All right, Pastor Kunz, look at me," he would say. "I went out into the world—to Chicago, to New York, to California. I was on a train. I went to the theater. I was on a Ferris wheel. I was on streets where there were many people. There I had money and I bought all the pretty things I wanted. The world was bright with music and I was free."

Reflectively he stood in the dirt path. Joshua Volkner and his children had gone into the schoolhouse. Everyone had disappeared. He was alone. Before him lay the uninhabited yard. There the gate. And beyond that the tempting road rose like a mighty angel saying, "Come, Little Mike, come!"

He took a step. Nothing stopped him. No voice sounded to hold him back. Freedom was beckoning. All that Robert Volkner had he too could have. He would still have had his harmonica had it not been for the fear of personal possession. The elders were to blame. The rules and regulations which they had made were the cause of his sorrow. He had tried to guard the instrument too well. Gradually he placed the full blame for his suffering on the unyielding confinement of commune life.

He began to run, past the sheds, past the barn, past the carpenter shop and the separator house, out into the clearing of the commune road. *The gate is never locked. It opens easily. Nothing confines you, Mike, only the rules.* These thoughts were wrung from his heart as he threw off the chain from the gate. The chain clanked loudly. He pushed the gate open and stepped out. The world's road lay free and calling before his eyes. He felt the gate close. He heard the sharp click of the iron latch.

"Mike!"

The word stabbed through his thoughts. Tremblingly he turned. Sarah mother was running toward him. She stopped when he swung around. "Mike, what are you doing? Why are you outside that gate? Come back here and hurry! Quick now!"

Rachel, dressed for the wedding, hastened to her mother's side. "Please hurry, Sarah mother," she pleaded. "Come, Mike, come! We are all late already."

Sarah was at the gate and opened it. "You know you shouldn't be out there," she told him in an almost tender tone.

He came in and she hurriedly flung the chain around the gatepost.

"What was he doing out there, Sarah mother?"

"Doing?" Sarah said, busy with the gate. "Telling the world it is churchtime, I suppose. Listen! There is the first song. Didn't I tell you the pastor wouldn't wait? Get in there, Mike, so you are in your place before Rachel comes."

He turned submissively and the three went quickly to

the schoolyard. As the compelling strains of the singing
called Mike back to churchtime and his world, he was possessed by one vivid impression. There was a touch of kindly
understanding in his mother's voice which he had never
heard before.

He went up the schoolhouse steps, brushed back his
hair and opened the door. Down the length of the long
aisle he started to go. The pastor was setting the tone for
a line of the song as he stood behind the table, book in
hand. But when the late-comer entered, Pastor Kunz did
not refer to the hymnal. He sang from memory and his
unflinching gaze followed Little Mike every step of the
way. Four elders were in their places at the pastor's right
and three at his left. They sat on low backless benches,
feet squarely on the scrubbed pine floor, beards neatly
combed, their eyes on Little Mike as if they were already
preparing a pronouncement of eternal judgment. They
sang the song with spirit. It was the story of the wretched
plight of those who succumb to the *Weltgeist*.

Little Mike walked the length of eternity down the
center aisle. At his left sat the colony men and Joshua
Volkner and Robert. At his right were the colony women
and Grandmother Volkner and Elaine. In each section
the worshipers sat shoulder to shoulder in the crowded
room, hands folded on the school desks, their eyes following him all the way. In the first three rows at his
right sat the younger girls. At his left the boys were
packed solidly in their places, the youngest in the very
first seats and those his own age just behind them. All of
these places were taken, and he had to go all the way to
the very front and then walk to his left where a bench had

been put against the side wall. Here Jake Linder had
reserved a place for him. Here was sanctuary. He dropped
awkwardly into the seat just as the song ended and an
expectant hush fell over the room.

Rachel and Sarah mother now came down the center
aisle and took their places in the women's section. The
somber faces of the elders relaxed. The pastor stroked his
beard. Rachel glanced nervously across the aisle to where
David sat. Relieved that he was being forgotten, Little
Mike settled back against the wall.

Pastor Kunz rose gravely to his feet. Slowly he paged
through the hymnal, held it close to his eyes and began
intoning the wedding song line by line:

> "It is not good to be alone.
> Vouchsafe these words, O God of grace."

The congregation repeated each line, copying the *Ansager's* doleful mood, together with the melody:

> "Bless thou and seal the marriage vows
> Which shall be offered in this holy place."

The schoolroom throbbed with the antiphonal singing.
The women's high-pitched, fervent voices mingled with
the deep, resonant chanting of the men. Little Mike and
Jake and all of the children joined in, taking their cues and
their words from the leader:

> "It is not good to be alone,
> The heart's desire begs admittance to another's love."

He imagined himself playing the song on the harmonica, bringing to Rachel's wedding the sweet sound of an organ. But as he thought of it, he brought only sorrow and longing to himself, and instinctively he looked for Sarah mother in the crowd, wondering what she was thinking as she sang. Would she tell Michael father that he ventured outside the gate? Would she report him to the elders?

> "Share with a loved one peace and pain;
>   Send forth together holy thoughts from earth
>   to heaven above."

At the end of four verses Pastor Kunz laid the hymnal aside and picked up the Bible. The room was very still as he said, "The Apostle Paul instructs us how a husband and wife shall live together according to the will of God. In the fifth chapter of Ephesians he writes: 'Wives, submit yourselves unto your own husbands as unto the Lord. ...'"

During the tedious reading Jake whispered cautiously, "Did you find it, Mike?"

Mike shook his head.

"I thought when you were late," Jake ventured, "maybe you were looking for it."

"No, I wasn't."

"Look at Robert Volkner's wrist watch. I can see it plain."

Mike shrugged. His mind was straying. Why was he not more frightened at what Michael father would say when his mother told him the reason for their tardiness? What if his mother had not come when he stood outside the gate? Why, then he would have been able to own things without fear. He could have walked through the world playing a harmonica as much as he pleased. No colony boss would tell him how he should dress or how he should act or what he should memorize or how and when he ought to pray, just as no one dared tell Joshua Volkner that he had to do this or do that.

Tremulously the pastor finished his reading. "For this cause shall a man leave his father and mother. . . ."

He closed the Bible and put it aside with a respectful sigh. Then he folded his hands and began to preach in a singsong tone.

"Today when the union of two young people blends into the tradition of our faith, I want to remind you of the glory of our way of life. And I want to warn you of the *Weltgeist*, the ever-dreaded spirit of the world."

The pastor's accusing glance passed over the listeners as if to assure himself that Joshua Volkner was in range of his words. He closed his eyes.

"Here we have a life that is beautiful and free," he chanted in deep earnestness. "We are safe and protected from temptation and harm. But—" his voice filled with ominous warning—"outside the commune is the everlasting ambush of the Prince of Darkness. His legions increase. He grows desperate with his lust for conquest. He refuses to rest while there is a remnant which still serves the one true God. We are that remnant."

Pastor Kunz pressed his hands tightly against his breast. His body swayed slowly from side to side.

"It is the *Weltgeist* that says, 'Come into the world and surround yourself with personal possessions. Come out where there are no rules or boundaries or restrictions. Come and satisfy your sensual appetites and desires. Come and forget about God.' "

He opened his eyes and pointed a finger at Rachel and then at David. "And what does the *Weltgeist* say to you? 'Come into the world where divorce is not forbidden and where the vows of marriage are a mockery. . . .' "

Little Mike sat engrossed as the swaying figure continued. He had heard the pastor preach many times. Each night when he sat in the service he waited restlessly for the final amen. But now for once he hoped that the sermon would not end. It was calling to him as his mother had called and, though he resented it, he again found himself obeying. The unsteady sense of standing outside the commune boundary, the daring of starting up the road that led to the world were receding. For the first time in his compulsory churchgoing, he was trying to understand what the speaker said.

He did not comprehend it all, but the tone of lament with which the pastor exhorted his people left no doubt as to the rightness of the Hutterian cause. As the pastor argued, Little Mike continued to yield. Phrase by phrase he was wooed back through the gate and up the commune path. The pastor gestured with outstretched arms; the furrows of his bearded face deepened as he pleaded for commune loyalty; his voice broke with passionate entreaty.

"Do not be misled by the monster *Weltgeist*, the great deceiver. He lies in wait ready to enslave you. But here you are safe and free."

Now the pastor nodded to the elders and they rose to their feet.

"David Wiese, Rachel Neumann," Pastor Kunz announced, "you will come and stand before the congregation."

Rachel was pretty. She wore a blouse that was soft and pink. The blue apron over her long, full skirt matched the blue of her head scarf. She carried no flowers. Michael father had said, "If she has flowers at her wedding everyone who gets married should have them. Roses for which you must pay a price are already tainted with the world."

David looked very young. His hair was freshly cut straight around his head and his black suit fitted him nicely. His cheeks were crimson and he smiled at the elders who responded with a gentle light in their eyes. They seemed almost to smile as Rachel and David stepped in front of Pastor Kunz. Rachel nervously smoothed her dress. David stood with his hands properly at his sides, his face lifted to the pastor.

"I ask you, my brother," the pastor charged, "do you accept this woman willingly and readily as a gift of God?"

"I do."

"Are you willing to lead her in all that is right and good that she may be led closer to the Lord by you?"

"I am willing."

Little Mike could not imagine himself in such a ceremony. But when the pastor reached the momentous question known as the special dedication, he suddenly became an interested participant.

"I ask you, David Wiese," the pastor continued searchingly, "if it should ever come to pass that you should abandon the church and this community and be enticed by the spirit of the world, will you let it be enough that

this happens to you and not desire or ask your wife to follow you?"

"It will be enough that I should go," said David.

Little Mike turned his eyes in Joshua's direction. What
was the worldling thinking as he heard this? How did he
feel as he sat in the congregation knowing that he had
departed from the true faith? Joshua rested his chin on
his hand, his eyes wise and watchful. Robert sat at his
side with arms resting casually on the desk.

"Should you ever embark on this terrible and unexpected undertaking," probed the pastor, "do you promise
not to trouble us before the magistrates to induce them to
have your wife come to you?"

David's voice was resolute. "I so promise."

The pastor turned to Rachel. "Are you ready to accept
this man as your husband, willingly and without complaint?"

Rachel said softly, "I am."

Little Mike suddenly wondered what the Neumann home
would be like with her away. Only now did he realize that
the closely knit family to which he belonged was being dis-
rupted. Rachel would be gone. True, she would live only
three houses from him. He would see her every day—almost as much as he always had—but a feeling of loneliness
touched him.

"Since it is ordained by God that the husband shall be
the head of the wife, are you willing to obey him in all
things righteous and godly?"

"I am willing."

Michael father sat with his arms folded over his black
hook-and-eye coat. He looked proud and pleased. Sarah
mother watched the ceremony solemnly.

"The husband is usually healthier than the wife," quoted the pastor, "but if sickness does come to him, will you serve him as well as in health, in sorrow as in love, never to part or leave him until the Lord severs you by death?"

"I promise."

"Then," said the pastor, "give each other the right hand and kneel before me."

As the couple knelt, the elders and all the worshipers went to their knees. For once Little Mike did not close his eyes as was the custom. He watched intently while Pastor Kunz laid his hands on the heads of the couple and said: "I bear witness that you are now married as pious people according to the ordinance of the Lord and the example of the fathers. May the God of Abraham, Isaac and Jacob bless you, and may you live together peaceably and well throughout your life! This I desire from God through Jesus Christ. Amen."

The worshipers returned to their seats. David Wiese took his place among the men and Rachel walked back to sit once more among the women. The pastor spoke a closing prayer and the service ended.

Out in the schoolyard, close by the commune road, Rachel and David received the congratulations of the people. Little Mike tarried in the crowd. He heard the oft-repeated "Well, Rachel Wiese, God bless you in your new home!" while the men wished David good luck and a good family. But as he passed the Volkners, he caught Elaine's anxious whisper to Joshua: "Why didn't she carry the roses? Don't they even kiss each other? Shouldn't there have been a wedding march? Won't they go on a honeymoon?"

Little Mike walked away, feeling an unanswerable sadness. It was the loss of the harmonica, of course—but it was something more. He felt tied like the pet lamb was tied each Sabbath so that it would not roam wantonly through the yard. He felt cooped up like the geese who were reminded it was Sunday by being kept inside the gooseyard. It was always Sunday with him. He was always caught—by rules, by discipline, by fear.

He walked once around the Neumann house and then decided to go in. He went into the children's bedroom, closed the door and flung himself on the big bed where Rachel used to sleep. Rachel had seemed very happy as she stood with David in the yard. Apparently she was undisturbed by whatever it was that caused Elaine Volkner concern about such unheard-of things as a wedding march, a honeymoon. Rachel was as happy as if she had a personal possession, yet she would never understand if he went to her and said, "Help me *find* my possession." "What is the matter with you, Mike?" she would say in a voice that was already the voice of Sarah mother. "You know what Pastor Kunz said in his sermon. And what were you doing outside the gate? You just better be good."

He tried to figure out what life in the world was like. If a boy worked hard he earned money. Then he could buy the things that brought him happiness. But what happened if one boy made more money than another, or had prettier things? That was hard to figure out. As he lay on the bed thinking about it, he said to himself, If I only had my harmonica I wouldn't care if every boy had one. Even if theirs were nicer than mine or even if they could play theirs better, I would not care.

He heard the opening of the outside door and recognized his mother's hurried steps. She went into the other bedroom to see that Baby Leah was all right. Now the outside door opened again and Sarah's mother returned to the front room. He heard her speak in a matter-of-fact voice.

"Well, Joshua, did you come to ask why Rachel did not carry the roses? Even if she didn't, it was nice of you. Nice but too much in the way of the world. There they are in the fruit jar on the table. They must have cost a pretty price."

"That's more talk than I've heard from you, Sarah, in all the time I've been here."

"Oh, you haven't been here so long."

"We're leaving soon after dinner."

"But not Mother Volkner. She stays awhile."

"Yes, I hear that everyone is begging *her* to stay."

"Would it do any good to beg you?" Sarah wanted to know. "Of course not. Your world is not ours, and ours is not yours. That anybody can see, so why waste time with it?"

"Tell me, Sarah, did you ever regret that my world, as you call it, did not become your world, too?"

"You better go to dinner."

"Did you?"

"Twenty years ago seems like another life to me," Sarah told him, and Little Mike heard her move about as if she were busying herself with duties in the room. "We were two different people in those days, Joshua, so why talk about that?"

"I wanted to ask you how you felt about it, Sarah, and

I'm glad you've told me. So you never regretted that you didn't run away with me as I wanted you to do?"

Sarah's voice was a tone of dismissal. "I never think about things like that."

"Never?" Joshua asked.

"What good does it do?"

"Sometimes a person can't help it. Sometimes it helps one to figure out how life works."

"That I don't understand," Sarah said shortly. Then she sighed. "Look at this room. To clean it up will take all day. Colony life makes easy housekeeping, they say. The elders should look at this."

"But, Sarah, this is a special day."

"Oh, it's not so special. This time it's Rachel. Next it will be Ruth, then Little Mike, then Anna, then——"

"That is, if we assume they will all stay and be good Hutterians. That is, if they never walk outside the commune boundaries."

"Oh, Joshua, you want to make out that we are prisoners. We are freer than you. Everybody knows that."

"Come, ride to Yankton with me! Come visit us in Chicago. Come, let us sit together at dinner. Rachel may carry the roses. Little Mike can go with Robert to a movie. Let me give you and Michael a radio so that you can listen to music. Wear a dress to make you as lovely as you really are. Go and buy yourself what you like. Free? No, Sarah, you are no freer than you were the day that I begged you to leave."

"I didn't want to leave."

"Yes, you did. We were in love. Terribly in love."

"You didn't love me enough to stay. I didn't love you

enough to go. Ah, such talk is foolishness! Twenty years
— Go to dinner."

"I loved you too much to want you to stay here and be
put into the Hutterian mold. Let's put it that way. You
wanted to go but you were afraid. To save yourself you
flew to Michael."

"I love Michael."

"You flew to him for protection from the greatest desire of your heart. Forgive me, Sarah. But haven't you
ever wished—?"

"Who knows what a person wishes?" Sarah interrupted
impatiently. "Wish for nothing that you cannot have and
all your wishes will come true."

"For at least two years I never stopped thinking of you,
Sarah. Often I almost came back, because of you. I suppose we were different from most Hutterians. We loved
each other, but not as a matter of convenience. We
wanted to marry because it would bring us happiness. We
were different. You were different, Sarah."

For a long moment no one spoke. Little Mike lay on
the bed, his heart pounding at Joshua's words. He heard
his mother ask quietly, "What is she like, Joshua, the
woman you married?"

"Would you like to see a picture of her?" Then in a
moment he said, "This was taken just this spring."

Sarah was silent for some time. "She's young," she said.
"She's pretty. She looks like Elaine. What is her name?"

"Helen."

"How were you married? In a church?"

"No. In the garden of her father's home."

"Did you give her a ring? An engagement ring, too?"

"Yes."

"How did you meet her, Joshua?"

"How did everything happen to me out in the world? Not by arrangement as in the commune, but by chance. A tourist picked me up on the highway the night I left here. He was going far, he said. To Chicago. I went with him. By chance I got a job. Or was it by some divine direction? Who is to say? One day, I told my employer the story. The next Saturday he took me home with him. He had a daughter. We saw each other off and on for nearly three years."

"I suppose she is rich. Yes, I can see from the picture she looks well-to-do."

"Her people were rich at one time. But we had some bad years. Things were not always easy. We had a great deal of sickness, too."

"Why didn't you bring her with you?"

"You wouldn't believe it from the picture, but she doesn't get around too easily. She must walk with crutches and has ever since she was a young girl. You see, there she is standing near the car and it is sort of make-believe that there is nothing wrong."

"And that is why she didn't come?"

"Yes, that is why."

Little Mike listened. The voices of people in the commune yard were far away. It was very quiet in the front room, but that quiet was near and real.

Then his mother spoke gently. "I'm glad you came, Joshua. It was good to see you and I'm happy that you talked to me. We have chosen our lives——"

"In our respective worlds," Joshua added. "But, Sarah,

give your children a chance, if you can. Give them a chance to go out and make something of their lives. Let them see what the world is like. Should any one of them ever want to go, let me know and let me help, for a change is coming to the commune life sure as can be. The time is not far off when the young people will insist on getting out, and they'll have the courage to go. No fences will hold them, no elders, no rules, no fears."

"Spare me from that day!" Sarah exclaimed.

"Oh, now, Sarah, the world is not as bad as Pastor Kunz has painted it."

"Spare me from having *my* children break our tradition," Sarah said as if pleading with herself. "You know, Joshua, this morning at churchtime there was Little Mike standing outside the commune gate. Oh, he wasn't running away. It was just boyish foolishness, I suppose. But I saw myself again as I stood once with you. If the sins of the parents are visited on the children—— No, it was nothing like that. He was just trying to be smart. But Michael is right: every generation goes a little farther than the last."

"Of course. That's inevitable."

"But I don't want it to be my child. Let someone else start it. Let it not be mine."

"But maybe it will be your child. What you didn't do, Little Mike may have the courage to do. Do you remember the Sunday afternoon we walked back and forth along the commune fence looking out into the world? We put thoughts into words that I've never forgotten: *In every life there is a dream gate through which one ought to go with all his wishes, soon or late, and take the free road where it leads.*"

Sarah's voice was low. "Yes," she said, "I remember. And if Little Mike is thinking about the world and his wishes, that is my fault." Then she added impatiently, "There is something else I remember. I was in the commune the night when your parents found a note. I know what they went through."

"Yes, I know that, too. But there can be no growth without pain. There are times when the individual must think of himself——"

"Listen! There is Michael. Yes, Michael! Yes, I am coming."

"Well, come and hurry!" called the voice of Michael father from the outside doorway. "Come, Joshua Volkner! Today you can eat with us. Come and see how it feels to have good solid food instead of the world's fancy dishes. And you can have a glass of wine. That's traditional at a wedding, you remember. . . ."

The words died away. The house door banged. In the commune yard the people were merrily inviting one another to the wedding feast. In the parent's bedroom Baby Leah cooed happily. Little Mike lay on the bed and it seemed to him that the voices he had heard in the outer room were still echoing.

CHAPTER 12

*A*T sundown Joshua was packing his bags in the teacherage. Little Mike stood in the room near the small-paned window. From here he could watch Robert and Joshua as they put their things into the suitcases, and he could also see the automobile standing in the schoolhouse yard. Joey, sitting with Jake on the feather bed, closed his eyes and sniffed the air.

"Smell it," he said. "It's like sticking your nose in the clover patch."

"That's Elaine's powder." Robert laughed. "Hey, Dad, you're spilling it!"

"Elaine should have packed these things herself!" Joshua exclaimed. "Hurry, Bob, we want to make a few hundred miles tonight."

But he gave Robert the powder box.

"Here, Joey," Robert invited. "Hold out your hands."

He sprinkled the powder liberally on Joey's palms. Joey sucked the fragrance through his nose.

"Put it on your face," Jake dared.

Joey rubbed it over his cheeks and hair and rolled on the bed in delight. "I smell like a skunk," he squealed, "only not so stinky."

He quieted when men's voices were heard at the door.

"Don't think this is a bribe, Joshua Volkner," an-

239

nounced Michael Neumann, entering with a large cardboard carton in both arms. "You know it's traditional to
show our guests we are glad they came."

"When visitors were too worldly," Joshua commented
good-naturedly, "we used to say 'Give them gifts and be
glad they're going.' What is all this?"

"Two hams, some hunks of speck, some three-pound
loaves of Hutterian bread and a roll of butter."

"Here," said the Bee Boss, "are two pails of honey.
You'll never get any like this in Chicago. This is number one white, purest and clearest in the country."

"I'm sure you're right about that, Rudolph, and I ap-
preciate the gifts. Thank you, Michael, for your thought-
fulness."

"It's all good colony stuff," Michael assured him. "But,
as I say, don't think this is done to influence you. If you
won't help arrange it so that we may buy the Jordan
Ranch, then all I can say is you don't have much love
and honor left for your parents and relatives. If I were in
your place, believe me I'd use my influence."

"I intend to see what can be done, Michael. I'm leaving
right now so that I may be at a director's meeting tomorrow night. The matter will be presented—trust me for
that. But I've been wondering whether you realize that
the ranch is a three-thousand-acre tract with good buildings and improvements——"

"We know that," interrupted the Bee Boss. "Why do
you suppose we have our eyes on it?"

"Well, then, you know it runs into considerable money."

"Big figures don't scare us," Michael said.

"Besides," Joshua explained, "we have drawn up plans

for the experimental project. I have a roll of blueprints in the car and the other day I went over them with some agriculturalists on the Jordan place. You see, we feel that if we can determine scientifically which crops and seeds are best for this section——"

Michael flung up his hands. "That," he exclaimed, "is all foolishness. Hard work and common sense are all the scientific methods that anybody needs. Give us a chance and we'll show you how to operate without blueprints or experts. There's nobody around here who can compete with us the way it is. Why are our brethren having such a hard time in Canada? Because their neighbors are jealous. They say, 'These Hutterians raise more crops with less machinery and make more money with fewer modern conveniences than we do with all the equipment we've got. They don't want the better things of life. They won't become Canadianized. All they do is work.' Since when is it a sin to work, I'd like to know? God said that work was honorable. People say we are expanding too fast. Doesn't the Bible tell us to be fruitful and multiply? We are being criticized for not taking part in war. But the Lord says that whoever takes up the sword will perish by the sword. It amounts to this: Because we live according to the Gospel and not according to the world, we are being persecuted."

"America isn't persecuting you," Joshua protested.

"No, but it is trying to make us a part of its system."

"Ah," Joshua exclaimed, "there you said it, Michael!"

Little Mike heard his father groan as if someone had marred a piece of his handiwork. But Joshua called to the Householder and James the Teacher, who were at the door: "Come in, gentlemen! Here's a man whom I heartily recommend as an elder. Carpenter Michael has hit the nail on the head. The American way stands at the commune gate and will force it open. Force it? No, you are already opening it of your own free will."

"Don't twist my words, Mr. Demas," Michael warned. "I said that America is trying to make us a part of its system. I did not say it would succeed."

"I'll say it for you," Joshua hurried on. "All during my visit we have spoken English. Robert found the boys as able to speak it as he. Twenty years ago that was unheard of. Soon you will be changing the songs from German into English, too. Then the old traditions will be foreign and strange. They are strange already to many of your young people. I see changes everywhere. I noticed a tractor in the shed and next to it was a combine—a small one, but a combine nonetheless."

"That's a used one," the Householder explained uneasily, "and we don't know whether we'll keep it or not. We haven't tried it out yet."

"Used or new—" Joshua shrugged— "it's another trend, another step toward assimilation. Machinery is coming in. The spinning wheels are merely symbols, nothing more. I saw modern tools in the cabinet shop. I noticed factory-made shoes and there are not as many hooks and eyes as there used to be. Ask my mother about the Canadian colonies. She'll tell you they have running water, electric lights, even milking machines——"

"But no luxuries," James the Teacher broke in.

"Well, that all depends on what you call a luxury,"

Joshua told him. "In one commune they burn gas. In another they have cement sidewalks. Hutterians are beginning to read magazines and secular books. Mother told me that some of the children sing popular songs. Why not admit it? Your young people are looking across the commune borders. Every war brings the world closer. You cannot isolate yourselves any longer. Every world event tells you that what affects the nation affects you. It's a new age and the fences out there won't hold it back."

Through this oration the boys watched the speaker with wonder. No one spoke. Little Mike seemed to feel the shadows pass over him as dusk touched the teacherage with gloom.

Michael father stood with his thumbs latched into the waistband of his black pants. His eyes were troubled and defiant. Stubbornly he said, "At times like this a person feels things that he can't put into words, but he knows that his feelings are right just the same."

James the Teacher nodded. "It can be put into words, Michael. A deep conviction is our answer to Joshua Volkner's exaggerated claim. We have been taught not to take seriously any established world order. They all pass away. The Kingdom of God is the only reality and that is here to stay."

"Good!" cried Michael, driving his fist into his open hand. "That settles the matter. Mike, run and get a match so that Joshua Volkner may get some light on the subject! Let us light the lamp, gentlemen, and drive out some of this darkness."

"I have matches," Joshua told him. "I'll light the lamp.

But we must be on our way. Robert, you and the boys take the box and the honey and your bag down to the car. Find Elaine and tell her we're ready."

"Your daughter is over at the newlyweds'," said the Householder.

"Yes, listen!" Michael spoke up. "That's where the singing is coming from. You remember that song, Joshua?"

Michael began to sing a verse:

> "I trust in God for everything,
> For everything, let come what will.

"Open the window there, Little Mike!" his father ordered. "Let's hear these young Hutterians. Open!"

Little Mike raised the window of the teacherage. As the voices came in more clearly, Michael sang:

> "I wait and let God have His way,
> His way not mine, in everything.

"That, Joshua Volkner," he affirmed, "is what I feel about the matter of the Jordan Ranch. Do what you can for us at the Chicago meeting tomorrow night. Use the influence you have, whatever it may be. But I tell you this: God is looking out for our interests. He knows that our brethren are depending on us and He'll take care of everything."

"Yes," said James the Teacher, "and when I listen to those young Hutterians sing I hear them carrying the songs of the fathers into a new generation. Change? Assimilation? Those old fences are still strong, Joshua."

The men nodded and were pleased. James the Teacher had spoken as if he meant it.

Robert instructed the boys. "Okay, Joey, you take the honey. Jake and I'll carry the box. Mike, you bring the suitcase."

Joey grabbed the honey pails. "Follow me," he ordered. "Follow the powder face."

He led them out, but Little Mike was sure that not even Joey's enthusiasm at being the leader could compare with the thrill he felt at carrying Robert's suitcase. The handle was smooth leather, soft to his touch. As he walked he swung the suitcase freely, but once for a moment he picked it up and held it in both arms. The leather had a rich, pungent smell.

> "I trust in God for everything,
> For everything, let come what will."

Joey was taking them past the home of the newlyweds where the singing emanated.

"There's Elaine!" Robert exclaimed as they stopped at the window.

They set the box down, but Mike did not let go of the suitcase. Some of the singers were nodding to the rhythm of the song. They sat on the floor and on the bed while David Wiese took the part of the *Ansager*. Mothers with babies in their laps occupied the chairs and women lined the walls. Elaine Volkner was trying to sing along. The hymn throbbed through the dusk, and Little Mike, listening, dreamed of raising the harmonica to his lips. He visualized himself standing in the room playing a new song for the colony and for the visitors from the world. He looked at David and Rachel, their faces bright, sitting on the marriage chest with their hands entwined. He saw Ruth holding Mary on her lap and Anna rocking Leah on her knee in keeping with the music. He heard Rebecca Mueller start the song all over again:

"I trust in God for everything,
  For everything . . ."

"Come, Mike, come," Jake was saying. "The 'powder boss' is almost to the car."

Not even the suitcase made up for the harmonica. The suitcase was not his, and he had no use for it unless, like Robert, he would be free to come and go. Robert was whistling the song while he walked. Whistling was frowned on by the elders. What if everyone walked around the commune whistling? But there was a spirit of freedom about it and why not, since Robert would soon be riding through the open gate and out into the adventure of the world? Little Mike would have to go to his room as always at the prescribed hour. In the morning he would have to help his father in the cabinet shop, and it might be that he would not even have time to hunt for the harmonica.

Jake's voice drifted back to him: "Wouldn't it be fun to go along?"

"Crawl in the box." Robert laughed.

"In with the ham and the speck?"

"You'd have plenty to eat."

"I wouldn't think about eating," Joey called. "I'd think about sticking out my nose and getting air."

"Wouldn't you want to see the big cities, too, Joey?" Robert asked. "Or do you just want to smell of them?"

"If I did go," Joey said, "how'd I get back? Or should I stay away twenty years?"

"Someday Joey will make his own automobile," said Jake. "Then we'll all go."

Robert opened the trunk. A light went on inside.

"Look, Mike!" Jake called.

"I could lay down in there," Joey figured, peering into the trunk as Robert made room for the box.

It was large enough to hold a boy, that was sure. Little Mike figured that it was almost the size of his bench bed.

"You can lie right in there," Robert told Joey. "I'll prop up the top and you'll have plenty of air."

Joey said, "Guess I'll stay."

In the trunk light Mike saw Jake turn to him. How easily we could go away! he seemed to be saying. In just a little while the commune would be far behind.

Mike nodded, wondering if Jake guessed what he wanted to reply: Should we do it, Jake? Would we really have the courage to do something like that? Would you be ready?

"Okay," said Robert. "Let's lift the box in."

Jake helped him put it into the trunk. Joey handed him the honey pails.

"There's still lots of room," Robert observed.

"There's your suitcase," Joey reminded him. "Or does Mike keep that?"

"That we'll put in the back seat," Robert explained. "I'll take it, Mike."

The suitcase was handed to Robert without comment. He opened the car door and a light flashed on. Joey jumped up and down joyously as Dan Mueller and Paul Wiese came out of the shadows.

"Come for the big trip!" Joey announced.

"When does it start?" asked Dan. "I want to see that."

"I want to see how the car turns around in the dark," Paul added.

"Come on in," Robert invited. "Look how soft." He bounced up and down on the seat.

"It's not allowed," Paul said.

"I guess since we helped bring the things," Jake decided, "we can go in and see how it feels to sit on the cushions."

"Hey, Mike," said Robert, "you get in the front——"

"Behind the wheel," urged Jake.

"Steer it!" yelled Joey.

"You're the chauffeur," Robert told him. "I'll sit back here and tell you where to go."

Mike opened the front door and got in.

"Out goes the light," said Robert. "Now no one will see us."

Mike closed the door. Jake ran around the car and got in beside him. The others could not resist; they climbed onto the back seat with Robert.

"Let her go!" Robert cried.

"Chicago, Car Boss!" chanted Joey.

"Step on 'er!" said Robert.

"Step on 'er!" echoed Dan and Paul.

Mike gripped the wheel and stared out into the dark. Once he had pictured Joshua trying to take him out of the commune, and he had trembled at the thought. Now in make-believe he was driving through the schoolyard, the gate opened by itself, he was on the outer road.

"Take it slow here—loose gravel," Robert called. "Stop

sign, driver. Now we're turning on Highway Sixty-nine."

"Highway Sixty-nine," echoed the boys.

"Okay, the highway's yours," Robert yelled and the boys on the seat with him repeated his words. "Step on it! Yankton coming up. Honk, honk! *Woo-a-woo-a!* On into Iowa. Now across the Mississippi. Hi y', Mississippi! Hi there, Illinois! Stop, we got to pay toll! Honk, honk! Watch that traffic, driver! Good work. Little more speed. *R-r-r-rr*." They made the motor roar. "*R-r-r-rr*. Hey, you've been driving without your lights!" Robert reached over the front seat and snapped them on. As they flashed across the commune, Mike shouted, "Chicago!"

Jake was jubilant and the boys in the back bounced up and down on the seat. But Robert said, "How can you go anywhere when Dad has the key?"

That was not Mike's feeling. It had been a most wonderful ride and when he stood again on the solid ground of the commune, he was sure that Jake agreed with him. As they walked across the yard, he stayed close to Jake, knowing that this friend understood best what had gone through his mind. Flight would not be too difficult or too terrible.

Loud and excited voices lured the boys to the teacherage. Men crowded the entrance and only Robert was admitted to the room.

"Go on away!" ordered the Town Man. "This is men's business."

The words from within were sharp-spoken, deep with emotion, arresting, but Dan and Paul decided to go back and sit near the car. Jake said he was going to join the singers at the Wiese home. Mike went around to the open window of the teacherage. From here he could see his father and Joshua hemmed in by the seven elders and other colony men.

"I know which way the wind is blowing," Michael was saying, calling on everyone to give attention. "Men in the world are used to having their palms greased. All right, Mr. Demas, how much?"

"That's world language all right," Joshua agreed. "But you have me wrong, Michael. The ethics of the grain business wouldn't allow——"

"Ethics!" Michael broke in.

"Ethics?" cried one of the elders. "How can there be any ethics in a godless world?"

"Come, come!" Michael urged. "How much? What do you want to help us get the Jordan Ranch? What's your price?"

Joshua's gaze traveled over the circle of bearded faces. As his eyes lingered on each man he seemed almost to speak each name: Caleb Wiese, Daniel Mueller, Rudolph Kunz, the Town Man, Shoemaker Graebel, Blacksmith Linder—the elders.

"All I can do, gentlemen," Joshua said with finality, "is put the matter up to my associates."

"And what does that mean?" asked Elder Wiese.

"They'll discuss it and come to some decision. You elders can understand that procedure."

"But what are you personally going to say at the meeting?" asked the Householder.

"I'm not sure you could finance the deal even if we would sell," Joshua said. "We paid three hundred thousand for the ranch."

The men made a clicking noise.

"That's too much," Michael told him.

Joshua shrugged.

"Then, of course," said the Householder wryly, "you will want a profit on top of that?"

"What do you think?" Joshua said shortly. Then he turned from the men to Robert. "Take my suitcase to the car, Bob, and get Elaine."

As Robert turned to obey, Joshua continued: "Even without a profit, the ranch is worth a lot of money. I think it's more than you gentlemen can afford."

"I told you we've handled big deals before," Michael boasted, and went on to say how Old Portage Colony had financed many communes in the past.

Suddenly Little Mike heard the voice of Pastor Kunz close to him. "Is there room at the window for one more?"

"Surely, Pastor," Little Mike said, startled.

The old man squinted at him. "What are you up to now, Neumann Mike? Well, come, there is place here for both of us."

Meanwhile Joshua was saying to the men: "If this were happening fifty years ago, even twenty years ago, I would urge my associates to sell you the ranch, and I'd tell you to pay for it as you pleased. For in those days and under those conditions you thrived. But things have changed. This is no longer a world for communistic enterprising."

"Why not?" asked the Householder.

"Because this is an age of self-expression, and that is one thing that communism must always stifle in order to survive."

"Don't we have self-expression?" Michael wanted to

know. "We are free to do as we please. Our children are free——"

"Yesterday Bob wanted to take some of the boys with us to Yankton——"

"Well, why didn't he?" Michael demanded. "Why didn't the boys come and ask for permission? That is all there is to it."

"That is not all there is to it," said Elder Wiese, "and I am glad it isn't. Self-expression, as you call it, Joshua Volkner, has brought the world into the terrible state in which it is today. Discipline is what is needed, discipline and obedience. Call us old-fashioned. We can show you a way of life of which we need not be ashamed. There has never been a divorce among the Hutterians. No Hutterian has ever been in jail. None has ever gone to court. If you have forgotten these things and if the moral standard among us is no longer in your knowledge, I'll refresh your memory."

"I haven't forgotten," Joshua answered. "But through the years I've become unusually skeptical of exclusive social concepts, the idea of a special people or a chosen group. Most of them have simply closed their minds and refused to investigate honestly the advantages of the American way. Their leaders have never provided them with a better life than they could have gotten on their own anywhere they chose to live. When I got away from behind these fences I wondered how many other groups in our country were trying to live under as strict a communal scheme as you practice. None! But I learned this: A hundred and fifty times someone had the idea that the American system was not good enough and that the only thing to do was to withdraw from it and live the communal life. Every such attempt failed. Only the Hutterian experiment stubbornly persists. Well, gentlemen, that's the story and I must be going. You've been very kind to me and I hope I've not been unkind to you."

The pastor leaned into the open window. "Just a moment, Joshua Volkner."

"Well, Pastor Kunz!" Joshua greeted him. "Have they crowded you out of this meeting? Come around to the door."

"I have nothing to say," remarked the pastor in a tired voice. "Nothing at all. I only want to reach across from my world to yours and put this book into your hands."

Joshua came over and took it without comment.

"A hymnal of the Hutterian Brethren," the pastor was saying. "Long ago a mother brought it to me with the word that her son was gone. His name is written inside. Though the boy has changed, the hymns have not. And I thank God, Joshua Volkner, that there are still other boys with us who do not change."

The pastor laid his hand on the shoulder of Little Mike. "Our children are our answer to you," the pastor told Joshua. "There is nothing more to say. The weakness of the world is in its low standard of ideals. Our strength is in our people and the high principles which we practice. Go your way and let us go ours. I am sorry only that you must travel by night, but perhaps by now you are used to that."

Joshua opened the book at the name written on the inside cover. Little Mike watched him with wonder. If the pastor had expected that the hymnal would bring the world-

ling back to the commune he was to be disappointed. Joshua
was smiling to himself as he turned the pages. Then he
raised his eyes and said sincerely, "Thank you very much,
Pastor Kunz." He pressed the book in both hands. "Well,
I will do what I can in the matter of the Jordan Ranch. But
I wish one of you could be there to answer all the questions
which the men of the world will be asking me. Come along
to Chicago, Pastor Kunz. Maybe you can convince my associates both about your people and your principles."

" 'If they hear not Moses and the prophets,' " the pastor
quoted, " 'neither will they be persuaded, though one rose
from the dead.' "

"That they wouldn't understand," Joshua replied seriously. "But come along."

Pastor Kunz shook his head. "I have only one journey
to take and where I am going I will not need to answer
questions put to me by men of the world. There everyone will be on my side. Good-by, Joshua Volkner, and
God go with you!"

He extended his hand to the worldling. Joshua clasped
it warmly. "Good-by, Pastor Kunz."

Little Mike turned from the window. There was no
sound in the room or in the commune; no singing, no
voices. The picture he carried in his mind grew: Joshua
Volkner with the hymnal, Michael father with a look on
his face that was solemn thought and no feeling of victory
at all, the elders with expressions that no one could ever
read. The silence was what he remembered and felt, as
if God wanted things to be very quiet so that He might
think. Little Mike walked away, feeling almost as if he
were Michael father walking, only that there was nothing

sure or confident about his steps, and he had no thought of telling anyone what to do.

The car horn sounded. At the schoolhouse the car lights flashed on. Robert Volkner ran past him and went to the teacherage window. "Come on, Dad!" he called. "Sis is at the car. We're all ready."

The singers who had been at the David Wiese home came out. Men and women left their houses, drawn by the headlights which Elaine was switching on and off. The boys came running from many directions. Elders and bosses, Michael father and the men accompanied Joshua through the yard.

Little Mike stood in the crowd near the car. Robert caught sight of him. "So long, Mike!" he said. "I'll be seeing you."

"Good-by, Robert Volkner!"

"I had a swell time. Wish you were coming along. Don't forget, come if you can."

"Good-by, Joshua Volkner, good-by!" said the people.

Sarah mother stood with her hands wrapped in her apron. Joshua, shaking hands with almost everyone, came to her and said, "*Auf Wiedersehen,* Sarah Neumann."

They did not shake hands, but only to her did he say that; to all the others he said, "Good-by." Even to his mother, when he held her in his arms, he said, "Good-by," but he whispered something to her which no one heard. The pastor did not come to the car, but Selma Kunz stood near Martha Volkner supporting herself on her cane.

"Drive carefully," cautioned Selma. "The road is crooked until you get to the highway, so the Town Man says."

"Yes," said the Town Man, "but after that it is wide and straight."

"Good-by, Joshua Volkner, good-by!"

Joshua sat in the front seat and Elaine sat next to him. Robert delighted the boys by curling up in the back seat and pretending he was already asleep.

"Look out, everybody!" warned the Householder. "Watch there, children, get out of the way!"

The motor started. The sound was accompanied by a cry of delight from the children as they scampered out of the way.

"He's going to back up," said the Town Man. "No he's going right around the school."

"Good-by, Joshua Volkner!"

Michael said, "That car needs almost as much room as the colony truck. Say, Sarah, look at Mary there!"

"Mary, come back here!" Sarah called and went to bring the child back from where she had gone to follow the car.

Andrew Mueller had already run ahead, followed by a long line of children intent on seeing the gate open. Little Mike stood watching. In the white light of the car Andrew Mueller was a black form that sprang out of nowhere, flung open the gate and then disappeared. The car went through. The red lights moved quickly into the outer road. The sound of the horn sent a sensation of longing and loneliness into Little Mike's soul. Moment by moment the sound of the motor faded. The bright light loomed a few times far away and soon it was gone.

The gateman came back to the group. "Well," he said, "I wrapped the chain around it good. I guess that will be the last traveler to go out of here tonight."

CHAPTER 13

*T*HAT night Little Mike slept in Rachel's bed. Ruth and Anna occupied the big bed on the other side of the room, and Mary was sleeping on the bench near the window.

He lay in the dark and it seemed that he could still hear the sound of Volkner's automobile although it was hours ago that the gate had opened and closed. By now the colony bread and the colony honey and the colony meat were far out into the world. By this time Robert was sleeping on the soft cushion and moving swiftly through the dark in the path made by the car lights. Little Mike's thoughts would not let him sleep. He could hear the regular breathing of his sisters and suddenly he was startled by the sound of his mother's voice in the parents' bedroom.

"Michael," she said, and Little Mike could not help overhearing his father reply.

"Aren't you asleep yet?" he asked.

"I was just thinking, Michael, that the Householder could surely have asked the Volkners to stay until morning."

"He did ask them, but Joshua wanted to get back for a meeting with his grain-company men. And that is an important meeting for us, too."

There was silence. Then Sarah mother asked, "Is Joshua Volkner going to arrange things so that we may buy the Jordan Ranch?"

"He said he would do what he could. That was the last thing he told Pastor Jacob. You know, the pastor is a wise one. He did more to bring Joshua around in two minutes than we did all evening."

Sarah did not reply. Little Mike recalled the moments at the teacherage. He remembered again the pastor's hand upon him and he knew it was that touch more than anything that kept him from hiding in the car and leaving the commune forever. Would he ever go? Would he have the courage to do that? How easily he had been brought back from outside the gate! How he had thrilled at the pastor's gentleness at the teacherage window!

His mother's low words arrested him. "I saw a picture of his wife."

"Whose?"

"Joshua's."

Michael father said gruffly, "It would have been better to see the real thing. Why didn't he bring her?"

Sarah mother's voice was gentle. "She's lame."

"Lame?"

"She has been lame since she was little."

"Is that so? Why didn't he tell us that?"

Little Mike could not hear his mother's reply. After a moment she called his father softly by name. "There was something about Joshua's going away that first time long ago that I never told you, Michael. I have had it on my conscience. I know that secrets are not allowed, but this has been a secret for twenty years with me."

"What do you mean?"

There was a long silence.

"You know, Michael, Joshua wanted me to go with him that time. He wanted me to go out into the world with him. We loved each other . . ."

Her words were suddenly excited whispering, then they trailed into silence. Little Mike stared into the dark.

"That has been like a great weight on me," his mother was saying in a quick whispered voice, "because I never told you or anyone. Since he was here it all came back worse than before. I had to tell you and ask you to forgive me for hiding it from you."

"Hiding what from me? Don't you think I knew that?"

"Knew—what?"

"That you loved him . . . and all the rest."

"You knew that?"

"Of course."

"How?"

"How does a man learn such things? I just knew."

The words crept into Little Mike's heart; the uncommonly gentle voice of Michael father and his mother's confession drew him into their circle. Had his mother once stood outside the commune boundary as he had done early that morning? Was it possible that she could understand how he felt? Why then could he not simply go to her and tell her his secret and confide to her all that had happened? And Michael father, why did he always seem to stand far off when he was really not to be feared at all?

"Did others know, Michael? Has anyone ever said they knew?"

"No."

"And you were never angry with me?"

"Why should I be angry?" Michael asked with genuine surprise. "Didn't I marry you because I loved you?"

"Michael."

"Go to sleep, Sarah. It seems to me it must be long after midnight."

Little Mike closed his eyes. Words drifted in to him that told him his mother was telling Michael father how glad she was that she had not run away. She was remembering the blessings of the Hutterian life and she was talking about the children, from Little Sarah who had died to Rachel who had married, and she said it was all the way it should be.

There was a touch about the night that thrilled him, that made him reach under his pillow and take out the empty harmonica box. Ever since the loss of the instrument the box had been hidden in his bench bed. In the morning he would find a safe spot for it. Maybe in the morning he would have the courage to tell his father and mother the whole story. But what if they would say that it was good the instrument was lost and that things were supposed to happen that way? He opened the box and felt inside. He remembered the first time he opened it in this very room and how Joshua Volkner stood near him and said, "It is yours, Little Mike, all yours. It will be our secret." He closed the box softly and pressed it to his lips. Dear God, he prayed, on such a pretty night . . . His eyes were heavy.

On such a pretty night, he wanted to say, tell me where else I can look for it. In thought he traveled every step

from cabinet shop to high bank. Where could it be? He
thought of the wolf cave and the river. He saw Jake raking at the river's bend and Joey crawling under the schoolhouse steps. He was going down the stump root again.
The old stump should be wise enough to know all secrets.
It had stood on the high bank and watched the river flowing in and out of the world long before the first Hutterian came to Old Portage. It had held its place where God
had put it. It knew where it belonged even though its
roots were breaking out of the commune soil. Maybe they
wanted to be free. The stump stayed and never told its
secrets to anyone. Secrets it must have, many of them.
Suddenly Little Mike sat straight up in bed; a thought had
come to him as vividly as if he had heard a voice.

Quickly he got up and put on his pants. He hurried
to the door. In the front room he carefully moved a chair
to the high shelf and took some matches from the box. Then
he hastened out into the yard.

The commune lay lifeless and still. There was not a
sigh or sound of the wind, but the clouds swung in a
gray and white procession across the sky, like garments
being pulled along on the moving wash line by the Laundry Boss. The pale stars rode on them laughingly, reck-
lessly playing a new game while the pastor slept. Everything slept. Whatever hour it was, it was the hour for the
world to sleep.

He ran through the cold night air with the dream
thoughts spurring him on across the long way. Frantically
he made his way to the edge where the stump sent down
its dead roots to the river. He found a small stone near
the stump and struck a match. What a frightening light

it made! The grass around it was alive. The match made the dew sparkle. There were no golden chains so beautiful as these. Kneeling on his bare knees, he folded back the grass from around the stump. As the match flickered he dug his hands into the earth. It seemed to him that the river was trying to speak.

Once more he guarded a match in his hands and bent down. Close to the stump he held it. The tiny shadows danced and laughed up at him. "Come, Little Mike! Here under the stump look hard—down in the small hole where the stump is rotting." A single, small glint of something bright and shining returned the flicker of the match. As his fingers touched the instrument, the match dropped from his hand. Passionately he pressed the harmonica against his closed lips while his body shook with joy. He flung himself to the grass, pressing his possession so hard against his cheek that he closed his eyes in pain. Then he laughed softly and looked up. Above him the stars rode on and below him the river was singing.

Long moments later when he walked back to the house, a memory verse ran through his mind: "It is the glory of God to conceal a thing, but the honor of kings is to search out a matter." He was a king. He was David with his lovely harp and his bedroom was his royal chamber.

He crawled into bed without undressing. Apparently no one had heard him come or go. With a prayer of thankfulness he clasped the harmonica in his hand under the pillow and closed his eyes. He had no thought of sleep, for he was already thinking of the morning and of the story he would have to tell the boys. "Here is how it was, Jake, here is just how it happened." Jake would know what to do. Jake would probably say, "Since you found it, it's a sign that you should keep it now forever."

With this thought he fell asleep and at the sound of the commune bell he awoke with it still in his mind. After putting the harmonica into his pocket and the box under the feather mattress, he hurried outside intent on seeing Jake. But Jake was not in the yard at washingtime. Jake was not at breakfast. Anxiously Little Mike looked along the benches at the boys' long table.

"Where is your brother Jake?" he asked John Linder.

"He's sick."

"With his neck?"

"I don't know what it is."

"Is he bad?"

"Who knows that?"

A thought of guilt came over him, a feeling that God was still bent on punishment. Jake was sick. There must be a reason. There must be a fault somewhere, somebody's fault. Heaven would not let the beauty of the past night stand by itself; for every joyful experience there was always a time of payment.

Little Mike was one of the first out of the refectory and he started at once to the Jacob Linder home.

Matt Neumann caught up with him. "Are you going to hunt for the harmonica some more?"

Joey Kunz rushed to his side. "Mike, have you thought of any more places to look?"

He started to speak. Thrilled as he was, impatient to tell everyone about finding the instrument again, he could not bring himself to impart the news to anyone until he had confided it to Jake.

Across the yard came the voice of Michael father: "Hey, Mike, come along!"

Michael walked briskly from the refectory to the cabinet shop, and his order towed Little Mike along against his will. "We have to make up for the time the worldlings took from us," Michael told him. "The Bee Boss must get his new hives by lunchtime. When the day warms up a little he starts putting some bees into their new homes. So it's work for us colony carpenters and no excuses."

"But Jake Linder is——"

"Sick. So I hear. All the more reason he should be left alone."

Never had there been more work and never a longer morning. At every available moment he tried to watch the Linder home and interpret the commune activities in terms of Jake. Once he saw Jake's father hurry into the house. At noon he watched one of Jake's sisters take some soup from the commune kitchen. Little Mike determined to go over immediately after the dinner hour.

For once the men were through eating before the children and when he got outside the Farm Boss was talking about trying out the new combine that afternoon. Little Mike's questions about Jake were never answered. He started for the Linder home. Just then the farm truck roared through the yard, heading for the commune road. The Town Man jumped to the ground and opened the gate. The truck driver drove through while the other stayed behind and closed the gate.

Pastor Kunz came to the Householder quickly. "What's going on?" the pastor demanded.

"The truck is going in for the doctor. It's Jake Linder."

"Is he so sick that we must go for the doctor first thing?"

"Yes, Jake is that sick. I gave the truck man permission."

"Yesterday he was all right. I saw him with Joshua Volkner's son and with Little Mike Neumann."

"I know, but Daniel J. and Joanna had me in to see how sick he is."

"We have come to depend on doctors too much," complained the pastor, but he started for the Linder home to see for himself whether a man was justified in driving to town before he had been consulted in the matter.

Little Mike ran to catch up with him. "Is Jake going to be all right, Pastor Kunz?"

The old man shooed him away. "If there is anything you should know, you will learn about it in plenty of time."

Pastor Kunz entered the Linder home without rapping.

Little Mike stood in the yard helplessly as Joey Kunz and Dan Mueller ran up.

Dan said, "He must be dying-sick if they go for the doctor."

"Maybe it's only his neck that's sick," Joey added. "Maybe the rest of him is all right."

"Look," Mike told them: "there goes Jake's father to the kitchen for something and he's even running."

The voice of Michael Neumann called, "Come, Mike, the work is not done over here."

Hopelessly Little Mike turned to the cabinet shop. His father was bringing out the new hives and setting them on the ground for the inspection of the Bee Boss.

"Yes, hurry up," said Rudolph Kunz. "I need some help."

Little Mike came to his side reluctantly.

"You did a good job, Carpenter," Rudolph was saying. "And now if your son helps me——"

"That will show how the co-operative life works," Michael concluded. "Yes, Mike, you help the Bee Boss as long as he needs you."

"How is Jake going to be, Michael father?"

"Am I a doctor? All I know is that his father told me that Little Jake told him that he fell into the river on Saturday morning. So I suppose he's got a bad cold out of it."

"Oh, well," said Rudolph, "children get sick quick and they get well quick, too."

He picked up two beehives and instructed Little Mike to carry one and follow him. Then he strode forward in the direction of the apiary.

Little Mike walked resentfully, unable to forget his father's words. Jake had not fallen into the river. He got wet and cold when he waded in and rescued Mike two days ago. Jake did not tell his parents that; it all went back to the search for the harmonica. It was all caused by his personal possession, and when he admitted this to himself a shadow fell over the glory of finding it. How was it that a person never had happy moments for long? Why was every good experience followed by something bad? Was God the elders' God, righteous and just and never gentle and kind for long? How he wished he could always think of Him as he had last night when the dream came and told him where to find the instrument! It was a good God who

did that. It was an understanding God who let him take
the matches without waking his parents, who walked with
him to the high bank and knelt with him in the grass
whispering to him. God changed according to Little
Mike's feelings. His God made the stars ride in the clouds
and let the world sleep peaceful and calm; the elders' God
brought sickness to Jake. But there could not be two Gods.
There could be only one, and the touch of the harmonica
in his pocket made him fear more than ever that the One
was more interested in judgment than in joy.

The apiary looked somber and foreboding. It stood
within a fenced-in place at the orchard's edge. Long,
weathered boards enclosed the nearly two hundred white-
painted hives. The hives were in six rows and the lanes
between them led to the one-story, flat-roofed honey house
made of rough unpainted lumber. From the door of the
honey house a wire cable was stretched straight down the
center lane some six feet from the ground. From this
cable a carrier platform was suspended on two small
wheels. Rudolph's invention provided an easy way to
push the cargo out of each hive into the honey house.

As they neared the gate, the Bee Boss noticed that the
wire was loose, due to a sagging pole. He set the hives
down and marched off, straight through the lane without
so much as glancing at the bees flying around.

Little Mike closed the fence gate slowly. The beeyard
always reminded him of the colony cemetery; the rows
of hives might have beeen the unnamed headstones set over
the graves of the Hutterians. He remembered how one
of Rudolph's helpers once left the apiary gate open and a
mare strayed in. She knocked down several hives and the

angry bees covered her body with stings so that she almost died. All that saved her was the quick work of Rudolph Kunz, who forced open the horse's mouth, pulled out the tongue as far as he could and stuffed handfuls of salt down the animal's throat. Ever after the apiary was the symbol of righteous wrath.

Rudolph Kunz came back through the lane with a sledge hammer, a long stake and a roll of tangled wire. "Neglect a thing yesterday and you have two things to fix today," he observed. "I'll drive in an anchor that will straighten up this lazy post and it will stay tight as long as I'm Bee Boss around here."

He ordered Little Mike to hold the stake at exactly the angle he wanted.

Little Mike put his hands on the stake and braced himself. Rudolph swung the sledge in a great arc. Down came the iron hammer with a jarring thud.

"Hold it steady," Rudolph warned.

With unerring strokes he put the full force of his body into the swing of the sledge. The crack of the iron against the wood and the hollow sound of the earth giving way beneath the ground were reflections of Hutterian mastery.

"You can sit down and hold it now," he finally said, "though it's just about set."

Mike sat down. He held the stake in the space made by the spread of his legs. Rudolph spat on his hands. Once more the sledge came around. Mike glanced up at the stern, red-bearded face. Rudolph's eyes were large with a sense of power. His thickset lips were puckered as if holding back a cry at every swinging stroke. Little Mike thought he saw God standing in Rudolph's place. The hammer cracked against the stake. The ground trembled. Rudolph threw the hammer back for another stroke. Just as the sledge came around, Little Mike let go of the stake and jerked back in fright. Rudolph was thrown off balance by the unexpected movement. He tried to hold back the blow, but it struck the edge of the stake and glanced off into the ground at Little Mike's side.

"Dumbhead!" Rudolph cried. "Do you want your legs knocked off? Get up!"

Mike jumped up. "I'm sorry, Bee Boss."

"Sorry is a poor excuse for trying to get killed. Go home. You boys are all alike."

He drove the stake to the desired depth. Then he wrapped the wire around the carrier post, pulled it tight and fastened it to the stake.

"I was thinking about Jake Linder," Little Mike confessed. "Does a person ever get sick on account of God being mad?"

"You have to ask big questions, don't you? Little questions won't do. The smaller the boy, the bigger the talk. When you talk to me, ask me about bees."

Little Mike watched him as he rolled his sleeves high up on his arms and turned an old beehive upside down. Then Rudolph boldly ripped off the boards and exposed the busy swarm inside.

"I told you to go home," Rudolph told him.

"I'll help," Mike promised. "And if a bee gets on me, I'll remember how you said it won't do anything if a person doesn't strike it."

"That's such a first lesson it doesn't have to be taught in this school," the Bee Boss grunted.

Rudolph noted that a few bees had settled on his arm.

"There, you see," he said. "They are harmless. But now, look." He caught hold of a bee and held it for a moment between his fingers. "It's mad now because I made it mad and that's its nature." He lowered it to his bare arm.

"It'll sting you," Mike warned.

"Why not? It's got a right to."

The bee buried its stinger into his arm. Rudolph brushed the bee off. "It will die," he said fatefully. "But look. See how the stinger stays in the flesh and how it pumps up and down releasing its poison?"

"Doesn't it hurt!"

"A man shouldn't complain when he is punished for his own sin." So saying, he scraped the stinger off with his fingernail, reached into the hive, put a touch of honey on the wound and continued his work. So God, thought Little Mike, had the right to punish him.

Rudolph placed the new hive on top of the old one. Then he lighted a smoke box and gently blew some smoke into the lower hive.

"They'll go up," he predicted. "Queen and all."

He waited a moment, then calmly raised the new hive so he could look inside. "Yes, they are going nicely. If you want to do something, Mike, you can pound your hands on the old hive while I start on another one. The pounding will make the swarm hurry into its new house."

He demonstrated how he wanted it done by beating a loud and rhythmic tattoo on the box. Satisfied that things were going according to the rules, he walked far down the lane, almost to the honey house, to provide another bee colony with a new home.

Little Mike knelt on the ground and pounded the sides

of the hive with both hands. The bees flying around and the need for practically hugging the hive were not pleasant experiences. When a bee touched his cheek, the frightened feeling returned: Jake's sickness was his fault, the glory of the past night was only a shadow. God was very likely the elders' God. Rudolph had nothing to fear. He had no sins and no secrets. He had no personal possession that he was hiding. That is why Rudolph could kneel with his beard against the crawling bees and beat the hive as unconcerned as if it were a drum. Little Mike closed his eyes. In a moment he jerked back his head in fright. A bee was crawling on his neck. The clinging sensation shocked him into the remembrance of Jake and the growth on his neck.

"Bee Boss!" His whisper was choked from fear. "Bee Boss!"

He drew away from the hive. Bees were settling on his arms and gathering on the thin folds of his shirt. He rose tremblingly to his feet. "Bee Boss!"

Rudolph Kunz looked up. "Don't strike!" he shouted. "Don't do anything! Just stand still!"

Rudolph repeated these words as he hurried through the lane. Little Mike stood with his body tense. The sound of wings and the horror of being covered face and body made him cower helplessly. The heavy scent of wax and honey which the bees exuded was sickening. He cringed under the sudden fearful stinging in his arms and chest.

Rudolph Kunz reached out and took him by the hand.

"Come along," he ordered. "Keep your wits. The smoke box broke. Come with me."

Blindly Little Mike obeyed. The bees clinging to him, the stinging agony were conquered for the moment by the touch of Rudolph's hand and the sense of the beeman's presence. A thought leaped into his mind: Nothing bad happens unless a person deserves it. The elders' God rose up to accuse him. What did he deserve? No boy could hope to appease that righteous Monarch no matter how hard he tried; nothing could satisfy Him except justice according to the colony rules. God always won. God always had His way. God, like the fathers, was always right.

A bee crawled over his mouth. He moved his tongue. A needle pierced his lips. With a terrorized cry, he wrenched his hand from the grip of the Bee Boss, turned and started to run. Behind him came the angry shout: "Stop, you dumbhead!"

Frantically Little Mike beat his body with his hands.

"Don't run! Don't run!" Rudolph screamed.

The warning only drove him on as a searing fire swept through his body. He cried out desperately. His bare feet stumbled as he neared the apiary gate. He lurched forward. Something sharp struck his leg. Dimly he caught sight of a silvery object. The harmonica had fallen from his pocket. He pounced on it and put it back as the swarming roar and the burning pain convulsed him. The light faded around him as he buried his face in the grass.

CHAPTER 14

*W*HEN he opened his eyes he saw nothing. Only darkness. He was lying on hard boards.

"Mike?"

"Where am I?"

"In the honey house."

"I can't see anything."

"Well, you aren't a cat, are you?" But Rudolph could not hide the fear he felt. "Can't you see me?"

"I can see that you are near me."

"Well, it's dark in here. How else do you think we got rid of the bees? Your eyes will probably be swollen. Can you get up? Let's go out and see how bad you are hurt."

Rudolph reached down and helped him to his feet.

Little Mike clutched his pants pocket. The harmonica was safe. He had kept it all this time. It had stayed securely in his possession. Surely God wanted him to have it and when he thought of that he laughed happily.

"Quiet!" said Rudolph, putting a heavy hand on Mike's shoulder. "Go into fits and we will have something to explain to the colony."

"No fits, Bee Boss," Mike assured him. "I just feel good."

"I guess so. I fan my arms off thinking you will not come to; now you feel good."

They went outside and Little Mike closed his eyes against the bright light. Rudolph's arm went around him gently. Then the man put a hand on each shoulder and shook him in amazement. "Mike! Look at me! Open your eyes!"

"My eyes are all right," Little Mike told him and looked at him.

"Yes, yes, I see!" Rudolph's expression was fixed and anxious. "Let's look at your arms. Let's look at your body where the shirt was open. Take off your shirt. Where are the welts? These little red blotches are nothing. You were stung worse than that. By rights you should be in bad shape. But you aren't. You aren't in bad shape, are you?"

Little Mike looked at his arms and felt of his face. He was not thinking of pain. He was thinking that God had tested him and he had passed the ordeal. Something told him that the punishment of the bees had purged him of all the wrong he had done. But Rudolph accosted him incredulously. "I picked stingers out of you. I rubbed honey on you. But this is beyond anything I have seen in my years in this business. Look, here is where some stung me! You can see for yourself. But you! There is something in you that will make a wonderful beeman!"

"I'm not afraid to walk right through between the hives down the long lane," Mike boasted.

Rudolph appraised him a moment. "That's just what we're going to do," he decided, starting off. "Come on, walk with me!"

Little Mike hurried along at Rudolph's side. The bees, the humming sounds, the long rows of hives did not deter him. He saw the place where Rudolph and he had worked on transferring the swarms. He was no longer afraid. The Bee Boss was satisfied that a lesson in courage had been learned and he refused to hide his wonder at Mike's immunity. "It beats everything," he said over and over. "Did you faint from fear of the bees or did you stumble and hit your head?"

"I don't know. Was I fainted long?"

"About as long as a colony song."

"That is a long time, Bee Boss," Mike told him. "Especially if it is 'The Great Song.'"

Rudolph led him to the gate.

"Do you want me to help you now, Bee Boss?" Mike asked.

"No. I want you to go over there in the shade and rest until you are all right."

"I'm all right."

"We've got one boy in bed and that's enough for today."

"If you don't want me to help, I'm going to see how Jake is. Please let me go, Bee Boss!"

Rudolph pondered a moment. "Well, go then," he decided. Then he added, "Maybe it would be just as good not to say anything about the bees stinging you. I will explain that to whoever wants to know. I will explain about the smoker, too. It was a secondhand one anyhow, but if it had been working I could have saved you easy. Well, something saved you, so be thankful."

The heavens were smiling and carrying Little Mike along the path back to the commune yard. Joyfully he pressed the harmonica to his lips.

When he reached the yard he saw Pastor Kunz walk

slowly from the Linder home. Little Mike broke into a
run and reached the old man. Before he could speak, the
pastor raised a warning finger. "Beware, Mike Neumann,
beware! All you young boys better be good. I will have
no foolishness."

"How is Jake?" Little Mike faltered.

"Very sick." The pastor's tone left no doubt that God's
hand was somewhere in the happening. "And it is no
wonder. No wonder at all."

So saying, Pastor Kunz moved on. Jake must have confessed, Little Mike told himself as he stood uncertainly in
the yard. Jake must have explained to the pastor why
he was in the river. Under the stern questioning of the
Boss of Bosses he very likely told everything that had
happened. That meant he had been forced to tell about
the harmonica, too. The Linder home was suddenly a
place of judgment, and he opened the door hopelessly.

"Mike!" Jake's mother greeted him eagerly. "Jake
asked for you while Pastor Kunz was here. He called your
name over and over. That is all the pastor could get out
of him."

Little Mike moved to the parents' bed where Jake lay
with closed eyes. His flushed face caused Little Mike to
look at Joanna Linder with concern. She moistened Jake's
forehead and pulled up the blanket to cover the growth on
his neck. "Jake, Mike is here."

Jake made no move. Fearfully Mike put his hand on the
thin blanket that covered the sick boy's body. Beneath his
hand he felt the rapid beating of Jake's heart.

"Open your eyes!" pleaded the mother. "See, Mike is
here!"

Jake tried to wet his lips.

"All right, don't try then, dear Jake," whispered his mother. "The doctor will be here soon."

Two colony women appeared in the doorway, and Jake's mother went to them quickly so they would not disturb the sick one. "Don't you remember," she whispered, "he had a spell like this once—was it four years ago? Come outside. Maybe if we leave him and Mike alone—— Children, don't stand at the door. Pastor Kunz said everybody should stay away. Let Jake be quiet."

She ushered the women out and closed the door.

Mike leaned over his friend. "Listen to me, Jake, and I will tell you a great thing. I found the instrument. Think of that! Last night, real late, I thought about all of the places we had looked and something told me there was one more place where it could be. So I went back to the old stump. There it was! And, Jake, today God set the bees on me because He was angry about the personal possession. His madness was in the bees. But He kept the harmonica hidden in my hand and the Bee Boss never even saw it. You hear, Jake, even when I fainted he didn't see it, and when I woke up and stood up again he never noticed it. So God took back the punishment and He never even let me swell up. He just passed His hand over the sore spots and there were no welts."

Little Mike felt the beat of Jake's heart. Only the weak, hasty throbbing under his hand kept Jake alive. There was no movement. Only the quivering heart. Instantly and without warning God could take Jake away by simply bending down and saying, "All right, Jake, that is all." That would be the end as surely as when the pastor

spoke a word to the children, as surely as when the Farm
Boss said, "Drop everything and come to the field. Come,
it is time." He drew his hand away in fear. Jake moved his
lips.

"Mike . . . "

"Yes?"

"Do you have it?"

"Yes, Jake. Right here in my pocket. See, here in my
hand."

The frail body moved beneath the blanket. The black
eyes opened and looked up with an unseeing expression.
"Play me the song, Mike."

Mike lifted the harmonica to his lips:

> "Come, brothers, and let us sing of the true faith.
> Let us tell you of our history . . ."

He closed his eyes while he played and it seemed to him
that he was hiding in a secret place with only the music. He
thought of Jake lying on the sheep hill saying, "I could
stay here and listen to that for the rest of my life." He
let his father enter the holy circle of his thoughts, and he
let Sarah mother come in, too. The instrument was no
longer one small harmonica; it was a whole commune full.
The secret place in which the favored ones hid filled to
overflowing with the song. But then it seemed as if the
golden curtain around him was being pulled aside. Voices
were heard and the sound of people running and the noise
of the colony truck.

"Don't stop!" Jake whispered.

Little Mike played on, but as he did so he realized that

people had entered the room and were standing about curiously: Sarah mother holding Leah to her breast, the Householder and the Farm Boss, Elder Wiese and Blacksmith Linder, Martha Volkner, with Mike's sister Anna. But then he saw Jake partially raised up in bed and Jake's mother standing over him hopefully.

"Come, come, let the doctor in!" ordered Pastor Kunz from the doorway. "Is this sickness or a picnic? Out, please, all of you!"

"Jake," exclaimed the father, "you look better! When I went for you, Doctor, he looked like a dead one."

"Well, good enough," said the doctor. "But he's not well yet, so let's have everybody out of the room."

Jake reached out a hand, but the pastor pushed Little Mike out of the room with the others. In the commune yard everyone looked at him strangely, and Michael father came walking toward him swinging his arms.

"What's going on?" Michael Neumann asked while he was still some distance away. "I hear my son is a music maker all of a sudden."

The people gathered more closely, but a sound on the meadow road arrested them. The noise of a tractor and the clatter of machinery called forth an exclamation from the Householder. "Listen! There's some better music! There goes the combine for its first assignment."

Everyone's attention was directed to the two machines heading for the wheat field. With cries of delight the children sprang forward.

"Who said you should go?" shouted one of the men.

The children paid no heed. They were already being joined by others from all points of the commune. Joey

Kunz appeared out of nowhere leading a group of boys
screaming with delight toward the miracle. Everyone was
hurrying across the yard talking excitedly.

"The roar of the world is calling," lamented Elder
Linder.

"Farm progress is all right," contended the Householder.

"The tractor and the combine do look like monsters,"
said Michael Neumann, but he, too, moved with the people
toward the field. The kitchen crew and the laundry
workers and the women with children in their arms left
their duties. Even Elder Linder went with the crowd,
drawn against his will. Only Little Mike stayed near the
house.

Finally when the pastor came out, Mike pleaded, "How
is he?"

"You stay out of there," came the command, "and don't
bother him again. This is going to take prayer as well as
medicine and more praying than music making. I will see
you later, Mike Neumann."

The pastor could not resist the sight of the colony members converging on the wheat field. He started off quickly
as if he feared he would arrive too late. Little Mike
followed him from afar. Pastor Kunz had made clear what
would happen. He would summon Mike and demand the
meaning of the personal possession. Private ownership.
Forbidden music. Secrets in the commune. Familiarity
with the world. All of this had brought the sickness on
Jake. These thoughts were specters walking with him as
he joined the people in the wheat field and rushing over
him in the sound of the tractor motor and the noise of the
machines.

Householder Caleb Wiese stood with Pastor Kunz at the edge of the field and the people clustered around them. Michael father and a group of men stood in a separate group a short distance away. Everyone seemed anxious to have a part in the harvest scene. But only one man was actually needed: the Farm Boss did all the work. He drove the tractor which pulled the combine, and he operated all of the levers. The combine reached out its long sickle, and the cylinder devoured the grain. The blade lifted itself where the wheat was tall and lowered itself where the wheat was short; wherever it went it left behind a stripped and barren stand of trembling stubble.

"Look at it!" was the oft-repeated exclamation from the spectators, and the pastor shook his head in an expression of unbelief and wonder.

"What is a man to say?" he asked.

"It's plain that it saves time," Michael Neumann observed.

"That I can see," nodded Pastor Kunz, "but what are we going to do with all the time we save?"

Michael father had no answer to this, and no one seemed to care. For once there was something more important than the pastor's words. The Farm Boss had turned the tractor down the outside edge of the field and was heading back to the group. Soon he would complete the first trip around and be back at his starting point. David Wiese had the honor of driving up with the black team. He stood up in the grain wagon holding tight rein as the horses shied at the noise. The Farm Boss stopped the tractor, raised himself up from the seat and beckoned to David. The team felt the snap of the reins across their backs. Proudly Rachel's husband drove out into the field.

"There's one wagonload already harvested," announced the Householder.

The wagon rattled over the uneven ground.

"No more work of binding or shocking or threshing," explained the Town Man to all who would listen. "That machine does away with all that in one operation."

The crowd moved forward. Everyone wanted to see the automatic spout as it raised its long neck and hovered over the wagon. Out came the golden grain as neatly as if the miller were pouring it out of a sack. A cheer went up. Rachel watched admiringly as David took the shovel and leveled the wheat out in the wagon box.

"Yes, yes, Pastor," Martha Volkner observed, "that's how it is done in the Canadian colonies. Only there the combines are even bigger and they are self-propelled."

"This is big enough for us," the pastor admonished. "When I was a boy there was work to do at harvesttime. Now everything is only watching and pleasure. In those days we followed the men with the sickles. Twelve abreast went through the fields. The women and children were the gleaners. That was Bible-fashion."

"But slow work, Pastor Kunz," said Rebecca Mueller.

"And this is fast work," the old man replied, annoyed. "What does that mean? More time for people to fall into temptation. Tying bundles by hand is a thing of the past. Shocking grain is suddenly out of date. If we are not careful, work will soon be out of style and then we might as well take down the fences."

"The world, the world," murmured Elder Linder.

No one was listening. David Wiese came in with the first wagonload of grain, the tractor roared, and the combine began methodically snipping off the wheat. The Householder figured that two acres could be harvested in the few hours before nightfall.

"All right," said the pastor, clapping his hands for attention and trying to make himself heard, "we have seen enough. Everybody back to his work! Let's make the time count."

"Once more around!" pleaded young and old. "Let's see one more load come out of the field!"

Another team was being driven up ready for the signal from the farm boss. No one made a move to go until the wagon box had been filled. Then at the insistence of the pastor and the elders the spectators turned their backs on the wheat field.

But Michael Neumann did not return with the rest. Little Mike, who stood just inside the swath of stubble which had been cut by the combine, saw his father approach and pause near him at the edge of the field. The meeting which the combine had postponed was inevitable. Joey and Dan and Paul and the other boys still played in the field, but Little Mike stood motionless under his father's piercing gaze. The wheat spears were sharp under his bare feet, but resentment and quick planning were sharper in his heart. In desperation his hand sought the harmonica in his pocket. His fingers covered it. If his father tried to take it, he would run away. He would run as fast as he could and never return.

"Come, Mike, we'll go to the cabinet shop."

His father and he stood alone. The others were so many friendless shadows spreading over the commune. Behind them the metallic, rhythmic sound of the machines mourned their dirge over the death of the grain.

"I said, come along," Michael repeated.

The hum of the tractor was to Little Mike the call of Volkner's car. It throbbed in his mind. Why had he ever let it go away without him? But then he would never have found the harmonica. He would not have experienced the wonders of the past night. When he remembered how he heard his parents speaking at the midnight hour, he looked at his father with a new hope.

"I'll come," he said.

"You'll come?" Michael exclaimed. "Whatever made you think you wouldn't? We have something to talk about and we have work to do. Just hope and pray that we don't have to build a coffin for Jake Linder."

At the heartless severity of these words, Little Mike felt tears rush to his eyes. But Michael turned abruptly and started to the commune. "Come along!" he commanded.

The invisible bond that tied him to his father drew Little Mike out of the stubble and led him along the meadow road. It kept him always a short distance behind but always in his path. Shoemaker Graebel met them but did not speak. The Hog Boss and a helper glanced at them. They passed a group of boys with Joey among them but they said nothing. Their glances asked Little Mike what he was planning to do when the blow fell. "Why didn't you tell us that you found the harmonica, Mike? Then we would have stood by you." A group of women scrubbing the narrow porch of the separator house stared at him accusingly. Everyone was against him.

Suddenly Michael Neumann stopped in his tracks. Little Mike stopped, too, and followed his glance. Near the door of the cabinet shop the father of Jake Linder was waiting. At his side was the doctor. Michael quickened his steps so that Little Mike had to run to keep up with him. He ran past him, up to where the doctor stood. Terrified, he cried out, "How is Jake? What has happened?"

"Where's that harmonica?" asked the doctor.

He could not answer but his hand went to his pocket.

"Come with me then," urged the doctor and held out his hand.

"Why?" asked Michael Neumann. "What's the idea?"

"Little Jake tosses and turns and asks for Mike and the music," Jacob Linder explained. "So the doctor said he'd get him."

"You mean the music might help?" Michael prodded.

"There's a good chance that it might," the doctor told him. "So, come, my boy."

Michael Neumann nodded, but his face was puzzled and he said uncertainly, "Well, go with the doctor, then."

Little Mike had never known such a moment. Jake was calling for him. The harmonica was being asked for and Michael father had given his permission.

"We'll go in quietly and you play a soft little tune," the doctor said as they neared the house. "Play what you think Jake would like best to hear."

They went in. Slowly Little Mike moved to the bed where Jake lay tossing and crying to himself.

"Let no one else come in," the doctor instructed Jake's mother.

No one, not even Jacob Linder, was to be admitted. The only person the doctor wanted was the "Harmonica Boss" and now he nodded to him. "Go ahead."

In a moment Little Mike was softly playing the "Morning Song." He finished a stanza and played it again. The doctor whispered to him to continue. But after a few moments the playing stopped. He had opened his eyes and caught a glimpse of Jake. In the darkening room he saw his friend lying so white and breathing so heavily that he was afraid. Jake had stopped swinging his arms and he was no longer mumbling; he might have been dying for the way he looked.

"Do you know any other songs?" the doctor asked. "This is doing our patient more good than medicine."

Outside the supper bell rang with a new feeling, as if in deference to the sick one. An infinite silence was shed over the room as the player put the harmonica to his lips. Jake's mother anxiously stood by with hands wrapped in her apron. The doctor urged Mike on. Inspired by this confidence the instrument began a new song and soon the room was softly pulsing with the hymn tune that Little Mike had longed to play when he heard it at David and Rachel's window. With tender care he played:

> I trust in God for everything,
> For everything, let come what will——

As he felt his way into the melody he became another aid in the recovery of his friend. He relived again their afternoon on the sheep hill, the moments on the high bank, the appointment of the "Harmonica Boss," his walks with Jake, the sight of Jake on the riverbank. He heard Jake say again, "Why does God always punish with sad things?" He remembered how Jake had said, "If you want to pray, go ahead. I will keep on raking." This music was Mike's prayer and in it he breathed his requests to

God. He offered promises that he would do whatever God wanted him to do if only Jake got well. But could a person bargain with God? Could a person compromise with Him any more than one could with the pastor and the elders? Added to this conflict was the remembrance of Jake lying white and motionless and fighting against death. What if death was heaven's way to work its judgment?

His eyes burned beneath his lids. He wanted to cry out rather than play. Could no one tell him how God could be softened and changed and made to understand? The hundreds of memory verses were no help. The training under James the Teacher had taught him nothing to serve him in this moment. One voice was terrifyingly real to him. He heard again his father's voice in the field of stripped and barren stubble. "Hope and pray that we don't have to build a coffin for Jake Linder."

The doctor was speaking: "All right, my boy. That will do. Our patient is resting. We'll see how things go on from here."

"Thank you, Little Mike, thank you," said Jake's mother. "You go and eat now."

He went outside. The commune yard was deserted and the only sound was the drone of the tractor, hastening to use up the hours before nightfall. He noticed that he was holding the harmonica in his hand. For once he had not put it into his pocket and as he looked at it he realized that it was no longer a secret. Everyone knew about it now. Only a little while, he thought, and the pastor or Michael father would demand to see it. And then what? The commune road was a river flowing out into the world.

He walked to the schoolhouse and stopped where the

path of Volkner's car was written in tire tracks in the
yard. Here it had stood. Here Robert had said good-by.
"So long, Mike, wish you could come to Chicago." The
commune road was a highway with a gate that opened
easily.

How could he leave his dearest friend, leave him to call
for music and find no answer, leave him to die? He was
the one responsible for Jake's sickness. How could he
go? He was the one who had the harmonica, the only
one who could play it. Was this enough to hold him here?
Shadows were covering the commune yard and darkness
was falling beyond the hedges on the outer road.

He drew a deep breath and started toward the gate. The
colony truck was a sudden, arresting noise in the yard.
He swung around and saw the truck drawing up to the
Linder home. Frightened, he watched. Nothing must
happen to Jake now. When the doctor came from the
house and climbed into the cab, he knew there was nothing
to fear. Jake was well enough for the doctor to leave.
Light of heart, Little Mike hurried to the gate. Without
waiting for permission he untied the heavy chain and
threw it free. He pushed the gate open and in a moment
the truck moved through. It stopped and the Town Man
jumped out with a hasty glance at the commune.

"You, Mike—" he beckoned— "the doctor says you
should come along. That's not the rule but he wants to
talk to you about Jake and I'll take it on myself to explain. We'll only be gone a little while."

Had he heard right? A ride beyond the commune
grounds? Hurriedly he pushed the gate shut and threw
the chain around the gatepost. He rushed to the truck and

climbed in between the doctor and Thomas Moessner. This was no make-believe. The motor roared and he was moving through the dusk. Here Volkner's car had gone, flashing its lights and frightening the dark. Here Robert had boasted of lying down to sleep and Little Mike remembered how he had envied Joshua's son when the black car disappeared into the night. Now the Town Man was his "chauffeur."

"Looks as if Jake will get along all right," the doctor was saying. "The harmonica music helped him, but it can also upset him if he begins to be afraid of what the elders might say. So I wouldn't play for him again unless——"

Little Mike only half heard. If he was thinking of Jake at all it was only because he would have so much to tell him when he returned. When would that be? Just now he was setting out on a never-ending journey. The thrill of coming from the hedge-enclosed road into the vast portions that made up the world held him transfixed. He gazed out at the open country. He felt like spreading his arms as Joshua Volkner had done in the meadow and exclaiming, "Freedom!"

It was almost too dark to see the broad expanse of farmland, but he could see enough to know that fields did not end at the commune fence. He could see the outline of private farm buildings and he noticed people moving in the yards, people who could come and go as they wished, people with houses close to the road where they could step out into the world without opening a gate at all. He saw a pheasant rise out of the ditch and fly away frightened. A boy on horseback made believe he wanted to race the truck down the road. He felt the full force of the boy's spirit. He felt the greater power of the truck as it drew away and left the boy whipping the horse with the reins. The immensity of space possessed him as the Town Man drove over the winding graveled road and onto the highway. Now the dark sky looked deeper and wider than ever. There was a fearful bigness about the world, and he could understand why God had so much trouble in keeping His eye on so much country all the time.

Cars sped past them, blinking their lights and occasionally honking their horns.

"What's all the traffic tonight?" Moessner asked.

"Carnival night," said the doctor.

"That so? Doesn't look like a good night either. But of course, if people want pleasure, they'll go no matter what kind of weather."

"Always seems to rain when the carnival comes to town," the doctor answered.

Little Mike marveled at the way Thomas Moessner knew just what to do. Moving lights and cars did not frighten the Car Boss. He was sure of every move and his bearded face was set. The hissing sound of the passing cars and the glare of lights as they swept against the increasing dark made the highway as wild a place as Pastor Kunz had described. This was what the prophet had meant when he spoke about "chariots jostling each other in the streets." This was the "madness of Babylon." This was the land of the Prince of the World. But that is as far as it went. To Little Mike the world was as beautiful as it was frightening, and as he stared at the scene he wondered where one would find sin and evil and the crowds of people who were lost. Where was the Devil who prowled the fenceless fields and pounced upon those who dared set foot outside the commune boundaries? Calmly the doctor smoked.

The farther they went the longer the line of cars became. They poured out of space like wheat out of the combine spout. In the sky the black clouds rolled and fumed, but it was useless for the night to try to conquer the highway; the twinkling lights wove a path that ran through the hollows and climbed the knolls. The cars were all going one way, the way the Town Man was going. Little Mike tried to imagine what Jake would say about this spectacle or what Joey would do if he saw the sight. Everything was motion and light and every moment was an adventure.

They were crossing a low hill when Little Mike suddenly sprang forward with both hands against the windshield. The Town Man did not scold and the doctor only laughed. Far in the distance a huge wheel with lights was turning against the sky.

"Yes," said the doctor, "there it is."

Thomas Moessner made a clicking noise with his tongue.

"Be thankful that Pastor Jacob doesn't see this," he murmured.

"Why?" the doctor wanted to know.

"I saw that carnival last year," Moessner recalled, unable to conceal the touch of excitement in his voice, "but I never saw it at night. Think of what it must cost and think of the time that's going to waste there. And think of all that goes on in a place like that."

"Yes," mused the doctor, "but isn't it fun! What do you think, Mike?"

"It's a Ferris wheel," Mike breathed.

"That's only part of it. Look! Now you can see the merry-go-round and the two lanes of booths like city streets. They've got lots of things this year. It's wonderful! But don't turn in with me, Thomas. I've got to go to the office."

"I turn in?" Moessner cried. "Don't think that I'd stop at this Sodom!"

"Oh, you must stop on your way back," said the doctor mischievously. "As Town Man you should know about these things. Let Mike ride some of those contraptions. And go yourself. It'll do you good."

"Don't give us ideas on how to get into trouble," Thomas warned. "If we went up on that wheel it would break in a thousand pieces."

"Oh, no, it wouldn't! It's inspected and safe."

"That wouldn't make any difference in this case."

"Come now, Thomas, leave such talk for the pastor. You've got too much sense for that."

"I know what would happen," the Town Man retaliated darkly. But he divided his attention between the highway and the lighted grounds.

The line of cars was turning in and the truck was forced to stop. Now Little Mike could see the magnificent sight. It was the pastor's description of paradise come true. The rows of lights were the streets of gold and the music, harsh and bold though it was, proclaimed eternal freedom. The flashes of color and the glitter of moving things were heaven's trappings. At one end of the grounds stood the fabulous wheel. Near it was a large rink on which people were roller-skating. Farther on was the merry-go-round and not far from that a lighted pole with swinging airplanes that dipped and turned. The lanes were thronged with people. Boys dashed through the crowds with balloons on strings and the wind hurled the balloons around crazily. In one roped-off place tiny automobiles driven by children bumped into each other. Little Mike heard the happy shouting and the music, and he was sure that no one, not even Michael father, had ever seen such a sight.

"Turn in now if you want to," the doctor gibed. "I'll get home someway."

"Give me the commune any day," Moessner said with a tragic shake of his head. "What *do* people see in there? What good does it do them? What is there to learn?"

"Go and find out," said the doctor.

The Town Man sat with his arms over the steering wheel, mumbling about the awfulness of what he saw. But he made no move to go. Suddenly the cars behind him honked. He jumped into action.

"What *do* people see in there?" The doctor laughed.

Moessner sighed aloud. "The world, the world—Joshua's world."

Happily Little Mike turned round and knelt on the seat so he could look through the narrow window panel. He imagined that the confusion of music and noise challenged the rising wind. Joshua's world was defying the elder's God. The whirling machines carried the people. The music was for them. The big wheel turned, churning the shadows. He watched it as long as he could, cupping his hands round his eyes. What he would give to have his friends with him! "There's your wheel, Joey, high as the mill. There are the seats, Michael father, working just as you said they would. There's the music, Jake; it's the big harmonica playing."

His hand covered the harmonica in his pocket. He had something in common with the Ferris wheel boss, wherever that man might be. His thoughts ran from the little wheel of sticks and wire that Joey had tried to build to this huge wonder. It was a symbol of the greatness of the world. It was an evidence of the world's power. Who in the commune could make such a wheel? Who could make the lights shine so brightly?

A hand touched his. The doctor motioned him to silence and pressed a coin into his hand. Little Mike stared at it and started to give it back. "Carnival money," the doctor whispered and pushed the boy's hand away. Fearfully Little Mike clasped the coin. The truck had entered the town and Moessner drew up to the curb in front of a small office. When the doctor opened the truck door the music and gaiety of the carnival were loud. "Your harmonica is better than the calliope, Mike," he commented. "Good night, Thomas."

"Good night, Doctor. Send your bill to the Householder and we'll take care of it."

The wind tore at the car door and the doctor slammed it shut.

As the Town Man drove off, he observed, "The Farm Boss said it would rain before they got the wheat in and it looks like it. Well, it won't take us long to get home. I could take a road that would miss the carnival traffic and it wouldn't be much farther around."

"Go past it again, Town Man," Mike pleaded.

"Why, I'd like to know? I got a good eyeful and that's all I want."

"We could ride the wheel."

"I guess so! Anyhow, that takes money."

"Look!"

"What?"

"I got money!"

Moessner slowed the car. "Where'd you get that?"

"The doctor."

"You know you shouldn't take such things. What's the matter with you, Mike? Nobody has to give us money. Fifty cents! You give it back."

"He said it was carnival money."

"Oh, he did! Well, he should know better. As if any of us would spend our allowance on such bedevilment."

"This isn't allowance money."

"It's the same as a month's allowance, isn't it? And how much do you think you could buy at a carnival for that? Not very much. When I come in next time I'll hand it back. So give it to me."

Little Mike gave him the money. What did it matter? Thomas Moessner was grumbling about the doctor and the world, but he was not taking a different road. He was going back the way they had come, and already the carnival lights beckoned in the distance.

"Go slow, Town Man, please go slow!"

"How can I go fast with all these crazy people hurrying to spend their money? This is a lesson for us Hutterians. I wish the whole colony could see what we're seeing. Look at those lights swinging in the wind. Look at that tent. You'd think it would blow down any minute. But that doesn't matter. When the Devil calls, all the sinners come running."

The carnival scene was beginning to be clouded with dust, but that only made the wheel look mightier than before. It turned and sang just the same.

"Town Man, let's go in! Let's go in for just a minute!"

"You think I'd been seen in there?"

Little Mike held back his words until the truck was opposite the carnival grounds. "Please, Town Man!" he cried. "Please let me see the big wheel up close. Please let me hear the music from close by!"

Moessner turned angrily off the highway and stopped the truck alongside the road.

"You listen to me, Mike Neumann," he scolded. "I can't drive and have you pulling at my arm. This is why you boys don't get to ride to town with me—you don't know how to act. You see something and you must have it. Well, take a good look at how things are going in there. Look at those foolish people. Listen to them— laughing in God's face! Look at them riding that wheel and spinning on those things. Look at them on those wooden horses. Everybody acts as if they were drunk. Ah, Pastor Jacob, how right you are! Glitter and music are the Devil's playground."

He scanned the scene from one end of the lane to the other, groaning over its awfulness. Little Mike rolled the window down, and strangely enough Moessner said nothing. The music and the wind beat into the truck. Still the Town Man did not scold. Little Mike leaned out the window. The suddenly cold, damp whip of the wind lashed him, but his eyes were traveling with the Ferris wheel. His mind was bursting with the musical shriek of the calliope. The pastor and the elders had deceived him. This *was* the world, and it was all glory. He cast a vivid glance at the Town Man. Moessner was lost in thought. The lights were charming him, too. The music and the night were screaming their frantic calls.

Little Mike seized the door handle with both hands. The door flew open and the truck shook in a blast of wind. He leaped to the ground and plummeted down the sloping bank. Dimly he heard the shouts of the Town Man but his bare feet carried him quickly out of the sound and the wind drove him on. Dazzled by the brilliance, he was in the lane reveling at the sight of the hurrying people. He saw large trucks painted with broad stripes; red, white and blue. Along the stripes was printed AMERICAN SHOWS. The sawdust under his feet felt cold and wet and he laughed with excitement. He heard people talk about a storm but their words were lost in his wonder. The dust that blew about him was part of the adventure. The smell of things to eat, the sight of boys, the pushing, hurrying crowds were what he remembered.

Along the lane through which he went men and women stood at their booths shouting their prices, calling people to come and play. He passed the rink where the rumble of the skaters filled him with awe. Now several men pulled a large canvas piece over a booth full of toys. People stood gazing anxiously at the sky, but Little Mike raced on to the far end of the grounds where the Ferris wheel was turning. There he stopped. It was higher than he had imagined and the motor that turned it shook the ground. People sat behind the seat bars swinging in

space. Some were laughing and others were frightened at
the dust and the wind. The Ferris wheel boss stood with
his hand on the lever. The brim of his little gray cap was
turned up and he puffed at a cigarette. While Little Mike
watched, the lever was pulled and the wheel stopped. The
boss flung back a seat bar and let a couple out. They
joined hands and ran away quickly. From the other seats
came voices asking to be freed, but some of the riders
begged that the wheel should go around and the music
should start again.

Little Mike walked over to the Ferris wheel boss.

"Can I go up?" he asked.

"You get away!" he was told.

He saw the sign inviting the people to buy a ticket and
ride the wheel. He ran to the cage where a man was
hurriedly putting money into a drawer, and the money
on the counter was being held down with his hand to keep
it from blowing away.

"Can I ride the wheel?"

"No more rides tonight the way it looks."

"Please let me ride it."

"Where's your money?"

Little Mike put his hand into his pocket, remembering
as he did so that he had given the money to the Town
Man. He had no money. Only the harmonica and it had
never been so precious as at this moment. It was some
thing he could love and understand. The wheel and its
music were overwhelming and frightening in their greatness. No wonder that God was sending the wind and swinging the lights back and forth. No wonder that the people
on the Ferris wheel were now asking to be let go. The

grounds were growing dark with the wind and the saw-dust blowing.

The Ferris wheel boss threw his cigarette to the ground and stepped on it. "Take it easy," he shouted to the passengers. "I'll get you down."

One by one they were freed from the shaking wheel. Quickly they ran away. Into the confusion of sound came the noise of many automobiles starting and horns honking and parents shouting for their children. All along the lanes men with sledges were driving down stakes and tightening the ropes on the booths and the machines. But now the elders' God flung a lightning bolt across the sky. The frightened people ran and the skies scolded them with thunder. Papers and dust filled the air. The tent was shaking. The booth tenders pulled the canvas covers over their wares and lashed them tight but the rain started and pelted them.

Little Mike stood uncertainly, a hopeless questioning expression in his eyes. He heard the pounding of rain as it came across the grounds. It struck his face and stung his body. The terrorizing flashes of lightning were the hands of God. Then through the deserted lane where the wind ripped at the booths came Thomas Moessner. He might have walked out of the blinding skies and his call was a summons. "Mike! Mike!" Unmindful of himself he came like a figure out of the great Book, honoring God with fearlessness, having no thought for himself, concerned only for the one whose name he called. Black and rain-drenched, he tramped through the storm.

"Mike!"

People huddling against the canvas canopies looked at

him in amazement. His stocky body, his beard, his black hat blended into a figure that seemed to throw back the lightning.

"Town Man!"

Little Mike ran calling. In a moment his hand was linked in Moessner's. Together they ran out of the grounds and up to the colony truck. No cars were moving but the Town Man started the motor. The wheels spun in the wet ground. Little Mike trembled with the cold, waiting for Moessner's anger to be loosed. A flash of lightning snapped off the carnival lights and plunged the scene into blackness over which the wind shrieked. Now only the eerie streaks of God's wrath revealed what once had been motion and brilliance. The lightning showed Little Mike the altered face of things: the outlines of people and the drenched lanes in a mixture of water and tightly closed booths. At the end of the lane the great wheel stood colorless and dead. Joshua's world had been transformed in fury while the power of the Hutterian God paraded his justice in the skies.

The truck moved onto the highway. It rocked in the wind, and the rain pelted it, but the Town Man sat hunched behind the wheel driving stubbornly over a highway flowing with water.

The harmonica lay in Little Mike's pocket wet and cold. He took it out and wiped it on the blanket that covered the seat.

After a long silence Moessner spoke. "But for you we would have been home before this storm and we would have nothing to explain." He waited for a reply, then added, "You have taken your first and last trip with me."

"I know." Mike nodded.

"All right, then you know. So make up your mind where you belong. You can't have the carnival grounds and the commune—you ought to know that. And which is the right place is easy to see. Even the lightning doesn't seem so bad now we're getting close to home."

"I only wanted to see the wheel," Mike told him.

"The wheel," Moessner said disgustedly, and his voice made clear how forsaken the wheel had looked in the darkness, stripped of its splendor and music. But Little Mike could not help recapturing again the excitement he had felt when he first saw it as it turned rhythmically, carrying the happy people. Would he ever see that again? Would he ever hear the music? A gentle feeling spread over him when he asked himself these things. He closed his eyes, pressed a hand over the harmonica and listened to the blowing of the wind and the rain.

Moessner cleared his throat. After a moment he spoke in a distant, thoughtful tone. "Did you ride it?"

Little Mike's eyes flew open at the words. "No," he said. "That takes money."

The Town Man was satisfied. "Be glad I took the fifty cents," he said, "or else you might have got on."

"And then what?"

"Lightning would probably have struck you."

"Just because I was on it?"

"Yes."

"But why doesn't it strike other people? Everybody got off. If they got off, why wouldn't I have got off, too?"

"Because you wouldn't have. I just know it."

"Joshua Volkner was on one often and nothing happened to him. And he even ran away from the colony. Why do such things never happen to him?"

Moessner's eyes were riveted on the road. "Who knows what might still happen to him?" he figured. "Or maybe God has given him up long ago. But God hasn't given you up. He has His eye on you all the time."

Whether that was good or bad, Little Mike hesitated to ask, for the storm was not over and the lightning still flashed threateningly.

CHAPTER 15

~~~~~~

*T*HE five-thirty commune bell awakened another Hutterian day. The yard had been pounded by the rain and the geese moved between the houses. From the Farm Boss came the assurance that the storm had not damaged the wheat. The warm sun would work its miracle and by noon the combine could resume its work. Voices of women foretold that it was milkingtime. In the refectory the kitchen crews were noisily stirring.

The night had been sleepless for Little Mike, and through the long hours he reviewed the happenings since he played the harmonica for Jake. Michael father had made no comment on the trip with the Town Man, but his mother was worried about him. "He is sick, too," she said, "and no wonder when you see how soaked he is." But his father answered that sickness and sin had the same symptoms. Late that evening the elders had prayed for Jake and the pastor anointed the sick boy with oil in the name of the Lord. Michael father had attended the prayer gathering. When he came home he announced that Jake looked better. Nothing was said about the harmonica, and it seemed that everyone was waiting to see whether Jake would recover before the business of discipline began.

Now as Little Mike came from his room his mother stood at her customary place by the washstand surrounded by his sisters waiting their turn. "The Garden Boss wants boys for working in the orchard today," Sarah informed him. "Go and report."

"How is Jake?" he asked. "Did you hear this morning?"

Ruth spoke up. "He's better."

Little Mike went outside where his father was hurriedly washing at the house bench.

"Jake is better, Michael father."

"Don't get any big ideas," Michael answered. "He is still sick. And you and I still have some matters to get settled."

"But if he's better, then the music——"

"Didn't the doctor say he would get better? All right. Come to the shop when you get washed."

Michael poured the soapy water into the commune yard. Little Mike filled the basin with water from the rain barrel. He splashed the water over his face and whispered a prayer of thanks for Jake's recovery.

Dan Mueller and Joey Kunz were rigging up a baby wagon and Joey called, "Hey, Mike, is it safe for us to come over?"

"Sure, it's safe. What do you mean?"

Joey approached Mike with a weighty question: "Do you think it is the harmonica's fault or the wheel's fault that Jake got sick?"

"How could it be the wheel's fault?"

"I've been building the wheel in secret," Joey confessed. "And Jake knows that."

"Who says it is any fault like that?"

"I just thought about it myself, and Dan and I thought about it together."

"There always has to be fault somewhere," Dan explained. "Nothing happens without there being a fault."

"But, Mike," Joey said with a sudden jump into the air, "how was it in town? What did you see? How was it going through the rain in the truck?"

Mike held back his desire to tell them about his great experience. How much of that would he ever dare tell? How much would the Town Man say? Hastily he dried his face on the long towel. "The harmonica made Jake feel better," he contended. "If I could I would go and play for him right now, but there is already too much trouble."

"Do you still have the harmonica?" asked Dan.

"Right here," said Mike, touching his pants pocket.

Dan and Joey gazed at him in wonder.

"Didn't Pastor Kunz take it?" Joey wanted to know. "He looked to me last night like a harmonica taker when I saw him."

"We all thought your father would take it away first thing," Dan marveled.

"You did?"

"Sure," Joey chimed in. "We thought that after everybody heard you play for Jake, that was the end."

"My father would have taken it and broken it right away," Dan had to confess.

"I don't know what mine would have done," Joey pondered. "And I don't want to know either."

"Michael father understands things better than anybody," said Mike.

"We all thought that he had taken it away and so we

kept our distance," Dan explained. "You know the saying, 'Blood on one finger covers the whole hand.' We were the hand because we were in with you. But your father didn't take it and stick it in the stove?"

"Here!" Mike said happily. "Try the pocket if you want to. There it is, plain as you can feel."

"It's there," Joey agreed. "Say, Mike, where did you find it anyway?"

"In the old stump on the high bank. Right inside. There where the stump is falling to pieces. There it was. The stump was just keeping it for me."

"If the stump did that," Joey figured, "then the elders ought to be kind to the harmonica, too, and no wonder your father was kind to it."

"You don't know Michael father," Mike boasted. "Didn't he tell us how to fix the wheel? Didn't he understand that? Well, he understands this, too."

"But it is a personal possession," Dan stammered. "And even after you played it right out the way you did, and even when your father took you to the cabinet shop, there has been no discipline?"

Mike shook his head. "No discipline."

"Then all I can say is that it will come yet," Dan concluded. "Don't you think so, Joey?"

"I can figure out building things," Joey decided, "but this I can't figure out in any way."

"Just the same," said Dan, "for a few days it will be just as good that we don't go too much in a group together with Mike. The blood has not stopped yet, I think, and the hands had better keep clean."

Mike stood listening. "I hear an automobile."

"It's the tractor in the wheat field," said Dan.

"No, it's an automobile and it's close to the gate. Maybe the doctor is coming back."

They ran to the commune road as a car drove up.

"Open the gate!" called the driver.

The boys hurried to obey, forgetting that it was really the business of Andrew Mueller to take care of these things. They let the car come in. Mike closed the gate while Joey and Dan ran behind the car as it headed into the yard. The car's uncommon speed halted the women carrying the milk to the separator shed. The men came hastily from their work. Michael Neumann hurried from the shop.

When Little Mike reached the car a large group had gathered and the driver was saying, "What a way to have to deliver a night letter in this day and age! The depot agent calls and says this is sent special handling. It's costing the sender four extra bucks."

"Householder! Pastor Kunz!" called the Bee Boss. "Here's a man from town with a telegram!"

"Somebody sign for it," said the driver. "Say, when're you folks getting a telephone out here?"

The Householder signed for the telegram and started to open it. Then he paused. "It's addressed to you, Pastor Jacob," he called.

The pastor was not to be hurried. He came with his customary stride and the men made way for him. "It's from Joshua Volkner, that's sure," he was told.

"He sent it special so it would be brought right out," said the Town Man. "I could have gone in for it if I'd known."

"Well, this must be big news," Michael proclaimed.

"Somebody go with me and open the gate," said the driver. "I've got to get back."

Andrew Mueller rode out with him.

Pastor Kunz turned the telegram over a number of times and weighed it in his hand. "These things carry only good news or bad," he said with a sigh and opened it without a show of emotion. He read the message to himself. "So!" He shrugged and handed it to the Householder. With loud questions, the men pressed forward. Some read the telegram over the Householder's shoulders.

Michael Neumann was the first to speak. "So, Joshua Volkner—your answer is 'no'!"

" 'The company has gone too far with its plans. . . .' " the Householder quoted. " 'Greatly regret . . . very sorry . . . if you find another location and I can be of assistance . . .' "

Everyone spoke at once.

"Not even to help his own parents!"

"He knew this when he left."

"He says he will write us a letter."

"There'll be another place somewhere that we can get."

Pastor Kunz made himself heard. "What is so surprising about this. Isn't it as I have always said? We can look for no help from the outside. The world must ever be at enmity with us and we must ever be at enmity with the world. Ring the breakfast bell! This does not stop a Hutterian day nor will it stop the growth of the Hutterian life!"

The Bell Man ran to his duties. Determined voices endorsed the pastor's words and the elders gathered around

the old man and the Householder, emphatically express-
ing their confidence and faith. Michael Neumann exclaimed, "The day will come when they'll be asking us
to take the Jordan place off their hands!" Few showed that
they agreed. They were ready to gird themselves for the
job that lay ahead, but they were not so sure about tomorrow. Little Mike felt that for once his father was not so
confident as he tried to appear. Michael father took the telegram and read it for himself. He handed it to the Town
Man who also read it and passed it on. The breakfast bell
was ringing.

Michael Neumann started to the refectory, turned
abruptly so that he brushed Little Mike with his body, and
said, "Come with me."

He led his son to the cabinet shop and they went in.
"There's a wall shelf to be made for Martha Volkner," he
said in a distant tone. "It must be finished so she can take
it back with her. We want to show the Canadian colonies
how we do things."

He turned the shelf bracket over in his hands, glanced
at Little Mike and laid it aside. "We should go and eat,"
he said.

He wiped a cutting tool with a cloth and hung it in its
place. "We should go," he repeated. Then, brushing his
hands together as if to wipe both the wood grime and his
thoughts away, he said, "Come along."

He strode to the door, timing his steps so that Mike
could come through while he held it open. Sarah Neumann was on her way to the kitchen with Ruth and Anna
at her side. Selma Kunz made her laborious way with her
cane. The Chore Men came from the barns and Martha

Volkner appeared leading a child by each hand. Dan and
Joey left their wagon at the kitchen door while they went
in to eat. Everyone was answering the call of the bell, but
Michael Neumann led his son straight to the Jacob Linder
home. He pushed open the door. Joanna Linder sat beside the sick boy on the bed, feeding him.

Jake raised his hand feebly, bidding her stop while he
called with effort, "Mike, come here."

"How are you, Jake?"

"Better because of what you did for me."

Mike bent over him and whispered, "Did you hear the
music when I played for you yesterday?"

"Sure, I heard it."

Michael stood in the room with folded arms, his black
hat low over his forehead. "Did the playing make you
better or worse?" he wanted to know.

"Much better," Jake answered.

"What do you think, Joanna Linder?" Michael asked.

"Well," Joanna admitted, "Jake is able to eat a little.
But there has been the praying for him, too."

Michael shrugged. "I am not comparing the music to
the praying," he made clear. "That goes without saying.
I just want to know if the music itself did Jake some
good."

Jake reached out a hand to Mike. "Did you bring the
harmonica again?"

"Now," interrupted Michael, "that isn't the reason or the
purpose of our coming." Then he turned to his son. "Did
you bring that infernal instrument?"

"Yes, Michael father."

"I want to hear it again," Jake said.

"Now, Jake——" his mother began.

"I am not for it," Michael intruded firmly. "If God wanted us to have harmonicas, He would have made our mouths that way. He would have given us harmonica mouths."

"If the playing makes me better, Joanna mother——" Jake pleaded.

Michael Neumann glanced awkwardly at Joanna Linder. Mike had the harmonica half in and half out of his pocket. Moments passed. He waited for his father to speak.

The silence taunted Michael. Silence was a sign that a man was no longer the master. A man should always have a ready word, especially when he was in the right. A man should always be in the right. Michael pushed back his hat resolutely and gripped his hook-and-eye shirt with both hands.

"Well, play then," Michael decided. "Don't say you can do a thing unless you can do it."

Little Mike drew the silver instrument from his pocket.

"Play soft," said his father. "It is no use blaring out so that the whole commune can hear."

The melody was low and stirring as Mike played for the two people whom he loved beyond everyone else. He did not close his eyes at once. He looked at Jake lying silently listening. He caught a glimpse of Michael father as the harmonica played the well-loved tune, bringing to mind the words, "I trust in God for everything." What was his father thinking? Was he, too, wondering where such pretty music came from? Was he asking why the elders would object to it? Little Mike pursued these thoughts while he closed his eyes. Then he played with all his heart.

He heard his father clear his throat. Michael broke into the song with as little rudeness as possible. "I see that you know it, Little Mike," he said shortly. "So, come."

He was already at the door. He was hurrying through the yard and Little Mike ran to catch up with him. Michael started to the cabinet shop, then turned to their home. From here he swerved in the direction of the kitchen as if to say, "Come, we must be seen at breakfast," but then he turned into the sunlit path which led to the river bottom, and that was the way he finally went with Mike at his side. As he neared the balanced rock, he walked slowly, then leaned against it in a sprawling fashion.

"Once," he said, facing Mike, "when I did wrong my father brought me down here. This is a good place. You have done wrong and maybe this is the best place for me to bring you. Why did you let Joshua Volkner give you the harmonica?"

"It made such pretty music."

"Why didn't you tell me that he gave it to you?"

"I was afraid you would not let me keep it."

"So you thought it would be better to do wrong than to have me tell you what was right."

"Is it wrong, Michael father?"

"If you have a harmonica, doesn't that mean that Jake Linder should have one, and Dan Mueller and Joey Kunz and Paul Wiese and every other boy just the same? All right, what kind of colony would we have then?"

"I would be glad for them to have one if they loved it too, and played it good."

"Oh, you would? Then pretty soon there would be no more singing. Out would go our songs. Is this what you want? You want to start a harmonica band? Mike, where is the sense in your head? Start with harmonicas and soon someone wants a horn. Soon someone wants a piano. Next comes a radio. Do you hear me, Mike? Look at me. Let me see that harmonica. So, this is it? It glitters. That is the first thing about things in the world. They must glitter. They must dazzle the eyes. Where is the box for this?"

"How did you know there is a box?"

"Answer me."

Mike scanned his father's bearded face in fright. His father knew everything. There was no need to hold back anything from the men. His father knew, the elders knew. Pastor Kunz knew more than any other perhaps. Then there was God. There was always God, and the men in the commune stood in God's place.

"The box is under my feather bed."

"All right, then I know where that is." Michael turned the harmonica over in his hand. "This is a personal possession. It does not have to be a harmonica—it can be anything. But whatever it is, it is a little rabbit that comes through the wall. It makes a small hole. Next comes the fox. He comes through the hole that the rabbit made. After the fox comes the *Weltgeist*. Down goes the wall. Do you understand what I am telling you, Mike? Look your father in the eye. The *Weltgeist* in this case is the harmonica. Can you understand that?"

"I like it so much, Michael father. But I will give it to the Householder. He can let anyone use it, just so I can play it once in a while."

"I am talking about more than the harmonica. I am

talking about the Hutterian life. Nothing is worse than
to want what you can't have instead of enjoying what is
yours. Across this river, over the commune boundary the
world is waiting to break through and destroy us. The
world is the Devil's world. The commune is God's world.
Joshua Volkner has become the world's disciple. Now
that he has lost his soul he wants you to lose yours. But
we will not let you lose it, Mike."

"What will you do, Michael father? What will the
elders do?"

"We will not give the harmonica to the Householder.
We will not give it to the elders either or to Pastor Kunz.
We will do what is the right thing and the great thing,
Mike."

Mike probed beneath the stern, unrevealing face. He
watched his father's downcast eyes follow the gleam of
the harmonica as he turned it over and over in his hands.
Michael's voice was suddenly so soft that it could scarcely
be heard against the river. "We will do what God wants
us to do, Little Mike. We will give it back to the world
and there will be no more trouble."

"Give it back to Joshua Volkner?"

Michael shook his head. "That is not necessary. He
would only want to have a long talk as to why this and
why that. He would only try more than ever to make us
believe that the day of God's people is over. No, Mike, we
will give it back to the world in an easy way. The Missouri will take it back for us. It flows long and far."

Little Mike gasped. A darkness more enveloping than
any that ever settled over the commune descended upon

him and a voice within him cried: *Run, Mike, run! Take your harmonica and run. Take the road that Joshua Volkner went. Out through the gate, Mike—anywhere, anywhere!*

His father's eyes were gentle. Slowly he said, "Tell me, Little Mike, how did you learn to play so good?"

The boy wanted to cry, "Enough, Michael father, enough! Do not hurt me any more!" But there was something about his father's voice that drew him against his will.

"I don't know how I learned. It just came. I just close my eyes."

"Music is a good thing. God wants us to sing. The Bible tells us that. But God does not want us to copy the world. Yes, Little Mike, you do play good. I must say you play very good. The music you make is all right. But I suppose it is easy. Is it easy?"

Mike turned away. He could endure no more. He looked at the path leading up to the high bank. If only he had someone to help him now, to take his hand, to speak the word and give him the courage he needed! If Joshua Volkner could suddenly appear! If only the worldling's voice would call to him, "Come, Little Mike, come!" There was no one. He flung open the gate in thought and stood on the free road. It was in thought only. He could not take even the first step. He stood rooted, immovable. Everything he had learned and believed restrained him: Four hundred years of tradition . . . the dread of the world . . . the elders . . . the Boss of Bosses . . .

He heard a sound. It was the soft, pleading tone of the

harmonica. He heard a whispered note. Then another. A
melody was being picked out. It sounded like a part of
"The Great Song."

He turned. His father sat with the harmonica at his
lips, his beard covering it, his hands over it, his eyes sug-
gesting a mischievous gleam. Michael Neumann groped
for the tones and succeeded in completing a line. "Ah!"
he exclaimed, puffing, "I make it sound like a saw going
through two nails in a plank!"

"No, you don't, Michael father! You make it sound as
good as I did."

"Oh, I do!" Michael mocked. "Thank you for the com-
pliment, Mr. Neumann Mike." Then, seriously and with
tender care, he said, "Mike, there come times in life when
we do things that are hard for us, but that are good for
what we believe. There are times like that and they are
not easy. But I want to tell you something that my father
told me, and someday—who knows?—you will tell it to
your son and he will tell it to his: 'The good of all is what
is best for one.' That is the heart of the Hutterian life. The
peace of all, the comfort, the security of all is what we
must look for. The world is lost. We are saved because
we lose ourselves in the community. And then when we
lose ourselves there, we find ourselves. You are too young
to understand. But maybe not. You seem older than you
are. I can hear that in the playing. I can see that in some of
the things you do. I can feel it when I think what happened
to you when the bees stung you. I know about that. And
I know all that happened to you last night at the carnival.
Listen, Mike, I do not say that your music did not help

Jake—I do not say that it didn't. But I tell you what will help him even more—to do your father's will."

He held out the harmonica. It caught the morning sun and as Little Mike took it he could see his face reflected in it. He saw his blue eyes and noticed there were no tears in them. He saw his tanned cheeks and he thought of the bees and God. There were no scars there. He saw his brown hair hanging down over his forehead. He turned the harmonica over, seeing again every detail and line. It was in his memory even more than in his hand. He would have it always. Ever and ever through the years, no matter what anyone would think or say, no matter what would happen in the commune, no matter what would happen in the world—this was his. He would hold it forever where the Householder would never see it and where Pastor Kunz's eyes would never penetrate. It was his and there was only one way to keep it, to guard it from everyone who did not understand. Breathlessly he met the steady gaze of the bearded man on the rock.

He clenched the harmonica in his fist and raised his arm. "I want to throw it, Michael father!" he burst out in a tearful cry. "Far! Far!"

He swung his arm. His hand opened. Out into the river sailed the silver instrument. Swiftly, silently it flashed for a moment and was gone. Empty-handed, Little Mike stood looking out over the water, repeating in a dull, toneless voice, "Good-by, harmonica . . . good-by!"

Michael Neumann did not turn his head. He stared hard and straight into space. Then he sprang from the rock and planted himself at Little Mike's side. His strong hand gripped the boy's arm. He stood gazing with Little Mike at the spot where the Missouri dipped and flowed unchanged, uncomplaining, neither sorrowful nor rejoicing, going its endless way between the river flats and the chalk cliffs and the willows, a thousand miles upstream and a thousand miles down.

THE END